GAR
12.18

KT-559-667

This book should be returned/renewed by the
latest date shown above. Overdue items incur
charges which prevent self-service renewals.
Please contact the library.

Wandsworth Libraries
24 hour Renewal Hotline
01159 293388
www.wandsworth.gov.uk

Wandsworth

9030 00006 2668 8

Legend Press Ltd, 107-111 Fleet Street, London, EC4A 2AB
info@legend-paperbooks.co.uk | www.legendpress.co.uk

Print ISBN 978-1-78719801-2
Ebook ISBN 978-1-78719800-5
Set in Times. Printing managed by Jellyfish Solutions Ltd
Cover design by Gudrun Jobst | www.yotedesign.com

Susanna is fascinated by human relationships. She can be found people-watching wherever she goes, finding material for her writing. Despite the writer's life, she has an adventurous streak and has swum with whale sharks in Australia, fallen down a crevasse in the French Alps and walked through the sewers of Brighton – not in that order.

Her passions include animals, particularly her dogs, walking in the countryside and tennis, which clears her brain of pretty much everything.

Susanna's debut novel, *Dare to Remember*, was published by Legend Press in February 2017.

She aims to keep writing, and never to get old.

For Sharon

PROLOGUE

On a strip of sand by a northern sea, salt water caresses pale skin. Bare legs are washed clean, buffed by gentle waves and a million grains of sand. A single shoe, its skinny heel pointing to the sky, lies lonely. Fabric swirls in the backwash, its pattern of leaves and flowers fading in the brine; yellow hair curls and curves like soft seaweed. The eyes, blue as the sky, stare out at the world, which has turned away.

CHAPTER ONE

The Baltic Sea, at last. She's never been as far as this, never seen this vast stretch of white sand, this huge horizon beyond which lies Scandinavia.

The hotel is flanked by sand dunes, each room overlooking the sea. It's off-season, the winter dragging on, but even in summer people come to escape everyday life. No children here, no tours, no live entertainment. Just views of the huge grey sea and the lowering sky, a long spit of sand that seems to go on for ever, birds screaming. No need to talk to anyone.

She feels the cold blast of sea wind on her cheek as if for the first time, relishes its beating and buffeting as she walks, takes deep gulps of oxygen until her head aches with the freshness of it. She breathes in the icy air. Gradually her mind empties of chatter, her body starts to recalibrate.

Until a small, energetic volcano far away interrupts the gentle flow of the hours.

*

"Good morning, madam," the man on reception says. "Have you contacted your airline yet?" His English is immaculate. A small brass badge indicates his name.

Anna's break is close to an end. "No," she says. "A couple more days."

"Haven't you heard?" His eyes widen with concern.

"There's been a volcanic eruption. Flights all over Europe have been affected. Would you like me to check for you?"

"Lithuania has a volcano?" As far as she knows, there are no mountains at all here.

"No, madam, not here… in Iceland. There's a big cloud of ash. A lot of flights to the UK are delayed or cancelled."

"I hadn't heard. When was this?"

"Yesterday, madam. It was on the news last night."

She'd gone upstairs early, read for an hour or so, and then slept. She's been avoiding the news, consciously cutting herself off.

"Yes, I would like you to check my flight for me, please. How long are the delays?"

"Nobody knows. Which airline are you booked with?"

She gives him the name and waits while he stares at the screen in front of him.

A couple approaches; the man waves at the receptionist, who ignores him, engrossed.

"This is ridiculous," the man says, glancing briefly at Anna. His neck is thick; an angry flush creeps up towards his cheeks. He taps impatiently on the wooden top. "Apparently planes were getting through fine at first, then someone panicked and now they've cancelled everything, without even knowing what the risks are. Idiotic."

The woman holds melodramatic fingers to her forehead, bracelets jangling. "Christ, we could be here for days, or even weeks."

She's right, Anna realises with a sinking feeling. If the ash cloud is too dangerous for flying, they won't be taking any chances.

"Do you need to be back urgently?" Anna says to the woman.

"Well, I certainly don't want to stay much longer in this dump," the woman replies, her voice rising in complaint. "I knew we should have left yesterday, but he wouldn't listen." The man looks away, an expression of disgust on his face.

Anna realises this is the first time she's spoken to any of her fellow guests. Strange how a crisis brings people together.

*

"Your flight's cancelled, I'm afraid," the receptionist says, an apologetic look on his face. "It's the same with all the airlines. I will keep checking for you though."

She sighs. "Thank you, I appreciate it." She leaves the couple waiting by the desk and goes through into the lounge, where a stove spreads its woody fragrance into the room. Soft sofas are scattered around, warm blankets on their seat backs, furred footstools beside them. Wooden coffee tables sit on textured carpets and a rack of glossy magazines hangs from a wall. The impression is stylish, opulent, warm. There's no one else there. Anna takes a seat by the window and dials the office.

A familiar voice on the end of the line.

"Jane, it's me."

"Anna, I was expecting your call. I hope you've had a good break?"

Anna's cheered by the businesslike voice, the sound of the real world. "I have indeed, thanks to you. It's been really good; I've managed to relax, as you wanted me to. But now I'm keen to get back and I can't."

"I know, what bad luck."

"It is. Listen, can you do some checking for me please?"

"Of course I can. Fire away."

"Can you book the first available flight home, if you can find one, and maybe look a couple of days ahead as well? We may need to take what we can get, so look at interconnecting flights too. And it might be useful to keep an eye on all the updates from your end."

"Okay. I'll get onto the airlines now. I'll call as soon as I have something to report."

"Great, thank you, oh, and I'll go to Vilnius tomorrow,

anyway. I want to be closer to the airport, and I won't get much done here. Can you find me a hotel please?"

She checks a couple of news sites to get the latest. It's not looking good. The volcano is top story, speculation rife about the fallout. There are images of the plume, dark and billowing. Europe's airlines are in chaos. People all over the world are hysterical, booking any number of flights over the next three weeks, aiming to travel as soon as the flight ban is lifted. It'll be chaos for much longer than that, with the nightmare of insurance claims and refunds.

She risks a look at Facebook, finds a barrage of stories and dramas from people in far-off places. Some are happy: *Yessss! We've got to stay!* Many, though, are stressed and anxious.

All the benefit of the last few days has gone up in smoke. Literally. With nothing to do but wait, she grabs her coat and boots and sets off for a last long walk along the beach.

*

There are no people here, no animals, just a few hooded crows hopping at the shoreline in the distance, a seagull coasting on the swell of wind high above, mewling at the empty sky. No plants to be seen, no trees, though beyond the white sand dunes on her left soft, fragrant pine forests line the length of the spit.

She walks, leaning into the wind, hat pulled down over her ears, eyes half closed. She watches her feet, one following the other, as if they are separate from her, marching alone. Beneath her feet the sand forms exotic patterns, fashioned by the sea breeze into whorls and ridges. Pure white shells stand proud like markers, each pushed upright into a tiny drift of sand by the relentless wind. When she turns to look behind her, as her hair whips around her face, there's nothing for miles but hard white sand and grey shoreline. Her footprints are already barely there, her presence wiped out. Ahead of her is more of the same. She revels in the open sky, the vastness of the sea.

She stops, plunges her hands into the cold water and cups them to her mouth. It's not salty, as they said. She wonders why. When she turns, the crows have landed close by. One, hopping delicately among shells and pale grey twigs along the waterline, cocks its head and considers her, its eye knowing, intelligent. What does it know? Its partner – friend? brother? – follows, mimicking its movements and for a moment they dance in harmony together, hop, look, peck, hop. When she starts to walk again, they fly up in formation, flapping their wings, balancing on the breeze, and land again ahead, keeping a sharp eye on her. She wonders what they're hoping for.

Further on, more birds arrive, investigating a pile of washed-up detritus, twigs and seaweed, chattering and calling to each other. Close by there's a casualty, a dead bird, its body wedged into the sand.

But it's not a bird, it's a woman's shoe, black and shiny, its sharp heel pointing towards the sky. It's out of place here, a landscape unsullied by the touch of humans

The crows stay with her as she walks, her hands plunged deep into her pockets for warmth, her feet tramping on, until the weather closes in for real and the rain starts to batter her face and the skin on her legs turns cold under the wet denim of her jeans.

When she turns to go back, the wind pushes her from behind, urging her on. She can barely see in the driving rain. She has no idea how far she's gone, and when she gazes back in the direction of the hotel, blinking against the drops that cling to her eyelashes, she can see nothing but grey sea and white sand. There's no sign of where she's come from, where she's been.

Half an hour passes and she's still not sure how far she has to go. Cursing herself for not taking more notice of her surroundings, she walks on until with relief she recognises, again, the pile of detritus. The crows have gone now; the wind has sent them off to calmer waters. The shoe still lies, incongruous, a pointer to the grim sky, the sand beginning to mount around it, claiming it along with the shells and the seaweed.

She's about to hurry on when something catches her eye. She hesitates. There's something odd about the ebb and flow of the seawater in and around the pile of seaweed. It sucks and pulls at a shape in the sand. She steps forward to take a better look, fighting to keep her hood in place, her hair tearing at her eyes and face. Leaning down, she pulls the brown slime of the seaweed away and recoils in horror.

Underneath is the white curve of a human leg.

*

For a moment everything stops. The wind seems to settle, the gentle rhythm of the sea slows. She can't breathe.

She forces herself to look again. The skin is translucent, there's no colour at all, as if the life has drained away into the sea. Steeling herself, she crouches down and pulls the slimy seaweed away.

The eyes of a young girl stare out at her, empty, lifeless.

Reeling, she collapses onto her knees, hands over her mouth, stomach churning. She reaches out a trembling hand and feels for a pulse on the alabaster neck. At the touch of the ice-cold skin she snatches her hand away as if scalded, scrambling backwards, her feet slipping and stumbling, away from the pile of seaweed, running, running through the icy rain.

*

At the hotel, she moves through the hours that follow like a ghost, the vision of the girl ever-present in her horrified mind. The police arrive in force and she loses all track of time. She's plied with sugary tea laced with brandy, her coat removed, a blanket wrapped round her shoulders. In the

13

lounge, she sits in front of the stove, which they stoke until the flames roar and crackle. When her hands shake too much to sip, someone holds the mug to her mouth. She can feel its warmth, the steam rising in her eyes. There seem to be a lot of them helping, moving around her, shouting instructions, until suddenly there are only two: a woman in uniform and a man.

They ask her a hundred questions, not many of which she can answer. No, she didn't see anyone else. Yes, she probably passed it on her way out, away from the hotel, but didn't notice it, what with the wind and the rain. Though she did notice the shoe. No, she can't put her finger on why it caught her eye on the way back. She has no idea how far she walked, no idea what time she left the hotel, or what time she came across the body.

The policewoman says very little. Perhaps she's there to provide comfort; a shoulder to cry on. The man, though gentle, is insistent. He asks her to describe, many times, what she's seen. At one point, early on, he leaves her and she hears loud voices in the foyer. The body has been found.

She asks when he comes back. He says they've found the body of a girl, and that she is certainly dead. That's when she starts to cry.

Soon after, some food appears, but she can't eat. She asks them to take it away. Just having it there makes her feel sick.

Eventually, to her great relief, the police have done their job. Handing her a card in case she thinks of anything more, they thank her and leave. The kindly receptionist takes her up to her room. She almost collapses when the door closes behind her.

It's one in the morning.

She raids the minibar and pours herself a long drink. There's no ice, and it's warm, but she doesn't care. Dumping everything on the floor, she collapses onto the bed and pushes off her boots, still stained with salt, ingrained with sand.

The images of the last few hours are not going to leave.

She lies in her clothes, the light on and her eyes open, knowing sleep won't come.

*

In the morning, her body feels brittle, her head ready to burst. She checks out early, brushing away the concern of the staff at the front desk. Yes, she was a little shocked yesterday, but now she feels fine, perfectly okay to drive. The police have her details if they need her, and she has theirs.

She needs to get back to the capital, to be near the airport. Quite apart from that, she's keen to get away from the sudden horror of the beach, forget that terrible image, occupy her exhausted mind with other things.

A cold wind whips her hair around her face as she climbs into the car. Flakes of snow melt on the windscreen as she starts the engine, the wipers destroying each wet smear as they flip from side to side. In Lithuania, the April weather is unpredictable. It's worth being prepared for anything here and she's glad she brought warm clothes.

The spit has only one road, linking the few small groups of houses – not enough to call villages – along its length. The car ferry that will carry her to Klaipeda, on mainland Lithuania, isn't far but she takes it slowly; she doesn't want to risk a breakdown or an accident when there are so few people around. Her reactions aren't what they should be after last night.

She turns the headlights on as a precaution and fiddles with the radio until she finds some music. As she sets off, the wind and sleet buffet the car.

She expects to see next to nothing on the road, but a few minutes into her journey flashing blue lights ahead interrupt her concentration. Two police cars, official crests on the driver doors, are parked up at angles on the dunes beside the road; an area alongside is cordoned off with flapping red tape. A black-clad policeman, muffled and hunched against the wind, talks into a radio, his arm draped over the open door of the car, a weapon on his hip. Another man is inside, a mobile phone at his ear.

As she passes, she risks a sideways glance towards the sea. A glimpse of figures moving around close to the shore, where a white tent flaps and billows in the wind. Like a snapshot, the scene is gone in an instant.

CHAPTER 2

She sits, cradling a glass of wine, scrolling through the news on her phone. It's early evening and at first she's alone in the hotel restaurant. An open fire blazes to one side; waiters come and go silently, preparing the tables.

As she waits for her food, a couple arrives and takes a table opposite, the man calling immediately for a waiter to order drinks. It's the couple she came across in the foyer at the hotel on the spit. She's not surprised; this is one of the better hotels in old Vilnius, popular with British visitors. She looks away, hoping that they don't know the story of her last twenty-four hours on the coast. She's still shaky, not ready to talk about it. She definitely doesn't want to discuss it with them. They don't strike her as the most sympathetic of people.

The man sits with his legs splayed, one arm slung over the back of the empty chair beside him, his eyes deep-set and knowing. It's hard to say how old he is, though his tanned skin betrays lines around the eyes and his hair is beginning to thin on top. His watch is big and expensive; his shoes look hand-made. He holds a large unlit cigar, a distinctive gold band around it. His wife – Anna would put her in her late thirties – is heavily made up, her blonde hair thick with spray, her lipstick bright. Jewellery sparkles from her hands and around her neck. Her eyes, behind heavy lashes, flit around the room.

Noticing Anna, the man looks over and says, in a loud voice: "Are you stranded here too?"

Thankfully he hasn't recognised her from the hotel, but there's no escaping his notice now. He's assuming she's British, therefore they have something in common. Repressing a sigh, she says: "Yes, indeed."

"Any luck with flights?"

The waiter arrives with a tray of drinks and places them with care in front of each. They sit waiting for her answer, like a double act waiting for a prompt.

"Nothing doing at the moment, it seems."

They nod. There's an awkward pause, which she feels obliged to fill. "What about you?"

The woman is quick to answer. Bracelets jangle as she gesticulates. "We need to be back for the weekend. Just our luck, bloody volcano. The one time I get him to take me on a trip, it had to erupt."

"It is a difficult situation for everyone," Anna says, wishing they'd go away.

"We don't know whether to wait and hope, or join the rush and get out as best we can," says the woman. Her husband ignores her.

Anna nods and smiles. She's grateful when her food arrives.

*

As she leaves the restaurant, she spots the British couple sitting in the bar. It's still early and she hesitates for a moment, wondering whether to stop for a drink. The man stands up, beckons her in. "Do join us," he says. "Let me get you a drink. What's it to be?"

Stifling an urge to refuse, she acquiesces. The man holds out his hand. It's huge, with chunky rings on the stubby fingers. In the other hand, he still holds the cigar, gold band glinting. It is now alight and spreading acrid smoke around the room as he moves.

"I'm Gavin, Gavin Strickland. This is Charlotte, my wife. Nice to meet you, even in these circumstances."

Charlotte's hand is limp and cool in hers and she has a smile to match. It fails to reach her eyes.

"I'm Anna."

"On holiday?" He takes a long drink and smacks his lips. They're red and somehow obscene. Sweat shines on his brow. They're sitting near the open fire, stoked high with new logs. Flames rumble and crackle in the confined space.

"Just a couple of days," she says. She doesn't want to invite unwelcome interest. "You?"

"I'm in business here. Casinos, clubs, that sort of thing." He fumbles in his jacket pocket and hands her a matchbook. There's a gold crown on the cover, and in shiny gold foil lettering, the words: *Princess – Clubs, Bars, Casinos*.

"Do you live here then?"

His wife smirks. "God no," she says. "Wouldn't live here if you paid me. Not enough going on." A look of disdain passes across Gavin's heavy features. It's lost on Charlotte. "Gavin comes a lot though, for work, here and to Klaipeda," she says. "Keeps a boat there, actually."

"Lovely place to sail, I'd imagine."

"It is, in the summer. We've just been to the coast, actually, but the weather was awful. He insisted on taking it out though. Didn't you?" She looks at Gavin, her painted-on eyebrows arching. "Came back after dark, freezing cold. I told him he was nuts." Gavin looks away, pointedly.

They don't mention the girl on the beach. Perhaps they left before all the excitement, or perhaps they're not interested. Anyway, Anna's not going to start that conversation with them.

Gavin frowns at his wife, turns to Anna. "Why Lithuania? Not the obvious choice for an Easter break."

"It's for work, too. I run an online business. Linen products. The factory's here." As usual, she's wearing clothes from her own company: soft linen shirt and jumper, linen scarf. Normally she'd point them out, mention the brand, but for some reason, she doesn't want these two to know too much about her.

19

Another couple appears, pulling up chairs to join them. It's clear they already know Gavin; there are kisses and handshakes. A waiter follows close behind, a tray of drinks balanced on his hand. He sets it down on the coffee table and replaces the ashtray, already overflowing with cigar butts. Gavin strikes a match, puffing wetly at his cigar.

He introduces Anna, his eyes slipping away from her as if she's already of no interest to him. The man, pale-faced with slicked-back hair, wears a sleek suit and shiny shoes. He has a distinctly Russian look about him, his English spiked with a heavy accent, his handshake a little too firm. The girl is beautiful, with high Slavic cheekbones and long slender legs, teetering on vertiginous heels. Her thin, gauzy dress is slit high. She's very young, perhaps not even twenty, and she looks strangely out of place here. Her hand in Anna's is like a child's.

Anna, already wishing she were elsewhere, forgets their names immediately.

The waiter places a tumbler and a glass of water before the girl. Condensation trickles down the side of the glass, pools around the base. She ignores it and his admiring gaze, and stares out into the room, away from the group.

"Is there news?" the Russian man says, his voice deep and gravelly. When he coughs, she can hear the phlegm rumble in his throat.

"Nothing," Gavin says. "They all seem to be running around like headless chickens, wondering what to do."

His wife bares her teeth in the ghost of a smile and sips at her drink; lipstick stains the edge of the glass. Anna smiles politely, excuses herself.

*

In the ladies' room, she's disconcerted to be joined by Charlotte at the row of basins.

"Fancy seeing you here," Charlotte says. "Time for a girl to refresh her face, I suppose." Rummaging briefly in her bag, she retrieves a gold-cased lipstick and applies it to pursed lips, turning them an unnatural shade of tangerine. "Can't wait to get back," she says. "I do like the comforts of my own home, don't you?"

Anna nods, drying her hands on a towel. She has nothing in common with this woman. But Charlotte carries on, oblivious.

"I expect you're missing your family, aren't you? Do you have children?" Now the mascara is out, the eyelashes thickening with even more layers.

"No, I don't." She wouldn't tell her if she did.

"We don't have any either, though we've tried. Turns out I can't have them. It's funny, I always thought I'd have lots of kids." She sighs into the mirror, her mouth turning downwards in a childish moue.

Anna is trapped, unable to escape the sickly honey of this woman's conversation, alarmed at the intimate nature of it.

"I keep saying to him, he's always travelling. I need kids to keep me occupied! He'd like them too, though he wouldn't see them much. Kids keep you grounded, I always say. Still, there's always adoption..." She flashes a look at Anna, whose hand is on the door handle, snaps her bag shut and fluffs her hair, pouting into the mirror. "Come on then, let's get back to the men."

*

"Oh, sorry, am I in your seat?" The invader jumps up from Anna's chair and smiles, a full-blown, eye-crinkling dazzler. It's impossible not to smile back.

He's young and slim, a laptop bag by his side. He's different from the others. In jeans and a jumper, he's more like a student than a guest in a smart hotel. As he shakes her hand, his look is intelligent and open. There's something about this man that changes her mind about staying in the bar. His name is Will.

21

"Are you stuck here, too?" he says, drawing another chair into the group.

"Yes, it seems so."

"Well, there are worse places to be stranded. Imagine if you'd gone to some outpost in Belarus or somewhere."

"True, though unlikely."

"Are you on holiday?" he asks. His voice is soft, with no discernible accent.

"I went to the coast for a few days, though I'm usually here on business. You?"

"I'm a travel journalist. I was researching tourism in Lithuania. Now I'm on 'Chaos hits European air travel'. There's always a silver lining." He grins at her. Across the table from them, the Russian whispers to the girl, who looks down at her hands, unsmiling.

"You must have some inside news, then?" Anna says.

"Not really. We need an east wind to take the ash out over the Atlantic, but at the moment it's hanging around, easing south and west if anything."

"Plenty of work for you, I'd have thought."

"Yes, an unexpected silver lining. But I'd rather be going back."

"To the UK?"

"To London, yes. I've done my stint on Lithuanian tourism for now."

The other men are now deep in conversation, speaking in low voices, their heads close. Gavin's wife flicks through a magazine, ignoring them; the Russian girl stares at her fingernails in her lap, her face blank. Her nails are long and manicured with dark purple varnish. It contrasts oddly with the delicacy of her fingers. Anna, noting the curve of her narrow neck, wonders again how old she is. When young girls dress like women, it's hard to tell.

"Do you know these people?" Anna says to Will, keeping her voice down.

He shakes his head, looks sideways at her as if reading

her mind. "No, we've just met. I have a habit of talking to everyone. Though these guys clearly have business to do." He flicks his eyes towards the men without moving his head. They are oblivious.

"Yes. Not for our ears, that's for sure."

When she finishes her drink and excuses herself, he stands and gives a small half-bow, smiling.

"Maybe see you again," he says.

"Maybe," she says, smiling back. "It's all down to the volcano."

*

When she sees the picture, she almost stops breathing. The girl smiles into the camera, her dark hair lifted by a breeze, her skin clear, luminous. She's young, full of life, carefree. She wears a white vest, the straps bright against the bones of her shoulders. Her eyes are narrowed against the glare of the sun. She holds one hand up as if to shield her face from the brightness; a shadow falls across her forehead.

For a moment she thinks she knows her. There's something about the angle of her head, the curve of her smile. She can't be more than sixteen or seventeen, her skin fresh and unlined, but there's a knowing look about her stare, a maturity in her eyes.

Her fingers shaking, Anna copies the story into a translation site and the words come alive.

Girl's body washes up on Kuronian Spit
The body of a young girl was discovered by a walker on a deserted stretch of beach at the Kuronian Spit on Tuesday. Police attended the scene and parts of the beach were closed off while a search was conducted. The body is believed to be that of Margryta Simonis, who was sixteen years old.

Ms Simonis, whose parents live nearby in Klaipeda,

*was known to have been working in Vilnius in recent
months. Cause of death is yet to be established.*

She's struck by the brevity of the piece. It's hard to
believe there are many unexplained deaths in a small place
like Klaipeda, and this was a child, washed up on a desolate
beach. A child. So precious to someone; a mother broken, out
of her mind grieving somewhere, a father, perhaps siblings,
friends too.

Surely this is an important story? It seems so strange. A
dead body washing up on a beach is chilling enough, but this
beach is miles from civilisation. Surely this is suspicious: a
terrible accident, suicide, perhaps even murder? Anna's not
given to melodrama, but this has to be wrong, so little space
given to the story compared with the many columns, over
many days, about the volcano.

It's tragic, seeing that young face: living, in a photograph,
and dead, in her mind's eye. She tries to remember who she
saw while she was at the hotel. There were certainly no young
people there. Perhaps she drowned, her body taken far from
the place where she died by deep, unseen currents. There's
so little information in the story, nothing about how she died,
what she was doing with her short life before it was snatched
away from her. She was only sixteen years old.

The outline of the girl's face softens through the hot mist
of Anna's tears.

*

The next day brings no further news on flights, and she spends
it working. Late in the afternoon, she walks around the city
to get some fresh air, but it's cold and drizzly and she soon
returns to the warmth of the hotel bar. As she approaches,
she's relieved to see Gavin and Charlotte leave with their
Russian friends, climbing into a taxi at the door.

The waiters fuss around, wiping the polished wood in

24

front of her and ordering each other around. She asks for a coffee, and when it arrives, a small glass of spirit appears from nowhere: "Complimentary, madam."

She's absorbed in watching the barman prepare some drinks, playing to his audience with theatrical gestures, when Will appears beside her and orders a glass of wine. "Would you like anything?" he says, turning to Anna.

"No, I'm fine, thanks." The waiter, seeing they've struck up a conversation, puts a second glass in front of her and hovers over it with a wine bottle, his eyebrows raised.

"Come on. You can't go home so there's no hurry, is there?" Will says, with a smile.

She relents. "Okay then. But I'm buying it."

"No problem," Will says. "Would you like to join me? I'm beginning to get bored with my own conversation." He executes a half-formal bow.

She carries her coffee and wine to a nearby table, where Will's laptop sits open. He closes it, puts it away.

"I've had enough of checking the news and the airlines," he says. "Not much point now, it's too late. I'll have another go in the morning."

"Do you need to get back urgently?"

"No, not really. I can work and file my pieces from anywhere there's a signal. It's being stuck that's annoying." He sips his wine. The skin on the back of his hand is smooth, the hairs on his wrist soft, like a boy's.

"So you're making the most of the situation, with your 'man on the ground' status?"

"I've done a couple of pieces. I need to go to the airport, see if I can find some interesting people to interview. I've got *The Times* waiting, if I can drum something up." He smiles and shrugs. "It's actually not that dramatic being stuck somewhere, is it? It would be much more interesting being in Iceland right now."

"You'd be pretty stuck if you were there, and covered in ash, to boot."

"True, but it must be a fascinating place, I'd love to go. All that bleak volcanic scenery and weather."

*

Talking to Will, Anna loses track of time, helped by the flow of wine from the barman. To soak some of it up, they order bread with olive oil and vinegar and nibble their way through an entire basket, the crumbs spilling onto the table around their glasses. She doesn't feel drunk; perhaps a little soft around the edges, but in no sense out of control.

She hasn't told anyone yet about the girl on the beach. She wants to forget, not to revisit the experience, or deal with other people's shocked reactions. But the image of the dead girl stalks her, flashing before her eyes when she least expects it.

Will asks her how she liked Klaipeda. It means only one thing to Anna now.

"It's a nice place, but…"

"But?"

"Something pretty horrible happened when I was there," she says, lowering her voice. "I found a body. A young girl." To her surprise, her voice falters. Just saying it has brought it all back. "She was on the beach, half in the sand."

"You found a dead girl? That is terrible," he says, concern reflected in his eyes. A small part of her notes how beautiful they are, deep, chocolate brown, full of empathy.

"Not quite the experience I was looking for on my holiday," she says, grimacing.

He nods and takes a gulp of wine, tidies the breadcrumbs into a small pile. "I think I'd be pretty traumatised if something like that happened to me."

"I can't get her out of my head. She was very young, her eyes were open. She looked… lost." She shakes her head, as if to dispel the image.

"Poor girl. Was there anyone else around? I mean, did you see anything suspicious?"

It's an interesting question. The idea she might have been in danger just hasn't occurred to her until now. "No, I'm pretty sure there was nobody there. The weather was foul, the beach was completely empty. She could have been there for hours. I nearly didn't see her. I'd already walked past the spot once and hadn't noticed anything."

He puffs out his cheeks and blows, shakes his head. For a moment he looks lost in thought, the smile gone. "What an experience. How were the police?"

"They were remarkably quick, actually." She plays with the stem of her wine glass, the scene at the hotel filling her mind.

"Did they give you a grilling?"

"No more than I would expect. I couldn't really help them. Which is good, in a way, at least they let me leave."

"So you didn't go back with them? To the spot where you found her?"

"No, they didn't need me to. It's a very long beach, but they only needed to track the shoreline to find her. She must have washed up from the sea. I wonder what happened to her."

"You never know, do you," he says. "Lithuania seems so quiet, almost boring. But you only need to scratch the surface…"

She's about to ask what he means when he excuses himself and heads for the men's room.

*

A group of people gathers at the bar, close to where Anna is sitting. Young girls in tight dresses and impossibly high heels, men in tight suits. The bar seems suddenly very full, noisy and hot.

There are four girls, all with long hair and heavily made up, their eyes smoky, their lips glossy and bright. Anna catches a heady whiff of perfume. Two of the men are leaning on the bar when the girls arrive with a flurry of kisses, hugs and exclamations. Two more men arrive shortly afterwards.

The women are young – early twenties, possibly younger – the men more like late thirties or forties. They all seem to be speaking Lithuanian, the odd word or phrase of English resonating strangely mid-sentence. Anna has always found this disconcerting; the flow of language disrupted by the banal sound of an English word: internet, World Cup, breakfast.

She's fascinated by the interaction within the group. The girls, young and beautiful, their clothes flimsy and revealing, smiling and laughing while the men touch their waists, stroke their arms. The champagne flows. She wonders if it's a celebration of some sort, then she begins to suspect the girls are escorts, perhaps even prostitutes, though she's loath to label them. She's pretty sure some of the group haven't met before. One of the girls seems shy and a little uncomfortable with the attention. She flinches when one of them strokes her neck. He doesn't remove his hand.

By the time Will reappears, the men are gesturing to the bar staff for their coats.

"I've been people-watching. What do you make of them?" She glances towards the bar and Will swivels slightly to take in the group. The men hold out coats for the girls in a gesture of exaggerated formality, the girls laughing and swaying slightly as they fumble with the sleeves.

The smile fades from Will's eyes. "You see the same thing all around Europe. Girls coming further west, from the former Soviet Union countries. Young girls, powerful men. Could be legit. Probably not."

"What does that mean?"

"It means there's a lot of exploitation going on. When the country's poor, the women and children bear the brunt."

The group's heading for the door now, the men smiling. Their polite gestures seem to Anna to be hiding something much more threatening. She resists an urge to intervene, to tell the girls to watch out, they're in bad company. They would surely laugh at her.

"Very often, the girls are desperate to get out," Will says, his eyes also drawn to the group. "Sometimes they're conned by scum who pretend they'll get them jobs or a rich husband. But they end up as slaves or in forced prostitution. Sometimes even dead, like—"

"Like my girl?" Somehow, importantly, the body on the beach belongs to Anna.

"It's much worse than you'll ever read about." He stabs at the ice in his drink with a cocktail stick; the table wobbles.

"Human trafficking, you mean?"

"Yes, and all the other crimes which surround it. Often the girls get dragged in, thinking they're going to better themselves."

"How do you know so much about it?"

"A fellow journalist takes an interest, that's all. He's written quite a lot on the issue."

The bar is eerily quiet now that the group has left. Rain lashes at the glass of the hotel door, bright flashes of headlights magnified in the dark puddles on the pavement outside.

"Do you think my girl was trafficked?"

"We can't assume that, and it's almost certain we'll never know."

His expression is guarded.

"Really? Why not? The police were there, and it did get into the news. It must have been murder. Surely they'd take that seriously?"

"It was in the news, briefly. It's the fickle nature of the media. Pages of coverage and broadcast time dedicated to the volcano. A mention in a Lithuanian newspaper about a body on the beach. It's tragic, but the volcano affected many more people than the death of a teenage girl, and a lot of money was lost because of it. It's all about money, when you come down to it. In some ways, they – we, the media – are as guilty as the traffickers."

"What makes you think those people were like that?" she says, nodding towards the door.

"I don't know, they could be perfectly respectable. But I've learned that very often things are not what they seem."

*

She's about to ask him what he means, but stops at the sight of Gavin squeezing the swell of his stomach past the diners on his way towards them.

"We meet again," he says, his lips curling into the semblance of a smile. Charlotte, in vibrant blue silk, drifts towards the bar. Anna is glad there's nowhere for them to sit.

"No luck getting home, then?" Gavin says. The question is aimed at them, though his eyes rove around the room as if he has no interest in their reply.

"Not yet. Just waiting it out," she says. She senses Will tense at her side. He makes a sign to the barman to get the bill.

"Actually we're just leaving," he says. "You can have our table."

She hesitates for just a second, before reaching for her bag under the chair and rising, Will ahead of her.

They pay up at the bar, the waiters and bar staff exhorting them to return the following day. Captive tourists are good for business.

"That was a bit sudden," she says, as they leave. "I take it you didn't want to talk to those two?"

"He's an arse."

She laughs. "Glad you like him."

They walk together to the lift.

"See you, then," he says as the doors part for her on the first floor.

"Quite possibly." She returns his smile.

The doors close with a gentle swoosh.

*

She's late getting up and there's an unpleasant dryness in her mouth. Last night she'd relaxed too much, drunk too much wine, stayed up too late. In the night, after a couple of hours of alcohol-induced slumber, the pale face of the girl had returned, haunting her until the early hours. Now she's wrung out and shaky from lack of sleep.

She makes coffee and climbs back into bed with her laptop, searches the news.

There's little to report on the ash cloud. It's moving slowly, but flights are still grounded all across Europe. She searches for the story of the girl, but there's nothing new. Frustrated, she flicks her laptop closed with a snap and stands, stretching out the stiffness in her back. Her stomach growls. She needs to get some breakfast.

As the lift doors open to the foyer, she spots Will, heading for the hotel entrance, wrapped up for the weather in a coat and scarf. She's about to call out to him when he's joined by another man, who greets him with a friendly clap on the shoulder before they enter the revolving door to the street. It's then that she realises, with a jolt, that the other man is Gavin.

CHAPTER 3

Anna likes men, their quick humour and their confidence. Since her divorce she's met many, but invariably they want more than she can give. She doesn't want a 'partner' in her life, she tells them, but too often they just don't believe her. A long time ago, when she got married, she thought that was what she wanted and for a short time perhaps it was true.

But when it went wrong – so badly wrong, and of her own doing – she decided that marriage and commitment of the relationship sort were not for her.

She's happy with her work and proud of her success. She likes men and she likes sex with them, but that's as far as she'll let it go. They're often affronted by her straightforward, not unkind, rejection of them for any future relationship.

In one interesting, typically short-lived, encounter, the man was taken aback when she said she wasn't interested in planning a future with him.

"But why not?" he said. "I tick all the boxes, don't I?"

"Depends what boxes you mean," she'd replied, knowing exactly what he meant. He was solvent, in fact wealthy, had a beautiful house, an apartment in the south of France, a good job, a smart car. Divorced, with children, whom he saw every other weekend and holidays twice a year. And he was a kind man, generous, sometimes funny. She liked him.

But it would take a lot for Anna to share her life. She's ambitious for her company. She has her freedom. She has no children and nobody is dependent on her. She's not going to risk it again.

*

In the bar, Will's at the same table. He pulls out a chair for her.

"Becoming a bit of a habit," she says. "How was your day?"

"Pretty tedious. You feeling any better?"

She's been feeling pretty grim all day. "Not much sleep, no. Maybe it's to be expected."

"You'll be better once you get back to England."

"I really hope so. Lack of sleep is so debilitating." She takes a long sip of wine, waits a moment for its warmth to spread through her. "I saw you with Gavin."

"Yes. He's still an arse."

"I'm sure he likes you too," she says, laughing.

"What do you think they do for fun?" he says. "Charlotte looks a bit grim."

"I had quite an awkward encounter with her in the ladies. Treated me like her new best friend. She insisted on telling me how they can't have children, they're thinking of adoption. Why would she tell me that? I'm a complete stranger to her."

"Perhaps she needs someone to confide in," Will says. "He doesn't strike me as a good listener."

"Or as good father material."

He smiles. "You never know. Perhaps he has a feminine side."

"I imagine she's a bored housewife. She probably makes cupcakes while he's playing golf. Do you think they're swingers?"

That smile again. His teeth are straight and white. "Not a good image. She's orange."

"Perhaps she eats too many carrots. They turn you orange if you overdo it."

33

"Huh. So what do I look like?"

She sits back and looks at him, imagining she's only just seen him. "Poker professional? Internet entrepreneur?"

He laughs. "Interesting. Name?"

She thinks for a moment, then says, straight-faced: "Tarquin."

His laugh is soft, infectious. "You're joking. Oh, you are joking. Thank God. Sorry to disappoint, though."

"Don't worry, I couldn't take anyone seriously if their name was Tarquin. Especially if they were a poker player."

"Glad to hear you take me seriously."

"I didn't say that…"

She takes a sip of wine, sits back in her chair and smiles at him.

*

When she wakes, the flat light of day falling on her pillow, it's late and he's gone. She squints sleepily at the empty space where he lay, lies still, remembering.

They'd talked until the early hours. He'd asked if she was married or with someone.

"No, neither," she'd said.

"Why not?"

"Why should I be?"

He shrugged. "There's no 'should' about it. I thought you would be though."

"I was married, some years ago, but it didn't work out."

"Sorry."

"Don't be. There were no children. He's remarried, which is fine." She picked at her index finger, a habit left over from childhood. "What about you, do you have anyone special?"

"Not right now. There was someone, but…" A shadow passed across his face, his eyes dropping from hers.

"But?"

"She died."

"I'm so sorry. Was she ill?" She said it gently, not wanting to stir up painful feelings.

"No. It's a long story." His voice dipped. The subject was closed.

"But," he said, the darkness lifting. "I'd like to get married one day, have children, settle somewhere. Did you want children?"

"Not at the time." It was the truth, if brutal. There was evidence to prove it.

"Do you now then?" he said. She noticed the tiny black flecks in the deep brown of his eyes.

Usually she would have bridled at such an intrusive question, from a man she hardly knew. But Will seemed different, his interest genuine. "I'm not the motherly kind," she'd said, avoiding his eyes. "Anyway, it's too late now."

"What? You're kidding me."

"No need to flatter me. I'm not sensitive about my age. I'm forty-five. And happy with my crow's feet."

"I wasn't flattering you. I would have put you a lot younger than that."

Ignoring the compliment, she said: "And you? You're just a whippersnapper, aren't you?"

"I wouldn't say that. I'm twenty-eight. Almost twenty-nine." He sounded like a small boy trying to impress.

She smiled. "Twenty-eight and three-quarters?"

"Stop it. Okay, I'm a bit younger than you. But I don't think age matters. If you're going to click with someone, you just do, doesn't matter how old they are, where they're from or what they think of global warming."

"It might matter about global warming if they have a diametrically opposite view from yours and you're passionate about it."

"You know what I mean."

"I do, yes."

"For example, if I found you attractive, your age wouldn't bother me."

She nodded, refused to acknowledge the obvious opening. "Good. Glad we sorted that one out."

He looked at her, a smile playing around his eyes but his mouth in a serious line. "And the clicking?"

Now he was probing.

"I'm not sitting here with you and a glass of wine because I want to be bored, let's put it that way."

"I'll take that as a click then."

When they'd finally left the bar, a little drunk, they walked together to the elevator, their shoulders touching. But as the doors closed with a swish, Anna felt the blood drain from her face, her legs weaken. Images of Margryta, those eyes, the white of her skin, flashed before her like leaves in a storm, one minute there, the next whipped away. Her balance gone, she fell against the metal wall, weak with fear, her bag and coat abandoned at her feet. When the doors opened, her legs wouldn't hold her weight and she began to sink to the floor. She was dimly aware of Will's voice, concerned, calling her name, his arms around her as he helped her out of the lift. At her door he took her key and guided her in.

"I'm getting you some water," he said as she sank on to the bed, head in hands. He sat next to her while she drank, his arm around her shoulders. Her hands shook each time she lifted the glass.

She jumps at a loud tap on the door, pulling herself from her reverie. Tightening her robe, she peers through the eyehole and sees Will's white T-shirt, a meaningless American slogan crawling across his chest. She opens the door a crack.

"Shouldn't open the door to just anybody, especially wearing that," he says.

"I didn't. I saw that t-shirt and couldn't resist."

As he walks in, he takes her arm and hugs her. It's such a natural gesture, it leaves her bemused; she'd expected awkwardness, even coldness. But his gentle hug and kiss on the top of her head have a strange effect on her. His charm disarms her.

"Listen, I'm so sorry about last night," she says. "That's never happened to me before. And thank you so much for looking after me. I don't know what would have happened if you hadn't been there."

He waves his arm, dismissing the apology. "Nothing to be sorry about. You had a panic attack, which is completely understandable given what's happened to you. And the lack of sleep."

"And wine. Probably should have left that out of the equation," she says, remembering with a grimace.

"I think you needed it."

"Perhaps. Anyway, I'm very grateful. And, as far as I remember, you were a perfect gentleman, to boot." He'd helped her undress as far as her underwear, had done the same himself and they'd climbed into bed. He'd held her close until she'd slept. And she had slept. No haunting images had disturbed her.

"Where did you go?" she says.

"Did you miss me?" He holds up a bulging paper bag. "Breakfast. We missed it."

"You spoil me," she says, laughing.

"That's just the way I am… Generous to a fault. Where's the coffee then?"

"I'll do the coffee, you sort out the rest," she says. "How do you like it?"

"With you, of course."

"Flatterer. Bet you say that to all the girls."

"I do. Not to all the older women though."

"Ha. Very funny."

*

As they finish their breakfast, he sits gazing at her for a moment, then takes her hand and leans forward. "Are you feeling better?" His eyes are on hers, questioning, serious.

She looks back at him but says nothing, understanding.

"Come here then," he says, as if she's spoken.

She revels in his leanness, the hard muscles of his stomach and arms, the curve of his buttocks. The blinds are half closed, the daylight soft around them as they move against each other. She closes her eyes as he kisses her neck, then moves down her body, his tongue tracing a path over her belly. She trembles, her heart pounding, her skin tingling at his touch. His tongue searches, explores, insists, then flicks and caresses until she cries out as her body stretches to its limits, pushes and shudders against him.

*

"Turn left here," he says.

They're heading for the airport, where Will wants to interview stranded travellers. Anna's driving, to keep him company, though the truth of it is, she doesn't want to let him go. But as soon as the airport doors open, she wishes she'd stayed behind. It's chaos. There are people everywhere: asleep on the floor, queuing at information desks. All the tables are strewn with dirty coffee cups and mounds of half-eaten meals. The air hums with anxiety. Will looks around, identifying his targets.

"I think I'll leave you to it," she says, stopping before they enter the thick of the seating area where people loll like stranded seals. "I'm going to go and find a quiet place to sit."

"I doubt there is one, but go ahead. I shouldn't be too long, it depends a bit on what I get."

"No problem. Text me when you're done."

He heads off towards a dejected family huddled on a small bench. She takes the escalator to the next level and soon finds what she's looking for. The executive lounge is almost empty, though refreshments are laid out as they would be on a normal day of travel. She settles down on a sofa with a cup of coffee and an English newspaper.

There are pages of reports from all over Europe on the

effects of the ash cloud. She's immediately engrossed, though there's nothing in the editorials to give her hope. Speculation is rife, but there's no new information about when the ash cloud might disperse.

And there's absolutely nothing about the discovery of a dead girl on the Baltic coast.

*

Outside the lounge, she stops briefly to text Will and ask how long he'll be. She stands for a few moments looking over the balcony at the mayhem below: bodies everywhere, bags strewn, bins overflowing. The air is tainted with the tang of sweat and stale food. At the information desks, airline staff squat in front of screens and long queues of people stream across the concourse. Announcements disturb the air: no luggage to be left unattended, please leave the fire exits clear.

She wanders through the upper level, the corridors stretching white and shiny along walls of closed doors, not a seat in sight.

At the other end of the upper level she pauses again to look out over the ground floor. Will's there, huddled in a corner of a bar, which crouches at the edge of the enormous room. He's talking animatedly to a suited man next to him, a black briefcase at his feet. He listens and nods from time to time. From a distance he looks like the Russian from the hotel. She wonders why Will would want to interview him; he's not a typical British holidaymaker. Although he's saying very little, it's Will who seems to be giving the interview.

As she watches, they finish their conversation. The man claps Will on the shoulder and stands, giving him a casual wave as he walks away. She waits for Will to check his phone, but instead he sits there for a while, hunched in contemplation over a coffee cup, seemingly oblivious to all that's going on around him.

She dials his number.

"Hey," he says. "Where are you?"

"Look up. Have you finished?" The figure below looks up and waves, hopping down from the stool.

"Yeah, just about. Come down and we'll get out of this chaos."

*

From the hotel room, she calls Jane again.

"So I've booked you onto flights tomorrow, Wednesday and Thursday. Surely one of them will go. I stopped there as I didn't want to waste too much money…"

"No, that's okay, thanks. We'll just have to keep our fingers crossed. Let me know as soon as there's anything."

"Of course. Don't worry, the company's still running."

By six o'clock it's raining and she's feeling stir-crazy. The weather in Vilnius, which suited her mood at the coast, makes everything harder. To go out she needs a coat, hat, scarf, and even then walking around is unpleasant, battling against the gusty wind and rain.

She's relieved when Will comes in search.

"This is beginning to get to me," she says. "No, correction… Total understatement. I'm probably the most impatient person in the world and I'm acting true to form. Sitting around doing nothing is my idea of hell."

"Let's go," he says.

"Where? What?"

"I know a little place…" he sings. "Come on, it's great fun, especially when the weather's bad."

The 'little place' doesn't look from the outside as if it's going to be great fun. Anna looks with a dubious eye at the rickety stairs and faded curtains and wonders where he's brought her. But inside a smiling Lithuanian couple greet Will warmly. He introduces them to Anna and they kiss her multiple times on each cheek. It's impossible to stay bad-tempered in the face of such a welcome.

40

The room is warm and bright, filled with colourful cushions and rugs; strange artefacts and bric-a-brac hang everywhere. A smiling waiter, talking incessantly, places a bottle of wine and a carafe of water on their table and pours them a drink. Food appears – there's no menu – raw vegetables, full of colour, dips in tiny bowls, a bread basket. People arrive and are fussed around and soon the four or five tables are full of laughing, eating, drinking people. In the corner someone starts to play the violin.

Anna glances at Will, who sits smiling at her, watching her reactions.

"Thank you for bringing me here," she says. "It's great. Sorry to be grumpy."

"Any particular reason? Apart from finding a dead body on a beach, being stuck somewhere you don't want to be, the work piling up, the prospect of a painful journey back, and, and…"

"All that, I suppose. Frustrating not being able to do anything about it."

He nods. "It's easier for me, I get good work from all this, even though it's news reporting, which isn't normally my thing."

"Did you get much joy at the airport?" she says, dipping her bread and savouring the olive taste bursting on her tongue.

"I spoke to a few people, got some views. Some strong opinions, as expected. Some of the airlines don't handle this kind of crisis at all well. People are rightfully angry. Thanks for the lift, it must have been pretty boring for you."

She reaches across for a dish piled high with vegetables. "I amused myself with the newspapers. So much coverage of the volcano, the ash cloud, the grounded flights, the politicians arguing about it. Nothing about the girl on the beach."

"That's the media for you." Will starts on a plate of smoked salmon, spooning the pink flesh onto pieces of rye bread.

"It's weird. Just that first story, with the picture of her alive. Don't you think that's a bit strange? I know I have a

41

special interest in it, as I found her, but from a journalist's point of view, I would have thought it was a good story, worth a lot more space."

He smiles, a crooked bending of his mouth. "As a journalist, I would agree. But as an editor, there's more money in volcanoes. Hurts more people in the pocket." He shrugs. "But I'm just a cynical journalist."

"Really? So they won't cover it again?"

"News stories have a limited life. It was probably on the local TV station – and there might be more in the press later, when they find more evidence – but the story might not reappear until they find out what happened. If they find out."

"I can't stop thinking about it. Her poor mother... To lose her daughter like that." She realises with a shock that her voice is shaking. "And she looks – looked – so different. So young, just a child. I suppose I shouldn't be surprised really, but I hardly recognised her."

"No. A dead body really isn't the person who lived." A shadow, fleeting, touches his eyes. It's gone so fast she's not sure what she saw.

*

A full week later than planned, Anna takes an early flight to Heathrow.

Will says: "I'll come and see you."

She says: "Yes."

She has no expectations, but this simple exchange makes her feel good. Thrown together in adversity, she thinks wryly as the plane's engines settle to a gentle thrum. She's flying back at last.

CHAPTER 4

The text lands with a gentle ping as she works. She ignores it, absorbed in a complicated spreadsheet which makes her head ache.

The second ping demands her attention.

She glances over at it, reading glasses perched on the end of her nose.

Up for a visit this weekend? Will x

"Oh," she says out loud. This is unexpected.

"What?" Jane asks.

"Oh, nothing. Just an unexpected text."

She hasn't told anyone about Will. It's three weeks since she returned and she has barely thought about him.

But she feels a prickle of excitement as she texts back: *Okay, come Saturday. Need me to pick up from train station? X.* She turns the sound off on her mobile and carries on working with half an eye on the small screen as it lies by her computer. After a few minutes, she's rewarded.

Arrive 4.00, see you then. Book dinner x

*

He appears at the station on time and just as she remembers him. Her stomach does a tiny flip when she sees him stride confidently out of the station and look round for her car.

He opens the passenger door and folds his body into the front seat. She leans towards him, breathing in the smell of his skin. He kisses her softly on the lips, holds her face in his hands. She's charmed all over again, tipped off-balance by the intimacy of his touch.

Then he smiles and says: "Come on then, let's go."

She gathers herself and starts the car.

*

They sit in a quiet corner in a café. Will draws his chair closer to hers as soon as the waitress leaves.

He's been back to Lithuania, briefly, to report on the aftermath of the flight ban, though in the event there wasn't much to report. Things have got back to normal remarkably quickly; It's the fallout for the airlines and the insurance companies that will take months to resolve.

It takes her a while to introduce the subject. But he's still the only person she's confided in, so the only one who understands.

"Will, I can't stop thinking about Margryta. I see her all the time, at night, in the street, in a magazine. It's like she's stalking me. And there's still nothing in the news. Did you hear anything while you were there?"

"Nothing, but I wasn't looking, to be honest. I'm not surprised you keep thinking about her. It was a traumatic experience."

A young girl arrives with their coffees, placing the cups and saucers carefully in front of them.

"I wish I'd seen more, been more aware of where I was walking," Anna says, taking a sip of coffee. It's bitingly hot and she licks her burning lip distractedly. "If I could remember something, at least I could go to the police with it. But my mind's a blank. The beach seemed to go on forever and I didn't really look, the weather was so bad. What do you think happened to her?"

He shrugs. "Who knows? Could have been any number of things. But I'm glad you didn't see anything, it might have been dangerous for you."

"It seems like nobody's interested. It's not right." She sighs, the memory of the girl still fresh in her mind.

"Honestly, Anna, I know you're feeling bad." He takes her hands in his. "It's not surprising. But I would leave it to the police. You can't be any help to them if you saw nothing."

"I can't just leave it at that, though. Perhaps I'll give them a call."

"Don't." His voice is serious now and there's a hint of concern around his eyes. "Believe me, Anna, there are good reasons why you mustn't. There's a lot of very nasty organised crime around. Drugs, money laundering, people trafficking. You only need to scratch the surface and a lot of horrible nasties can crawl out and bite you."

She stirs her coffee to cool it down, takes a sip from the edge with her spoon. The more she thinks about it the more she wants to find out.

"Please, Anna, take my advice," Will says. "It's not a good idea. Don't go to the police." His voice takes on a hard edge, startling her.

"Wait, are you implying the police are corrupt? Or involved?" She's had little or no dealings with the police in Lithuania, but knowing a little of the country's history, she can imagine they might be somewhat different from the police at home.

"It wouldn't be that unusual."

"Right. And the media?"

"Them too."

*

"Come on," says Kate, plumping herself down, her cup tilting. "Spill."

They're in the local coffee shop, stealing a quick break from work, mid-afternoon.

"I assume you mean Will?" she says.

"Stop being prim and spill the beans, before I have to take a half-day off work."

She gives in. "There's not that much to tell. We had a good weekend, got on well, he went back. We didn't arrange anything else."

"Sex?"

"Yes."

"Anna... give over."

She leans forward and speaks in a low, conspiratorial voice. "It was very good, thank you."

"Lucky you. Spoils of war, I suppose. You had to go all the way to Lithuania and get stuck there to find the perfect toy boy."

Anna laughs. "I know you're doing your best to wind me up. There's no need, I'm not going to give you the satisfaction. I don't care. It works for me and I'm fine if it ends here. Though actually..."

"What?"

"I would miss the mind-blowing sex..."

She's known Kate since her early twenties. A few years younger than Anna, Kate is confident and robustly feminist, with a great job in airline PR, a stay-at-home garden designer husband, Graham, and two small children. They seem to have the perfect partnership and Anna loves them both.

"Do you think you'll see him again?"

"Probably. He travels a lot, which suits me fine, and he knows I'm a workaholic. But he's a good guy, I like him. Actually, I really like him. We'll see."

She plays with her teaspoon, collecting up the last of the cappuccino bubbles from the sides of the mug. They pop gently on her tongue. It's true, she does really like Will, though it's the first time she's admitted it.

"He wants to settle down, have children." There's a cynical gleam in Kate's eyes. "No – not with me, specifically, and not now – just generally."

Kate nods. "As long as he knows who you are, then."

Anna laughs. Kate is probably the only person who knows who she really is.

"Something else happened while I was in Lithuania, though," she says. "It's really bothering me." Kate stares at her in surprise; Anna's not given to admitting her feelings. "I was at this beautiful place on the beach, really remote, on the Kuronian Spit, on the Baltic Sea. It's wild in winter, empty, no houses or cafés or anything. I walked there every day, in the rain and the snow. The weather was terrible, but it did me a lot of good. One morning…" She pauses, the scene vivid in her mind – the hard sand, the freezing whip of the wind around her face, her feet plodding – "I was out walking. It was blowing a gale and raining. I'd walked a long way. There are next to no landmarks on that beach so I don't have any idea how far I went. I had my hood up, a scarf and a hat round my ears and face and I could barely keep my eyes open against the wind. But I stumbled across a dead body."

Kate's eyes widen further and Anna can hear her sharp intake of breath. "Oh, my God, Anna."

"Yes. What made it worse was that it was a young girl, only in her teens. She was just lying there in the surf and seaweed. It was just by chance I noticed her."

"What a terrible thing to happen. You must have been horrified. What did you do?"

"I ran, as fast as I could, along the beach and back to the hotel. They called the police and that was that."

"What do you mean, that was that? Did they find her? Do you know who she was?"

"They found her. They interviewed me, though I didn't have much to say. I didn't see anything. I've racked my brain but the weather was so bad, I really wasn't paying much attention. She was only sixteen, Kate." There's a slight wobble in her voice as she meets Kate's shocked eyes. She's surprised again at the power of the memory to shake her, breathes in deeply to steady herself. "The media didn't give it much attention. It was right in the middle of the fuss about the volcano."

"Wow. I think I need another cup of coffee after that."

Kate rises, goes to the counter. Anna sits, playing with her teaspoon, the image of Margryta's staring eyes taunting her, only retreating when Kate sets a steaming cup of coffee down in front of her. She removes the used one and putting it on the next table.

"Are you okay?" Kate's concern is reassuring. Anna's been wondering if she was overreacting, if she was making the event into something bigger than it was.

"Yes, I mean, I can't stop thinking about her, but I'm okay. I'd really like to find out what happened to her, though. Somehow, seeing her like that... I feel connected to her now, whether I like it or not."

As she says it she realises it's true. She needs to find out what happened to Margryta Simonis, despite what Will says.

*

Margryta haunts her, in her waking hours and in the night. The terrible image of the young girl, her eyes empty, cold and lifeless on the deserted beach keeps coming back to her, sometimes when she least expects it.

She prints off the newspaper story with the photograph of Margryta, vital and alive. She tapes the cutting to the fridge door in her kitchen. She wants to see the girl as she was, alive, not as a lifeless body.

Despite Will's warnings, she must do something to find out what's happening. Going to the police is the obvious next step; she found the body, after all. What good it will do, she doesn't know, but the story has a grip on her and she can't escape it.

She stares out of the window of her office onto the busy street below, listening to Jane as she tries to make herself understood on the phone. After a couple of minutes Jane slams the phone down and collapses back into her chair. "Crap connection," she says at Anna's look. "And I couldn't understand a word of what the guy was saying. I'm taking a break. Cup of tea?"

"Sure." Anna's mobile buzzes. It's her mother.

"Can you come over later?" Her mum's voice is almost a whisper, as if she's trying not to be heard. "Dad's not feeling too well, it'll cheer him up to see you."

A prickle of concern focuses her attention on her mum's voice.

"What's up?"

"He's got a bit of a cold, his breathing's not good. He can hardly get to the bottom of the garden. What time will you come?"

"After supper. I'm not going to get away from work until then anyway."

She cuts the call with a sinking feeling. As an only child with elderly parents, she's beginning to feel the responsibility. So far she's avoided the subject of care, but if one or both of them becomes seriously ill, there is no way she can look after them herself. It would mean giving up the business — and anyway, she'd be no good at it. She's going to have to talk to them, sooner rather than later, about their options.

*

At the hospital they carry out multiple tests on her father's heart, feed him antibiotics and force him to rest. The doctor isn't taking any risks, and keeps him in for a week.

Back at home, her father recovers slowly. Though his breathing is still laboured, the colour is back in his face and he's a little more cheerful when Anna visits. She's relieved to find him up and about, though resting on a lounger in the garden, a blanket around his shoulders. When she steps outside, he stands up and the blanket falls to the ground. She stoops to pick it up and tries to rearrange it around his thin shoulders, but he waves her away and sits back down heavily.

"Don't fuss, please," he says, his words clipped short with irritation. "I'm fine now, just a bit of a cough."

"That's good, but please don't overdo it," she says. "I'm

away for a couple of days and I don't want to have to come rushing back."

"There'll be no need for that. Mum can give me CPR." He winks.

"Don't even think about it, she'd only hurt herself as well, and then what would I do, with both of you incapacitated?"

"There's life in the old dog yet." The twinkle in his eye is belied by a fit of coughing.

"I know, Dad, but seriously, no laying flagstones on the terrace or digging up the tree stump."

"Okay, okay, less of the nagging, eh? It's bad enough with your mum."

"I'll bring you some Lithuanian honey cake back," she says. "If you're allowed that much sugar?"

"I'm sure I can squeeze a little honey cake into the diet. Do me good."

"Hm. I wouldn't want to be told off for making you worse."

"Well, we just won't tell anyone, eh?"

When she goes home, she gives him a hug. It lasts much longer than normal. Afterwards she regrets it, in case he noticed. The idea that she has limited time with her parents, that this might be the beginning of a gradual and painful leaving process, leaves a small, persistent ache in her stomach.

*

When Will says: "See you soon," it seems like he means it. An unfamiliar flush of pleasure surprises Anna when he says it. It's the first time in a long while that she's looking forward to seeing someone again. She warns herself not to make too much of it, to get into something she can't sustain. She knows she works a lot, unable to balance her life like other people.

It's one of the reasons her marriage didn't last.

A fortnight later, from Poland: *Chciałbym żebyś tu był x*
    She smiles to herself, responds: *??*
    Wish you were here… in Polish x
    You're so clever. X
    I know x
    A few days later, she receives: *Dobrý den z Prahy x*
    Show off. X
    Then, a couple of days later, his text says: *Landing at Heathrow in three hours. Can I come straight to you?* Her fingers type: *Yes* before she's even thought about it. By her calculation, he won't arrive before seven at the earliest, so she can just keep going until he gets there.

    The taxi stops outside her flat, the door slamming. She presses the buzzer to let him in, opens the door to see him bounding up the stairs two at a time. Once inside, he takes both her hands in his without a word and leads her to the bedroom.

They take turns to shower. Anna calls for a takeaway and opens a bottle.

    "It seems like ages," he says as they sit down to eat.

    "It does. You've been busy."

    "So have you." They smile at each other and raise their glasses.

    "Good trip?"

    He grimaces. "I wouldn't say good, exactly. I was supposed to be doing a piece in Poland but it didn't work out. The guy failed to turn up and my other contact was away so it was a bit of a waste of time. But I spent the time usefully, did a speculative piece which I think I can sell in to someone."

    "It must be hard when things don't work out. Do you still get paid?"

"Nope. But some of the stuff I'm doing is pretty long-term, and it'll be worth it in the end."

"Such as?"

He waves a hand, as if wafting the subject away. "Nothing particularly special; country profiles, that sort of thing."

"I thought it was tourism you were doing, mostly?"

"That's the easy end of what I do. But I prefer the more in-depth stuff, it's far more satisfying than writing about hotels and beaches." Something in his eyes has closed; he seems wary for a moment. In that moment, she remembers that she doesn't know him well. But she'd like to.

*

He stays a full week at her flat. The next time, longer. Soon he stays there more often than at his London flat, though the journey from the airport is longer.

She likes to think of him there while she's at work. He's the perfect guest: self-contained, makes no mess, and leaves nothing there when he goes travelling, apart from a few newspapers, stacked neatly for her to read. There's no pressure on her to rush back from the office. He just carries on working, or goes for a walk, or prepares supper and waits until she gets back each evening. He takes nothing for granted. He uses a spare key, normally hidden outside the door, and returns it when he goes.

She begins to look forward to going home at the end of the day. She likes his presence, their discussions, his interest in the world. She misses him when he leaves. Will is a calm presence in her frenetic life, despite his travelling. Perhaps it's because he's been to so many places, seen so many different sides of life, that he's able to take most things in his stride. He talks to everyone he meets, shows an interest in their lives beyond what Anna would have thought was required of a journalist. She admires his ability to get on with other people, his realistic attitude to life.

Surprising herself, she starts to realise she needs him around.

*

So, when a few weeks later he mentions that he has to leave his flat in London, she says without hesitation: "You can stay here, you hardly stay in London anyway. If nothing else, it could save you some money for a bit."

He shoots her a quizzical look. "I wasn't fishing. You don't have to do that, I know you like your space."

"Listen, you're easy to have around and I quite like you."

"Thanks." He smiles. "I quite like you too, and I don't want to mess up our relationship."

"Why should it mess anything up? It works well, doesn't it?" She finds herself wanting him to agree, hopes she's not sounding needy.

"Yes, but it would be quite different if I moved in. It's your home, you own it, and I'm just a guest at the moment, which works fine. You might not want my toothbrush in your bathroom permanently. Once you find out all my bad habits…" He grins and draws her to him.

"Listen, I know you're away a lot, so I'll still get plenty of time on my own. Unless you're thinking of changing your job?"

"Not at all."

"There you are then. Don't worry, I'll chuck you out if you start to annoy me."

"I'm sure you will," he says drily. It's settled.

*

He's a man of very few possessions.

"Is that it?" she says, collecting him at the station. She was worried she wouldn't have enough room in the car. But he has one suitcase and a big backpack, both of which he lifts easily into the boot. "Are you sending the rest on later?"

"There is no rest," he says. "I've been renting a furnished flat, I travel light and I don't need possessions to weigh me down."

"Fine by me," she says, smiling. She'd worried, in a moment of brief anxiety about this decision to let him in, that there wouldn't be enough room for them both, that they'd feel the pressure.

But she need not have been concerned. He hangs a few shirts and trousers neatly in the space she's left for him, folds the rest into a small chest of drawers she's emptied, places a couple of books on a shelf with hers and one on the bedside table. In the bathroom, he fills a shelf with signs of the traveller's life: lines of sample bottles of shampoo and conditioner. A bathrobe from some nameless hotel hangs on the back of the door and a shaver sits in a holder next to the basin. Some battered running shoes live by the front door. Apart from these, she barely notices he's moved in. From his possessions, anyway.

It's as if he's always been there.

CHAPTER 5

"Already?" Kate says, stirring her coffee. The café is quiet this morning and they're sitting in armchairs at the front of the shop, looking out onto a rain-splashed street. People hurry by, umbrellas misshapen in the squally wind.

"It's not that quick." She feels her shoulders tense in self-defence. "And I'm not some young thing. I have lived with someone before, you know."

"Yes, but not for years, and you didn't like it." Though Kate says it lightly, with a smile, there's a serious note in her voice.

"It wasn't that I didn't like it, as such. It didn't work out." Anna's stomach always twists at the thought. She ignores the pinprick of guilt that never quite goes away.

"And that was why?" says Kate. She never pulls her punches.

Anna grimaces. "Because I'm a selfish workaholic. But this is different. Will travels so much, and the rest of the time he works, too. He's really easy to have around, when he's there. I like it. Him."

"Are you – no, now I'm really worried – you're not falling for him, are you?" She mimes inverted commas around the words 'falling for', ruby nails flicking.

"Just stop it, before I start to get annoyed."

She's had moments of doubt, for sure, inviting him to live with her. Always mindful of her past. At times, those rare moments when being alone feels like loneliness, she reminds

55

herself she's not deserving of happiness, she'll only mess it up.

"Okay, okay. I'm not trying to be funny. I'm just concerned about you, that's all. You barely know him, and you have been a bit… different, recently."

There's not much that escapes Kate. "Different?" Anna says, though she's not surprised. Despite the passing of time, she still feels the stab of shock over the dead girl, still sees her face in the night.

"I don't know. You seem a bit down at the moment, a bit vulnerable. Are you absolutely sure about this thing with Will?"

"Look, he's a good guy and I trust him. I like living with him. That's all I'm saying. And I'm fine."

"Okay," Kate says. "I'm glad you've found someone. But when are we going to meet this elusive man? Davey and Sai are gagging for a sighting."

Davey and Sai are among Anna's closest friends. Davey, a graphic designer, is an old school friend; Sai is his partner. He's funny, feisty, Asian and a talented photographer.

"I'm sure they are," Anna says. "They'll have to wait until next week, though. Will's in Eastern Europe again, researching tourism to the former Eastern bloc, or something like that."

He's away a lot, often two weeks out of four. Anna doesn't keep track of the dates, it's too complicated, and often his schedule changes while he's away. They keep in touch when they can. Arranging a regular social life to include him is nigh on impossible. She misses him when he's away, but it gives her a chance to concentrate on work, so she can give him more time when he's back.

"Perhaps he can find us a new au pair while he's out there," Kate says, with a grimace.

"What's happened to Magdalena? I thought she'd only been with you a couple of months."

Kate sighs. "I know, but her younger sister's a problem, she's fifteen and a bit of a handful, I think. She's disappeared."

"Run away?"

"They're not sure. She was hanging out with some older kids in the village and one night she just didn't come home. It's been days now, and she's not answering her mobile. She could be with a boyfriend, but at the moment they just don't know."

"They must be really worried. What's Magdalena going to do?"

"She has to go home straight away, her mum's frantic and she's on her own. Magdalena doesn't know if or when she might be able to come back, though she loves her job with us, and we love her too. I'll just have to find someone else. Selfish of me, but it's pretty bad timing for us with the school holidays coming up."

Anna thinks, not for the first time, how different her life would be if she had children.

*

They all come to meet him, sitting around their favourite table, beer bottles and glasses already half empty. Kate and Graham, Davey and Sai. She'd hoped to get there before them, but they'd obviously had the same idea.

"Sorry," she says quietly to Will as they weave through the tables towards the group.

"It's fine," he says, flashing a smile at her. "I think I can cope."

They sit opposite each other, Will squeezing next to Kate on the bench by the wall, Anna on a chair between Graham and Sai. More glasses appear out of nowhere and wine is poured, a beer ordered for Will.

"You should be a model," Davey says to Will, without further introduction.

Will laughs. "Not sure I'd be any good at that."

"Ignore him," says Anna, nodding towards Davey. "He's a creative type. Doesn't have a clue."

"You're a journalist, I hear," says Kate.

"Yes, travel journalist. I write about places other people take their holidays. Sometimes more serious stuff like country reports, opinion-pieces maybe."

"So Anna tells me. Who do you work for?"

"Myself, actually. I'm unemployable," he says, with a smile. "Otherwise known as freelance."

Kate smiles back. "I'm in airline PR myself, so I know what it's like. It's a tough life, being wined and dined while travelling the world."

"It is. Though you don't always get to see the really interesting parts of a place."

"Like what? I think I'd be happy with the sun and the sea and the nice hotel." It's a long time since Kate has taken a proper holiday.

"Like the culture, the way people really live. You only see the happy, glamorous side, even if you know there's more to it."

"Where have you been recently, then?" They're all listening, wanting to know more about Will.

He shrugs and shifts in his seat. "The Baltics, Poland, places like that," he says. "I try to go for the unusual, not just the normal tourist destinations. It's more interesting."

"But do you think people might be hiding things from you? As a journalist, that is?" Kate says.

He hesitates. "I do, yes, sometimes. Some people are nervous around journalists, they don't want you digging around."

"What sort of things would they be hiding, though?"

"People trafficking, for one," Anna says, without thinking. It's still front-of-mind, the mystery of Margryta.

Will glances at her, hesitating, his eyes darkening. "Yes. Along with drugs, money laundering, all the usual organised crime," he says. "Actually, where I've been recently, in Eastern Europe and the Baltics, sex trafficking is a real problem."

"Huh," Kate says. "My Polish au pair just left us because they think her sister's been taken by traffickers."

"Really?" Anna says, surprised. "I thought she'd run off with a boy. Is it true? Has she been kidnapped?"

"Magdalena emailed me this morning. They don't know, but that's what they suspect. The police are working on it, and they're looking at every possibility now. The boyfriend was involved in some kind of trafficking racket. Apparently, it's not that unusual in Poland, that's why her mum was so scared."

"That's dreadful. Her poor mum," Anna says. "I can't imagine how frightened she must be." She's reminded again of Margryta's family, the devastation her death must have caused. "When I was in Lithuania last time – Kate knows this, but not the rest of you – when I was stranded there because of the volcanic ash, I found a body. A young girl, washed up on the beach." Anna says.

"Anna, that's awful!" Sai says. "What happened to her? Did she drown?"

"I don't know how she died. The police took over when they arrived and they haven't contacted me since. All there was in the press was a short report, which said nothing. But she was only sixteen when she was found, and wearing a thin dress and heels. It was hideous weather. It must have been suspicious, the beach there is long and empty, nowhere near a town or a village. I think she might have been trafficked."

"We don't know that," Will says. He looks away, rubs at his forehead as if to soothe an ache.

"You're right. It could have been anything, it's just interesting, the stories of the two girls."

*

"Don't get too excited, Mum. There are no wedding plans."

"I'm just glad you've found someone nice." But she can hear the thrill in her mother's voice.

She doesn't mention the age difference. Neither does she warn Will about her mother's obsession with getting her daughter hitched. Not to mention her lack of grandchildren.

She almost laughs at her mother's reaction when the front door opens. Will turns on his best dazzling smile and her mum is hooked. He's in shorts and trainers, though it will soon be autumn and the temperature's dropped in the last few days. He looks about twenty.

He puts her parents at ease immediately and soon he's out in the garden with Anna's father, helping to move a few things around.

"Go and get your father back in, please, Anna, he won't listen to me but it's too cold out there for him," her mother says.

Anna walks him back in. He's still pale and short of breath, and takes her arm for support without comment. They stand at the window and watch while Will carries a pot into the greenhouse at the end of the garden.

"He's a good man." A rare acknowledgement from her father.

"He is," she says. "Early days."

Her father nods.

They stay drinking coffee in the kitchen for an hour or so, Will chatting to her mum about his travels with his normal good humour.

Her father tires quickly, though. Anna goes through to the sitting room with him; he wants to rest for a while. He smiles and takes her hand. "She likes him," he says. "You need to rescue him before she gets the videos out." She laughs, pats his arm and leaves him in peace.

"They're great," says Will as they drive back.

"Sorry about the grilling from Mum."

"No, she's sweet." He leans against the passenger door, looking out into the street. "She'd love to have grandchildren, that's for sure."

"Sorry, should have warned you. She slipped that one in without me noticing. It's a pity I have no siblings to take the pressure off."

He's quiet for a while, watching as a small girl in blue jeans skips along on the pavement, curls bouncing, holding her father's hand. "It would be great to have a proper family."

"You never talk about your parents, or any siblings," Anna says. A stab of guilt reminds her she's never asked him before.

"My parents died in a car crash when I was fourteen."

"I'm so sorry." She beats herself up, in her head, for not knowing.

"It's okay. I have a brother, Josh, ten years older. He looked after me, brought me up, really. But he lives in Australia now with his family. I see him every so often, but it's not like having close relatives."

"Does that bother you?"

She pulls up outside the flat and parks the car neatly. "Not usually, I travel so much. My work doesn't sit well with too many responsibilities. Anyway, I can blag a trip to Australia to see him sometimes, all expenses paid. It has its uses, being a travel journalist."

*

The wind swirls around the trees across the road, leaves clinging with slender fingers to the whipping branches. Will sits, gazing out of the sitting-room window.

He runs his fingers through his hair and draws breath, exhaling slowly.

"I need to tell you about Olga," he says. It's a statement, not a question.

"Who's Olga?"

"My girlfriend, the one who died."

She closes her laptop, curls into a corner on the sofa.

"She was Lithuanian, about nineteen when we met, in Vilnius. I was working there for a few weeks. We met in a bar near the dive where I was staying. I went there to eat almost every day, mainly because it was cheap and cheerful and I liked the owner. Olga was there most evenings, sitting at the bar. We got talking one night, and I fell for her. She was so… alive and… beautiful."

"What happened?"

"She always seemed to be going somewhere. She'd come to the bar early, then leave, saying she was meeting friends, going dancing, always going on somewhere. She never asked me to join her." He moves closer to Anna, his arm across the back of the sofa.

"At first I didn't think about it. Naive, I know. But then I started to wonder. I wanted more time with her. One day she had a bruise on her cheek. She got angry when I asked about it. When I pushed she cried and told me what was happening to her. She was being forced to meet men, for sex, by an ex-boyfriend. This man – I think he was a lot older than Olga – was giving her money. She had a little brother, just a baby. They were very poor, they relied on the money. Her dad had left, they had very few options."

Anna takes his hand, unsure how to comfort him. "What did you do?"

"I tried to persuade her to come back with me to England, where she could get decent work, but she said she couldn't leave her family. I offered to help them, to get them away from this man who was controlling them, though I didn't have much money myself. I thought she could come back with me, we could find a flat, she could work in a café or a bar. We would have managed."

Will stands up, goes to the window and leans, his forehead against the glass. She follows and twines her arms around his chest, holding him close. They stand for a moment, silent, her head on his back, listening to the thump of his heart.

"One day she came to me excited, so happy. She'd found a job in the Netherlands, just a few weeks' work, helping a family with children. She thought it would get her away, she could stay in western Europe. She thought she could send money for her family. What she didn't say was that her ex-boyfriend was arranging it all."

She takes his hand again, draws him back to the sofa. He sits down, resting his elbows on his knees. She watches as he runs his hands through his hair.

"We had it all planned. I was going to join her in a couple of weeks, once she'd settled in, find work there to be close to her. Then we were going to try to get her a proper job, and the right papers. It all sounded plausible, and stupidly I took it all at face value. But it was all a sham. The address she gave me, in Amsterdam didn't exist, it was all made up."

"What happened? How did you find out?"

"I couldn't reach her on her mobile. Usually we talked every day, texted all the time. I went to her family's house, in a tiny village near the border with Belarus. Her mum knew something, but she was terrified, wouldn't let me in. She pushed me away and shut the door. Olga had gone. She'd just vanished. I flew to Amsterdam and went out looking for her night after night, going to the worst places, the clubs, the dives, talking to the prostitutes to see if anyone knew anything."

"Will, that's awful. Did you find her?"

He shakes his head. "I drew a complete blank. She wasn't there. I don't think she ever was. It turns out she'd been taken to Minsk, in Belarus. She was probably dead all the time I was looking." His voice is low, shaky with emotion. "Her body was found in an alley a few weeks after she disappeared. She was dumped in a rubbish bin like a piece of meat. Actual cause of death was an overdose, but there's no way it was self-administered."

Anna's feels her mouth drop. She's aghast. "She was murdered?"

"I think so. But I can't prove it."

"Did they find the ex-boyfriend?"

"I don't think they even tried. I tried myself, although I knew it was dangerous. Olga's mum wouldn't tell me anything. She probably couldn't. Nobody would help. The police wouldn't speak to me about it, either in Vilnius or in Minsk. It was a shocking cover-up."

"Oh, Will. No wonder you didn't want me to pursue the Margryta story."

He turns to face her, grasps her hand in both of his. A muscle in his cheek twitches; his mouth is a taut line. "Do you see, now, Anna? It's a horrible, brutal business. Those guys are ruthless, and the authorities do nothing to stop it happening. You must not get involved."

She imagines the girl lying naked in a dark alley, abandoned, alone, the image like a still from an old movie. She's touched by Will's openness. "So is that how you got to know that other journalist? The one who writes about trafficking?"

He nods, looking down at their interlocked hands. "Yes, his name is Mark. He was working in the area at the time as a crime reporter. He wrote the news story when her body was found. I asked him to help me find out who killed her, but we hit a brick wall."

"And what happened to Olga's family? Did you keep in touch?"

"I see them whenever I can, when I'm in the country."

"How is her mum managing?"

"I help them out sometimes, financially, that is. The ex-boyfriend backed off after Olga died, though I think he's still around. Daria, that's Olga's mum, is still too scared to talk about him. The little boy, Sasha, is about four now. He's very sweet, seems to be doing well, though it's not easy."

"It's good of you to help them."

He shrugs. "It's not much, I wish I could do more. I'm worried about her. She's not well, she has no money and she can't work and look after Sasha."

"How about we go and see her together, perhaps next time I go over? I might be able to help her too, and it would be nice to get out of Vilnius."

"I think she'd like that."

"Let's do it then. Coffee?"

As she prepares their drinks, she wonders at the order of events that have introduced her to a world she'd barely heard of just a few months ago. Magdalena's sister goes missing in Poland, kidnapped by traffickers, not long after Anna finds a body washed up on a remote beach in Lithuania. Anna meets Will, whose past is scarred by another story of a young girl caught and destroyed by a terrible web of crime. Three young girls, two dead and one missing.

"Where is Mark now? Are you still in touch?"

"We email every so often, but I haven't seen him since then. He lives in Lithuania, in the countryside near Kaunas. He married a local girl." Kaunas is where Anna's factory is located, in central Lithuania.

She takes a deep breath. "Will, I know I said I would stop. And I know this probably isn't the right time. But do you think I could contact Mark? I'd like to see what he thinks of Margryta's story. He might be able to shed some light."

Will tenses. "What is it with you, Anna?" he says, his forehead creasing. "You talk about her as if you knew her. Why don't you just leave it to the police?"

"I don't know. I just… I feel a connection. I can't get her out of my head. Perhaps it's post-traumatic stress of some kind, but I don't think I can forget her until I know what happened," she says. "Please, just let me ask him. He's in Lithuania, he must know more than I do about what goes on there. I promise I won't do anything dangerous. He probably won't know anything anyway."

Will nods, slowly. "Okay. I don't know what he's up to now, but I'll give you his email address. Just for his opinion, okay? No more than that. Please."

"I promise. And, Will, thank you for telling me about Olga. I know it was difficult for you to talk about it."

As he draws her to him, a thud of guilt reminds her of her own veiled past.

The truth waits, like a monkey on her shoulder, ready to pounce.

*

She feels strangely wrung out. With Will away, the flat feels cold and unfamiliar. She still has that dragging 'something's wrong' feeling.

Too unsettled to go to bed, she scrolls through the TV channels. A report catches her attention, about people trafficking into the Baltics. Is Will in the Baltics right now? She can't remember where he's supposed to be, but in the moment of thinking about him she misses him. She dials his number but there's no answer. She sends a text: *Call me. I miss you x*

The report plays on. Russian girls – some of them no more than children – are taken through the Baltic countries to other parts of Europe, where they're promised a better life. There they find they're prisoners, forced to work as prostitutes or housemaids to pay back extortionate amounts to the traffickers. The report says that the governments of all the countries are working together to limit the trade, though it's been going on for many decades, buried deep in the criminal underworld. Some government departments have been accused of colluding with the criminals to hide the truth.

A young girl is interviewed, sitting on a bed in a dark room. Her lank hair frames a white face, her eyes echoed by pools of darkness in the room behind her. She talks in a child's voice as an interpreter speaks over her. The flat English intonation of the voiceover does nothing to dampen the impact of the story she tells. She was taken when she was twelve, offered by her parents, out of work and desperate, to people who promised she could get hotel work in western Europe. She wanted to help her mother and father by sending money back, but she never got the chance. Her passport was taken from her, she was kept in a room with eight other girls, raped by her traffickers and forced to meet other men for sex.

She's one of the lucky ones, rescued by a charity who will help her to get home. But she's frightened of the men who took her. They've threatened her parents. They may all have to leave her home and hide. They have no money, no prospects and no hope for the future.

Margryta's face floats into Anna's mind, her eyes staring accusingly, as if reminding Anna that her murder is unresolved. Guilt stabs at her, as if she's somehow let the girl down.

She pulls up her laptop and types *People Trafficking Baltics* into the search engine. After a few clicks she's absorbed in news stories, blogs and images, headlines swimming before her. She searches back to the time when the body was found, when the volcano erupted. The original story pops up again. Then, suddenly, from a link at the bottom of the page, she spots a news report from the local TV station.

A reporter speaks to the camera, standing in a street. The picture of Margryta – the one Anna's seen before, from the newspaper – hovers in the left-hand corner of the screen, above his head. He gesticulates towards the end of the street. The scene changes. A couple sit close together on a sofa, in what looks like their sitting room, talking to someone left of camera. They hold hands. Their faces are stricken, tragic, their eyes dark with sorrow. A caption pops up underneath: *Agne and Valter Simonis*. In her other hand, the woman holds a framed picture of Margryta.

The piece lasts around three minutes. It's in Lithuanian, but she doesn't need to understand the language to know what it concerns. She checks the date. It was filmed shortly after she found Margryta. The reporter's name is Jonas Kipras. Referring back to the online story, she finds it was written by the same journalist.

She sits back in her chair, thinking. Will warned her off pursuing the story. But the strong connection she feels with the girl won't leave her. A sixteen-year-old ends up washed up on a remote Lithuanian beach. Since that first week, there's no news coverage at all. Why not? There's something horribly wrong about it.

She goes back to the original story, enlarges it and prints

off two copies. One she attaches with magnets to the upper door of her fridge, the other she places in a plastic folder, which she labels: *Girl on the beach*. Then she crosses it out and writes *Margryta Simonis* in large letters. Finally she emails the picture to herself, opens it on her mobile and saves it to her images.

*

Hi Mark,

Apologies for the unexpected email. You don't know me, but I'm Will Russell's partner (we live together in England). I run a business here in the UK selling linen products made in Lithuania.

I persuaded Will to give me your contact details. He told me you helped him when he was looking for his girlfriend, Olga, and that you were researching organised crime and sex trafficking in the area. Will was reluctant for me to get in touch; he disapproves of what I'm doing out of concern for my safety, but I think you might be able to help me.

I'm trying to find out what happened to a Lithuanian girl called Margryta Simonis. You may have seen the story in the papers. I was the one to find her body when I was walking on a beach on the Kuronian Spit. She was only sixteen, and her death seemed suspicious to me. The news coverage has been really sparse. There was just a small piece early on in the press, a report on the local TV, then nothing at all. It might have been the timing, as it coincided with the fallout from the volcanic eruption in Iceland, but I still think it's strange.

I feel compelled to find out what happened to her, but I'm struggling to get any information. I might be completely wrong, but I'm thinking this girl may have been trafficked and died as a result. I know this is a long shot but there's a chance you may have some suggestions or indeed connections who might be able to shed some light on this case.

I'd be really grateful for your thoughts.

I look forward to hearing from you.
Best regards,
Anna Dent

Dear Jonas,
I hope you don't mind me getting in touch with you. I run an online business in England, selling linen products. My manu-facturing is in Lithuania, so I travel there often.

In April this year, the body of a young girl, Margryta Simonis, washed up on the shore. You covered the story at the time. I would like to find out what happened to her, but I have been unable to find any further information.

My interest is purely personal, so I am reluctant to approach the police for information. I wondered if you had followed up on the story at all, and if so, if you could tell me anything more? It seems strange to me that nothing has appeared in the media since the original story.

I'm planning my next trip to Lithuania and will be there for a few days, travelling to the factory and staying in Vilnius. If you can spare the time to meet for a coffee, I'd be very happy to come to a convenient meeting place.

I look forward to hearing from you,
Best regards
Anna Dent

Dear Mrs Dent,
I would be happy to meet you. Please call me on the number below and we can agree a time and a place.

Regards,
Jonas

*

On the evening of her return to England, she joins her friends in the bar. She senses the excitement in them immediately. It's busy tonight and there's an air of celebration in the smell of wine and the hum of conversation. She has to navigate knots of people standing around the bar before she can get close.

Davey and Sai sit close together on one side of the table, Kate opposite them. They fall silent as she approaches, their faces bright with untold news.

"Something's going on, isn't it?" Anna says to Kate, throwing her jacket over the back of the empty chair. An open bottle of wine sits in an ice bucket on the table and she reaches over to pour herself a glass. "What's happened?"

"Nothing's happened," Kate says. "But Davey and Sai have news… You tell her, go on."

Davey looks at Sai, who nods and pops his fingers at him as if bursting a bubble.

"We've been together a couple of years now, as you know," Davey says. "And, well, he's okay really." He flashes a look at Sai and grins.

"Hang on let me guess… You're getting married?"

"Yes! Yes we are. And even better than that, we're going to adopt!" Davey says, his eyes shining, watching her face.

"God, he couldn't wait to tell you," Sai says. "We only made the final decision yesterday. He'd make a terrible spy. Can't keep a secret if his life depended on it."

Anna gets up to hug them both. But when she sits back down, a strange sense of isolation chills her, like the draught from an open door. For a moment, time seems to stand still and all the bustle and the noise of the bar fades to a muffled rumble.

Of course, it's good news. They will make great parents and they're the perfect balance for each other. But for some reason the news has shaken her. There's a bitter taste on her tongue, and she's relieved that the others are too caught up in celebrating to notice her discomfort.

It's only towards the end of the evening, when they've dissected adoption in a hundred ways, that Kate changes the subject.

"We like Will, by the way," Kate says. "I can see why

you're together. He's very personable, very self-contained. He's obviously bright. And he seems to care about you."

"He is very easy to have around. I care about him too." More and more, she has to admit.

"Where's he gone this time?" Kate says.

"Actually, you know what, I don't really know. I think back to Lithuania, or maybe the other Baltic countries. He seems to be in demand there at the moment." Even to her, it sounds odd that she doesn't know which country he's in.

CHAPTER 6

She watches as Will chops onions, slicing them into neat semi-circles, his eyes half shut against the sting of the spray. She studies his profile, the line of his nose, the hair, grown surprisingly long in only two weeks, curling up over the edge of his shirt. Each time he returns, it feels new, having him living with her. She stands close, breathes him in.

"Do you know," she says, looking up at him. He seems even taller, more slender than before. "I've realised I don't know where you've been. I've been so busy with work." She gathers the onion slices, sprinkles them into the pan. Oil spits as they land. She flinches at the sting on her arm.

"All over the place," he says. "Lithuania and other Baltic states, mostly, and Poland. I'm becoming an expert, it seems."

"Speaking of Poland, Magdalena's sister came back," she says. "It does look like she was kidnapped."

"Really? What happened?"

"I don't know, exactly. Kate got an email from Magdalena. Apparently she was taken somewhere, with a couple of other girls. Luckily, they realised what was happening and managed to escape."

"They were lucky," Will says.

"You could call it that. Sounds like she was pretty traumatised."

"Poor girl. I hope the police catch up with them."

"Magdalena doesn't think they will – it seems to be a big problem where they live."

Anna finds a candle and a holder. The candle's been lit before; the wick is bent over into the wax in a loop. She strikes a match and watches, mesmerised, as the flame takes hold. She sets the candle straight. It flickers and glows, its fragile plume softening the gloom in the corners of the room, glinting on the sheen of the wine bucket. Two more candles and the room fills with a golden glow. Satisfied, she returns to Will.

"So, plenty of travel stories in the Baltics?"

"I'm getting to know the area pretty well now," he says, putting plates into the oven to warm. "The hotels, restaurants, tourist attractions, they all want me to visit. I'd be there for months if I agreed to everything they want."

"I'm surprised, I mean Lithuania's not a place I think of as a holiday destination."

"Parts of it are beautiful. And luckily, it's not just tourism I'm doing out there. I've got some work doing country reports. Social change, stuff like that. I'm getting some interest from the nationals." He opens the fridge, chooses a bottle of wine from a groaning shelf and crunches it into the ice bucket. She sees him register Margryta's picture on the fridge door, but he makes no comment.

"I wish I knew what happened to her," she says, pouring the wine.

For a moment, Will looks disconcerted.

"Anna, we talked about this. Don't get involved." She's surprised at the hard edge in his voice. It sounds like an order.

"I'm not, Will. But I can't just forget it."

"I know. I understand it was horrible for you. But I don't think you should be concerned with this. You have no idea what happened to that girl. It could be trafficking, but it could be something completely different. A domestic incident even. Honestly, leave it to the authorities."

"I know." But the impulse is too strong to dismiss so casually. "But it's important to know the truth, surely. For her sake, if not for mine."

"Look I know you have this urge to find out what really happened to her. But it's not your responsibility. Please, Anna. Leave it to the police. I'm sure they're investigating it properly." His eyes are pleading, insisting. "Promise me."

"Okay," she says. She should leave it. She has no obvious reason to get involved, and she could get into trouble just asking. He's trying to protect her. But, even as the promise drops from her lips, she knows it's false. She just has to know.

She has no intention of cancelling the meeting with Jonas Kipras. She'll just see what happens. Will's probably going to be proved right, the girl wasn't trafficked, she died for some other reason entirely. But there's no harm in finding out, and Will need never know what she's up to.

*

The building is old and ugly, its square metal-framed windows looking out onto a downbeat area of Vilnius, paint peeling from the frames. She crosses the road towards it, rings on a plastic doorbell above the name of the newspaper. The doors buzz and she pushes hard, expecting them to stick, but they're loose and she's thrown unexpectedly into a dim corridor.

There's no front desk and no signage, but she sees metal lift doors at the end of the entrance hall. She presses the button, unsure where she's going. It seems the logical thing to do. Once in, she's relieved to see a list of the floors and their occupants. The newspaper is on the third floor. The doors open onto a lobby where a young girl sits behind a desk. Anna approaches, gives Jonas Kipras' name and is waved towards a sofa to wait. The girl disappears through a doorway, her heels clicking busily on the wooden floor. After a couple of minutes a man appears and walks towards her, his hand outstretched.

"Anna?" He's dressed casually, his shirt sleeves rolled up. He's younger than she expected. A woollen scarf winds around his neck though the lobby is warm.

"Yes, hi, Jonas."

"Good to meet you." The hand that grasps hers is warm and dry.

"Thank you for seeing me."

He leads her through a large room full of desks. People stare at screens or type intently. No one pays them any attention. They go through into a windowless room, furnished only with a table and four chairs. A jug of water and two glasses sit on the table and without asking, Jonas pours her a glass.

"How can I help you?"

"You wrote this story." She pulls a sheet of paper from her bag. It's the original piece in Lithuanian, printed from the Internet. "And I saw your interview on TV with her parents."

He takes the paper and studies it, leaning back in his chair. He reads for a few moments as if he's seeing it for the first time.

"Can I ask what is your interest?" he says at last, still focused on the story.

"I found the body."

He pulls his chair closer in to the table. His eyes, pale and intense, search hers, as if he's trying to see inside her head.

"You found her? That explains it," he says, nodding. "That must have been a bad experience for you."

"Yes, it was. I'd like to know what happened to her. I couldn't find any more in the news. The story just seemed to disappear." It sounds faintly ridiculous, even to her.

"Just that? No more?" He leans forward, as if suspecting something more sinister.

"No more. Do you know what happened to her?"

"You are not a journalist? An official?"

"No, neither." Impatience prickles. She shifts and fidgets, resisting the urge to rush him.

He takes a deep breath, blows it out slowly. A faint whiff of tobacco reaches her across the table.

"I might be able to help you. I know a little bit more about this story." He sits forward again, as if he has made a decision.

"You do? Can you tell me?"

"Yes, but you must understand something first."

"Okay, I'm listening."

"The police are still investigating. If they know you are interested, they will ask questions."

"That's okay, I have nothing to hide. I do a lot of business here. It's all legitimate. My interest is purely personal."

He relaxes clasps his hands on the bare table. "Okay. She was sixteen, Lithuanian, from near Klaipeda." Anna nods. "She was out of school for the summer. A boyfriend found her a job working in Vilnius, waitressing – hostessing – in a nightclub. Girls can do well in the clubs, here. Her parents didn't like it, but she begged to be allowed. Eventually they relented and she took the job. She worked for a short time, then she disappeared. The parents reported it. A few weeks later…" He indicates the copy of the news story, slaps it with the back of his hand.

Poor girl. She did nothing wrong. She just wanted a good job, some money to enjoy herself. Maybe just to buy a few nice clothes.

"Was she murdered?"

He shrugs. "Police are investigating. But it looks like she was strangled. She died before she entered the water."

His words hit Anna like a blast of ice-cold air. She'd been expecting it, but still it fills her with horror. She sips her water, imagining a shadowy figure with the young girl in his murderous grip. "Did the police tell you this?"

He smiles, a wry smile that doesn't reach his eyes.

"We have… contacts."

Of course they do. "Why do you think they killed her?"

"We can't be sure. But… her clothes…"

"What about her clothes?"

"She was wearing just a little dress, high heels, no coat. It was very cold." She remembers the freezing temperatures, the wind and sleet on the day she found the body.

"What are you saying?"

"Perhaps she was kidnapped. For the sex trade. Maybe she tried to escape, get home, she was found near where her parents live." His face changes, as if he's remembered something. "You must not repeat this. We do not know anything for sure."

"I know. It's okay. Are you still following the story? Will you be writing about it again, when there's more?"

Another shrug. "It depends. If they find her killer."

"Do you know anything else about her? Her family, friends, what she liked doing?"

"I met only her parents. I think there's an older brother, but I didn't meet him. Margryta did well at school, she was clever. She seemed to be a popular girl, with many friends. There was a big crowd at her funeral."

"You went? Did you write about it?"

He smiles. "We are not so heartless, Anna. We don't take pleasure in people's grief."

"No, I'm sorry, of course not. Did you talk to her friends in Vilnius?"

"Probably the police talked to them." He scratches his head, shifts in his seat. "I have told you what I know. I have to go now."

"I understand, I won't keep you any longer. Just… Do you know what the nightclub was called, where she worked?"

He stands and pushes his chair under the table. The meeting is over. "I'm sorry."

She stands too. "Thank you for your time, I'm very grateful. Will you let me know if you find anything more about her? If you're following it up, of course." She scrabbles in her handbag. "Here's my card. I run a company in the UK. You can check."

"I can't promise. But, if we run another story, I will let you know."

The more she thinks about it the more she wonders how a young girl ends up dead, on a beach, in April, in the snow.

Anna's no further ahead in her search for the truth. It seems she'll have to wait for the police, or the journalists, to do their jobs. Perhaps the police already know who killed Margryta, but haven't caught them yet; perhaps there's much more to it, which is why nothing's being said. Or perhaps everyone's just moved on, it's old news and nobody cares.

But she can't bear that thought.

She can't ask the police. There's no reason why they'd tell her anything, she's not even a distant relative. They'd probably dismiss her as a mad Englishwoman with a strange obsession.

And they'd probably be right, she thinks. Kate, for one, is less than enthusiastic when Anna tells her she's been to see the newspaper.

"What's wrong with you?" she says. "You didn't know the girl. Okay, you found the body, which was horrible, but that's the only connection. You don't need to obsess about what happened to her."

"I know, I know. But there's something about this that really gets to me. She was so alone, nobody was looking after her, nobody cared. I want her to know that she mattered."

"You have no idea if anybody cared or not. What about her parents? If I didn't know you better, I'd say you needed to get a life. Or a job... Oh, I forgot, you have one," she says, her left eyebrow lifted high so it disappears behind her fringe.

Anna changes the subject. She understands why people think she's mad. But she can't help it.

*

As a small girl, an only child, Anna believed her father could do anything. And in turn her father seemed to think the same of her. He's the reason she grew up into an independent spirit. He always had unwavering faith in her ability to fulfil her dreams.

From her earliest memories, she was at his side whenever she could be. She helped in the garden, digging small holes with her toy trowel next to his large ones, placing seeds, one by one, into the spaces before covering them up. They marked each with a plastic tag so that she could watch them sprout the following spring. They'd walk the dog together in the park, a different dog in those days, of course. She'd throw a ball as best she could when she was small and it would often fall at her feet, but the dog loved it anyway. She climbed trees, her father lifting her to the first branch and standing looking up as she found her way higher and higher. They collected leaves in the autumn, wild flowers in the summer, insects and butterflies to identify when they got home.

Each evening he'd arrive home from work in time for tea with her, though tea was just that for him, a cup of tea while she ate her child-sized meal. Her parents would eat together later, after she'd gone to bed. She'd have a precious hour or so with her dad before then, and they'd play all sorts of games, outside if the weather allowed. He'd be in old brown cords – at least her memory saw nothing else – and a soft woollen jumper or a cardigan over his work shirt so that he could crouch on the grass or the floor to play with toys or read a book. At bedtime she'd beg him to read book after book, delaying the moment when he'd leave her room, and often her mother would look in to remind him of the time.

The strong bond had continued during her teens. Though she was wayward, she'd never done anything that would really upset him; she adored him far too much. She loved her mum, too, of course, but with her it was different. Her mum was gentle, kind, hard-working, but not the kind of mum who played football with her daughter or dug up earthworms to watch how they burrowed back down into the dark safety of the compost. Anna was a natural tomboy. She loved doing boyish things, and though she wore dresses when she needed to, and a skirt to school, she was far more interested in running, jumping, sport, animals, activity. She chose her friends carefully. They were the ones playing hockey or tennis, and cycling to places at the weekends. Holidays were for getting outside, climbing hills, tumbling around with the dog. She can't remember ever lying on a beach in the sun; the holidays she took with her parents involved camping and barbecues by the campfire.

She would have loved sisters and brothers to play with, brothers mainly, because they'd have been more fun. But in their absence, her father had provided everything she'd needed.

*

"Can I ask you something?" They're in bed and it's dark outside. Will's reading from a tablet, his free arm around her, her head on his chest. She's too tired to read, too worried about her ailing father.

"Of course." He puts the tablet down.

"What were they like, your parents?" He never speaks about his family and she knows no more than she learned that first time, when he told her how his parents died. But the prospect of losing her own father has reminded her that Will's family was torn apart by tragedy when he was just a child.

"My parents? Well, I was only fourteen when they died, so I can only remember through a child's eyes. My dad was an engineer, travelled all over the world for work, so we didn't see that much of him. He always seemed tired, but he tried to spend time with us when he was home. I remember playing football with him and watching sport on TV."

"And your mum?"

"An artist, taught part-time at the local junior school. I think she'd have been quite good if she'd had more time to paint. She was, well, she was my mum."

"You must have been devastated when they died."

"Yes. I missed Mum horribly. The last few years, it had been mostly just me and her, as my brother was so much older. He wasn't living at home at the time. He had to come back to look after me. It was pretty hard for him too. He had to put his career on hold and put up with me for a good few years until I could stand on my own two feet. I wasn't particularly nice to live with."

"I'm not surprised. It was a horrible thing to go through, so young. Losing both parents, suddenly." She sighs. "It's hard enough when you're my age, and you've had time to prepare for it."

He gives her a squeeze and kisses the top of her head. She can feel his breath in her hair, warm and comforting.

"You must have felt abandoned," she says.

"I was pretty angry at them. Selfish reaction, I suppose, but looking back, it was understandable. I was a bit like an only child, and they'd left me."

"You seem to have recovered pretty well."

He's quiet for a few moments and she lies there, breathing him in, his aura enveloping her.

A thought drops into her mind, icy cold. She shivers and props herself up, looking at him. Intelligent, knowing eyes look back at her. "That must have made losing Olga even more difficult," she says.

There it is again, the shadow flitting across his face. He pulls her back towards him and his words fall heavy into her hair.

"It was very hard."

*

Her father's death is gradual, if that's possible with death. When she looks back at the last few months of his life, she realises that his body was already closing down, his mind preparing. His gentle nature and his quiet lifestyle had disguised his slow decline; uncomplaining, he'd hidden the worst of his loss of strength from his family and by the time they noticed the symptoms of his failing heart, it was well on the way to stopping.

At the hospital, they ease his breathing with drugs; He's able to talk, to eat and drink small quantities. He insists on getting out of bed to go to the bathroom, but he needs help and he is exhausted once he gets back to bed. Anna and her mother stay every day for as long as they can, and Anna begins to worry about her mum's well-being as well as her father's.

But it's not for long. The doctor checks his heart and warns them, choosing his words carefully. "His heart's affected on both sides, and has lost a lot of its strength. The drugs could still help him, but he's very weak." He doesn't have to say more. They know what he has left unsaid.

She sleeps at her mum's. For a few days, she lives in a dreamlike world, waking every morning with a start and racing to the hospital, her mum sitting silent in the car beside her. Most days, Will joins them, holding her hand, providing coffee for them as they sit in silence, his presence a comfort to them both. Anna's life is reduced to the bleep of monitors, the squeak of nurses' shoes on shiny linoleum, the smell of disinfectant. And the constant listening out for the phone when they're not with him.

On a freezing morning when she has to clear frost from the windscreen before setting off onto icy streets, they walk into the ward to find him propped up, his eyes open, a nurse beside him. He smiles and takes their hands, one each side, and drifts back into a slumber, his breathing harsh and laboured. His hand in Anna's is almost too much to bear; so fragile, cold despite the stifling heat of the ward, thin. She feels the butterfly-wing beat of his pulse until it is no longer there.

*

A soft fog creeps around the fading street lamps as she walks towards the office. The damp air has left the pavements slimy and shiny. People pass her without looking, huddled into their coats, collars turned up. She walks unseeing, her mind a blank, heavy with the weariness that assaults her every morning.

Without warning, hot tears roll down her cheeks. Unstoppable, they gather at her chin and drip down onto her scarf. She can't move her hands to wipe them away. The street is a haze of billowing shapes, as if she's looking through a wall of water. The bones in her legs soften, seeping away through the soles of her feet. She grasps at the railing beside her, turns towards it, willing this to pass. But the ground falls away from under her, her feet scrabbling to hold on. She sinks to her knees, her hands gripping the rail, fingers curled around the black-painted metal, nails cutting into the palms of her hands. It feels as if she's being swallowed up into the earth and there's nothing she can do to stop it.

CHAPTER 7

Her father's clothes lie on the bed, suits piled, still on their hangers. A jumble of ties sits beside folded jumpers, waiting to be sorted. Without him to give them shape, everything looks a little tired, as if his belongings know their life is over too. Anna sits, taking in the smell of his clothes, remembering how he looked in those shoes, that coat.

It's eight weeks since the funeral and she's at her mother's, sorting out his things. It's not that her mum wants to part with them, but the items which might be helpful to others need to go, she says.

Her father's clothes are going to the charity shop. It's right that they should, and he would have agreed. But she doesn't want to lose even the smallest part of him. She's keeping a soft woollen jumper, fraying holes at the elbows, his gardening jumper. She'll wear it at home for comfort.

Since her breakdown, small things stop her in her tracks. Bad stories on the news break her heart. Her brain has lost its sharp edges, like glass turned into felt. She remembers very little about that day, only that one minute she was walking to work, the next she was in a hospital bed, Will beside her. She'd been unable to speak, eat or function properly for days. They fed her pills and food. The doctor prescribed anti-depressants, rest and therapy. She obeyed the first two for a while, but therapy was a step too far. Though she agreed to see her doctor and think about it, she never intended to go ahead with it and she simply ignored it once she was home. Both

Will and her mother reminded her, but she was adamant, and they knew her too well to insist.

She won't confide in a stranger. In anybody, in fact. Secrets hidden for years might emerge unbidden in psychotherapy.

In the following weeks, she slept for hours; she barely left the flat. Will worked quietly on his laptop as she dozed in the armchair by the window, a book unread on her knees. If he took a phone call, he left the room rather than disturb her. For once in her life, she avoided her emails and calls. Jane was under instructions not to bother her, to talk to Will first if there were any major issues for which she needed approval. Thankfully there were only a few.

After a month or so, the ground began to grow solid under her feet again, the walls became vertical and rigid rather than softly billowing. She went back to work a couple of hours at a time, to see how it felt. It felt okay.

Bit by bit she crept back into her old life.

*

But the balance of her life has shifted. Though she carries on, it's with a heaviness which goes everywhere with her.

She never really thought how she would be when her father died, she was far more concerned about how her mum would cope. As someone who's barely felt a wobble in her entire life, she expected to take it in her stride. Mourn, yes, for a while, miss him, of course. But she will be okay.

It's a shock to her that she is not okay. She's not at all okay. This is so debilitating, all-encompassing. She feels as if she's bending under its massive weight.

While Anna is out of balance, Will is rock-solid.

Unbidden, he takes to calling in on her mum when Anna's working, to check on her. He drives her to the doctor, helps with the shopping if she needs it, makes cups of tea and sits with her. He takes the situation on as if she's his own mother. He's uncomplaining and constant. At first she protests that he's neglecting his work for her, that he shouldn't spend so much time there. She tries to send him away. But she admits to Anna that he's a huge comfort to her, and soon she begins to rely on him.

This wasn't something Anna had expected; Will continues to surprise her. Perhaps his background, losing his parents so young, explains a lot. His sensitivity to Anna's loss, and her mother's, his sense of family. And his isolation, the private person who talks very little about himself.

In the evenings when she gets back from work, weighed down by grief, exhausted by the stress of pretending that life goes on regardless, he's there waiting, preparing supper, pouring her a drink. Every night he puts his arms around her and lets her talk, or not talk at all. He dries her tears at the end of the day when she can't hold them back any more.

*

Her parents' bedroom is full of memories. The bed, with its old-fashioned mahogany headboard, shiny with lacquer, used to seem enormous to Anna as a child. It looks so small now, too small for two people.

Anna stands with a sigh and goes to the heavy chest of drawers under the window. She pulls out the top drawer and stares at the contents. Cotton handkerchiefs, socks and boxes of cufflinks rub shoulders with old diaries and address books. It seems wrong to be rummaging through his personal things. She closes the drawer and wanders back downstairs to the sitting room. In the corner is her father's desk, waiting its turn.

It's a small, leather-topped desk with a couple of drawers and a single filing tray underneath on either side. She's already been through one side, where the household files are kept. The instructions for what to do in the event of his death are there, neatly drawn up in his loopy handwriting. He was meticulous by nature, which has eased the pain of sorting out his papers.

She opens the drawer on the other side and pulls out the

few hanging files that are left. One contains his notes on his family history; he'd started on a family tree but hadn't got very far, it appears. Another is full of newspaper clippings, random stories tossed together for whatever reason. Idly she flicks through the columns and articles, some of them faded with age, some quite recent, most dog-eared and torn.

There's a small cutting, ripped from a local newspaper. It's from about six months ago and there's a picture of a girl dressed in school uniform, a standard school photo. The girl had disappeared and there'd been a search, lots of people had joined in. Her frantic parents were interviewed on TV, appealing for her to come home, but eventually, after many weeks, her body had been found in a local beauty spot. It's not clear why Anna's father had kept the clipping, except that the body was found in a familiar place. But the story reso-nates with echoes of Margryta and all the emotions triggered by her picture.

It's unfinished business. For the first time since her father died, Anna feels a small flush of energy.

*

The café looks different, like everything since her father died. Not always in a negative way. It's as though her eyes are looking at the world from a new angle. She still feels a deep loss, a lack of balance which she attributes to bereavement, but there's also a new feeling, as if she's only now beginning to see, to understand what's important.

She plumps herself down at their usual table and waits, watching the door. People come and go as usual, punctuating their busy lives with shots of caffeine or sugar, treating them-selves or simply filling time. A young mother helps a small girl to choose a cake, lifting her up so that she can see the display. A golden ponytail, pink ribbon tied in a bow around it, bobs as she points.

Anna watches as they navigate a buggy between the tables

and the little girl clambers onto a chair. She's so small that she has to hold on to the back of the seat, bringing her knees up first, and then turn round before she can sit down. She manages it with ease, as if she does it often, and sits, waving her feet, waiting for her mother, who's gone back to fetch her cake. Her eyes flit around the room and when they meet Anna's, her face beams with a huge smile. Anna's pretty sure her happiness has more to do with the approaching cake than with seeing her, but nonetheless the smile, with its innocence, its lack of guile, affects her deeply and she's startled when Kate appears at her side.

"Anna? Are you okay?" Kate kisses her on both cheeks.

"Yes, I'm fine, really." The little girl is now engrossed in her cake, picking up small pieces with delicate fingers.

"You were on another planet," Kate says. "Not like you."

"There's quite a lot going on that's not like me at the moment."

"Grief does strange things to people."

"I suppose so. It certainly hit me harder than I expected. How are things with you?"

"The usual. Trying to juggle work and home. New au pair started, so I've had to keep an eye on her as well. She's doing okay now, but it takes a few weeks for them to get into the routine. I do miss Magdalena. She was so easy to have around."

"I'd forgotten she'd gone back. How's her sister now?"

A waitress appears and they order coffee. "Karolina?" Kate says. "She's home and still recovering. We sent them some money to help them, just until Magdalena can work again."

"That was good of you. Was she harmed?"

"I don't think so. Not physically, anyway. Though I think she's still pretty upset. She can't go to school and she's too scared to leave the house."

"Do you know what really happened? Was she trafficked?"

"I don't know, Magdalena didn't give us any details."

A wave of sadness passes over Anna. It's almost too much

to bear. Since her father's death, her emotions are fluid, so close to the thin veneer she has painted over her pain, they can seep through at unexpected moments. "Poor girl. It's just horrible to think how much of it goes on, all round the world. All for money. Kids being abused, exploited, their lives ruined."

Kate's face is grave. "Are you back on to the Lithuanian girl thing? I don't want to be harsh, but why can't you leave it alone, Anna?"

"I just want to find out."

"Even though Will warned you off it?"

"He was just being cautious."

"I'm not so sure. He knows it could be dangerous. How is he, by the way? Is he around?"

"He's fine, he's been great while I've been getting back on my feet after Dad died. I'm so glad he was around. He helped Mum a lot, too. He's away at the moment. Belarus, or somewhere like that."

"I'd be interested to see what he's working on, if he's doing tourism to Belarus." Kate smiles. "Not your normal tourist destination for the average Brit."

"Maybe it's not about tourism, he does other stuff too."

Anna watches as the little girl picks up the remaining crumbs of her cake with a small finger, pink tongue flicking. Dragging her gaze away from the child she finds Kate scrutinising her with a look of concern.

"What?"

"I think you're broody."

"No, I'm not." But deep down, there is something that she can't forget, woken by the sad story of Margryta.

*

Anna, for what's it's worth, here's an update from Magdalena on how her sister is doing. This doesn't mean I think you should get involved. Kate x

Hi Kate,

You asked how Karolina is doing. She is still not well. She is very quiet, sleeps a lot and she cries all the time. She is frightened to go out, and when we ask her why, she does not know. I think she is worried she might see someone, maybe one of the people who took her, I am not sure. She does not want to talk about it. The doctor says she needs therapy. I don't know if she will agree. At the moment she is not even going to school, but school can wait. My mother just wants her to be safe, for now.

We don't know how she was taken. She was seeing an older boy – she told us he was 18 but we think he was older – we never saw him properly, just a photo on her phone. He told her she was beautiful, gave her presents. She had expensive bags and a leather jacket. She thought he was her boyfriend and that she loved him. He had a smart car and his friends seemed very glamorous.

The police are searching for him, but he gave my sister a false name and she never knew where he lived. They met in bars and hotels, in other people's flats. I don't know if they will ever find him.

She escaped, with two other girls, from a house in the north-east, very isolated. They caught a bus and someone helped them call the police. We don't know any more, just that they are still investigating.

Kate and Graham, we are all so grateful for your gift. We can never repay you and I am sorry for that. We can only hope that one day you will be rewarded, in Heaven maybe, if there is one. I am not sure any more.

I hope one day soon I can come back to England to visit. Maybe I can do some little thing to repay you then?

I miss you all so much. Kisses to the children.

Magdalena xx

Reading Magdalena's email starts her thinking once again. She jumps up and goes to the bookshelf, pulls out her father's old atlas, a prized possession now. She flips through it, finds Poland and stares at the map.

The north-east of Poland borders on Lithuania.

Not that this means anything, she tells herself. There's absolutely no reason why the house where Magdalena's sister was taken should have anything at all to do with Margryta. Margryta went to Vilnius, in the other direction, to work.

But she was found on the Lithuanian coast, in the north, not far from her home town. Which isn't so far from the north-eastern border with Poland.

She barely acknowledges the pang of guilt; she knows she's deceiving Will, but the powerful feeling that she needs to know, for Margryta's sake, has re-energised her. She can't stop herself.

Hi Magdalena

You probably don't remember me, we met once when I came to Kate's house. I'm Kate's best friend.

I hope you don't mind me emailing you, but I'm trying to find out what happened to a girl in Lithuania who may have been kidnapped, like Karolina. This girl was called Margryta Simonis and her body was washed up on a beach on the Kuronian spit. She was only sixteen. By chance, I was the person who found her. This is why I'm interested.

I know your sister is still unwell and frightened. I'm so sorry about what happened to her and I'm very glad she's home with her family.

I just wondered if, when she's well enough, you might be able to ask her something for me. It's just for me, no one else, and it's because I want to find out what happened to this young Lithuanian girl. Did she meet any other girls in the house where she was taken, and does she know their names? Also, where exactly was the house?

I don't expect you to ask her straight away, but if there's an opportunity, and she does remember names, please let me know. Perhaps I can help this young girl's family in some way, or other lost girls.

If you don't want to ask Karolina, or you don't want to help me, I'll completely understand and I won't be offended.

All my best wishes to you and your family, and to your sister especially, for a speedy recovery.

Anna x

*

For the first time in her life, Anna's lost interest in work. Or rather, she feels rootless, and for once her work is unable to ground her. It's like a mild feeling of vertigo. She tries to shake the feeling off, but she has moments of deep melancholy. Everything's so fragile, so delicate. It can all change at any moment.

From a rational point of view, she knows she's lucky. She has fantastic friends. Many people go through life without such bonds. She still has her mother. And she has Will, a good man, who she loves, who loves her back.

They're invited to Sai and Davey's for supper. It's meant to be a low-key, informal meal, designed to create the least possible stress for Anna. She knows this, because Kate and Graham, also invited, have told her. They all want to help in subtle ways, coax her gently from her mental isolation, welcome her back into the fold. Before, she would have felt patronised by this. Now she feels touched.

The conversation inevitably turns to Sai and Davey's wedding. The ceremony will be simple and stylish. Neither man is flamboyant; neither wants enormous expense. But managing the expectations of their respective families is proving a minefield to be negotiated with delicate diplomacy. They're close to having a meltdown and are even thinking of disappearing to a Caribbean island to get married in private.

Anna lets the conversation drift around her. Will sits close, his leg touching hers, as if to let her know he's there. But she still feels separate, different, as if everything and everyone is the same while she's changed in some profound, unfathomable way. She watches the bubbles in her water glass glide, one by one, to the surface. They pop, each disturbing the surface gently as it disappears; some cling to the side of the glass for a brief moment before vanishing. She wonders where they go. One minute they have form, the next, none. Like her.

"Anna? Are you with us?" Kate is offering her a plate. A slice of lemon tart sits in the centre, a trail of red syrup encircling it.

"Yes... thank you." She tries to focus on the conversation, though a pulse in her temple threatens the arrival of a headache. Now they're discussing Sai and Davey's adoption plans, a long process which is testing their patience.

"Boy or girl?" Kate says. "I'm assuming you get to choose?"

"We'd prefer a girl, too many men already in this house," Davey says. "The younger the better. Although it's harder to find a baby. Everybody who adopts seems to want a baby. But to be honest, it doesn't matter to us at all. We just really want this to happen, as soon as possible."

"It's an admirable thing to do." Will says, stirring his coffee. "It's tragic, but everywhere, all the time, children are abandoned, or people just can't take proper care of them. It's brilliant that there are people like you, to rescue even one." How serious he can be, Anna thinks, how much he's seen of life. How little I really know him.

Going home in the car, she says: "You'd really like children, wouldn't you?"

"Yes," he says. "I would."

She stares from the rain-spattered window at the drenched streets with a deep, dragging sadness.

"Will?" In her armchair by the window she watches the wind whip through the trees in the square outside. Leaves bunch together like flocks of birds, whirling and beating at the air. People walk by, pushing against the wind with their heads and bodies. A woman's scarf rises up like a snake to a charmer. It occurs to her that she's like an old lady sitting there, watching the world from her high vantage point, as if she never goes out. She resolves to move the chair. Soon.

Will's laptop is open and he's reading something with intense concentration, biting his lower lip. She notices the tic of a muscle in his cheek as he bites.

"Will?"

He glances up as if surprised to see her sitting there. "Sorry, I was completely absorbed. Did you say something?"

"Did I say thank you?"

"What for?"

"For all the looking after you did. For me, and Mum, and not complaining. And generally being there. Just for everything. If I didn't say thank you, I'm really sorry, because you've been... unexpectedly brilliant."

He raises an eyebrow. "Unexpectedly? You didn't think I had it in me?"

"Not that, no, sorry," she shakes her head as if shaking her thoughts will make everything clear. "I'm making a hash of explaining myself. I just meant we have a certain kind of relationship, and this was way, way beyond what I would have asked of you."

A smile plays around his mouth. "A certain kind of relationship?"

"Stop repeating what I say as a question. You know what I mean."

Then he's serious. "I'm not sure I do. If you mean we both work hard and I travel a lot and you stay in the office until all hours, then maybe I do. If you mean we're not committed to each other in ways that mean we support each other through difficult times, then I disagree."

She picks at the fabric of the chair, stares out at the threatening sky. Clouds balloon into dark masses above the trees. Spots of rain click on the window.

Sometimes it's still a struggle to get her thoughts in order. This is all new to her. She hopes it's part of recovering and she'll soon get back to being as sharp and focused as before. What does she mean regarding their relationship?

"I just wanted you to know how much I appreciate you."

He sighs, puts his laptop down and comes over to kiss her. "Appreciate?"

"You know what I mean, Will." To her surprise, the tears rise and balance, ready to fall.

He puts his arms around her and holds her tight. "I love you, Anna. I think you know that."

"I love you too, Will." It's the first time she's said it to him, and she's frightened at the power of those three words. The tears roll, unchecked, down her cheeks.

It's the first time she's said it to anybody.

CHAPTER 8

Will's away in France and Anna's at home, nursing a cold and working, a box of tissues at her side.

But what she's really doing is nothing to do with the business. She's researching the trafficking of girls around Europe and Russia, and particularly in the Baltics. At last she's heard back from Will's contact, Mark. His email is friendly but doesn't give her much to go on. He's still working as a journalist but it's been some time since he covered trafficking of any kind; he's not sure how he can help her.

He suggests some websites to visit, a victim support charity. She follows the links but what she finds is general, much of it out of date. Details of the situation in individual countries are sketchy. She gets the impression there would be more if she knew where to look. The statistics seem unreliable. There's frequent speculation that trafficking may be more prevalent than the numbers suggest. But it's thought-provoking; a shady world she knows nothing about, where organised crime holds sway, and one kind of criminal activity paves the way for others.

She's planning a trip to Lithuania again, her first since her father became ill. It's a few months since she was last there and she has things to sort out.

But her real reason for going is to find out more about Margryta. She tracks back in her emails to find the address of the journalist and types.

Hi Jonas,
I'm planning another visit to Lithuania next week, on business, probably Tuesday to Friday. Would you be free to meet me on one of those days, please?

I look forward to hearing from you,
Best regards,
Anna

She sits back and takes a sip of her coffee, now almost cold. The search for more information has proven fruitless. There's been nothing about Margryta in the media for months. She's beginning to think the crime has been relegated to a cold case. Or maybe the police are hiding something, not releasing details until it's all sewn up. Her lack of knowledge about Lithuania – the culture, the police, the authorities – is frustrating, slowing her down. Without understanding how to deal with the police, she could end up either in trouble or at a dead end. She needs someone to help her on the ground.

A few seconds later, he replies.

Dear Ms Dent,
If you're still interested in the Margryta Simonis story, I'm not sure I can give you much more, but I'm happy to meet, as you're in Vilnius, and I will try to help. I suggest Wednesday at 11.00 for coffee. There's a café right opposite my office, if that suits you.

Regards,
Jonas

It's a start. She scrabbles in her wallet among the mess of receipts and business cards and retrieves the card, untouched until now, given to her by the police on the day she found the body. The name on the card is Vladimir Rostov; his title is Liaison Officer. There's an email address for general information and, she assumes, the main number for the Vilnius police.

She sits and looks at the card, wondering if it's worth a try. It seems feasible that, as the person who found the body, she would be interested in any news. But would they tell her anything?

There's only one way to find out.

*

Her flight from Heathrow is delayed by half an hour, so she buys a coffee and sits, watching people come and go, her mind drifting.

A family of four is settled at a table nearby. The two children are absorbed in their gadgets, their thumbs twitching, while the parents stare out at the ever-moving crowds. The debris of a meal is strewn on the table in front of them, but they seem oblivious. Anna gets the impression they've been sitting there for some time. From the look on the faces of the adults, they're unhappy about something, perhaps a delay, perhaps simply the stress of travelling with children. Or perhaps they're just annoyed with each other. The woman has a vacant look about her; lines etch the corners of her mouth. She looks as if she doesn't smile much.

The father fidgets, looking round from time to time at the departures board, checking his mobile, which never leaves his hand. At one point, he takes a call, stands up and walks away from his family, his free hand over his ear to block the airport announcements. The minute he moves away the children start whispering to their mother, who waves her hand at them as if to silence them and starts to tidy the table, piling sandwich boxes together with paper cups and plastic cutlery into a small pile which she gathers with both hands and deposits in a nearby bin.

When the husband reappears the family is instantly transformed. He says something to his wife and the woman's face lights up. The two children, a girl and a boy, jump up from their chairs and start to gather their belongings, chattering with excitement. Anna can't quite catch the language, but from their clothes and a certain look about them, she guesses they're not British, Eastern European perhaps, or Russian. She watches them as they head for the departure gates along with others, all walking in the same direction. She wonders where they're all going, what each is travelling towards.

With a start, she realises she's looking at someone she knows. It's the British man from the hotel in Vilnius. The one Will didn't like. Gavin. She's pretty sure it's him, but though she cranes her neck, she can't see his face properly, there are people walking behind him, shielding her view. He's quite a distance from her now, a suited figure getting smaller all the time, moving towards a walkway, the gate numbers hanging on large signs along an endless corridor. He stops briefly as another man joins him. They shake hands as if they were expecting each other and the second man, younger and more slender, the collar of his dark jacket turned up against his cheek, nods slightly as he greets the other.

A shock of recognition pulses through her. Surely that's Will?

More and more people join the walkway and she loses sight of the two men. Jumping up from the table, which clatters as she catches it with her foot, she grabs her bag and almost breaks into a run to catch them, knocking into chairs as she tries to negotiate the crowded café. People flinch and step back as she rushes past, but it's too late. She's lost sight of them amid the hordes.

As she stands there catching her breath, she wonders if she's imagining things. It did look like him, but it could have been someone with a similar silhouette. He was so far away, she might easily have been mistaken. And as far as she can remember, it's unlikely he'd be at the airport right now. He's been away for – what? – three or four days now. There's no reason why he'd be flying in to Heathrow and immediately back out again. None that she knows of anyway. It would be pretty strange if he was. And meeting Gavin? Unlikely, given his reaction to him in Vilnius that time. He certainly gave the impression then that he'd rather avoid him.

As she turns away, giving up the pursuit, she tries to remember where he said he was going. But she can't. He travels so much, often she can't distinguish between one trip and the next.

With a sigh she tells herself she's probably just seeing things. She sets off towards her departure gate.

*

Jonas is late. She's finished her first cup of coffee by the time he arrives and is relieved to see him. She was beginning to worry that her only concrete contact might let her down.

He arrives with a freezing blast of air from the door of the café, scarf flapping, windswept hair. He offers a cold hand and sits opposite her, indicating to the waitress. They order coffee and cake. He looks harassed and out of sorts.

"I'm sorry I'm late," he says. "I'm working night shifts at the moment. I needed to finish off my copy before I left. It took longer than I thought."

"What time do you finish?"

"Nine. I was very late today. One of the problems of the night shift. And lots of news last night. Big stories."

"Oh?" she says, and he smiles.

"You can see. In the paper and on the website," he says.

"Of course." She waits a moment as the waitress places the coffee and slices of soft sponge cake in front of them. "You know what I'm interested in. The story I was following when we met before?"

He nods, takes a sip of his coffee, wipes his mouth. A dark brown smudge stains the paper napkin. He takes a breath as if to say something, then lets it out, the words unsaid.

She waits, intrigued.

At last, he says: "The girl on the beach, yes. Margryta Simonis." She reaches for her bag, extracts a notebook and pen. She writes the name with care and underlines it. He watches her every move with a quizzical look.

"Is there anything new on the story?"

He says nothing, seems to be wrestling with some internal argument, trying to decide what to tell her.

"I'm still just doing this for me, for interest. No other reason." He turns his gaze to the notebook. "It's just so I don't forget, bad memory," she says, smiling.

He looks around. The closest tables are empty, wiped clean, waiting.

"We have nothing new. The police have asked us not to write about this crime for the moment."

"Do you know why?"

"Perhaps because they still have to catch the killer. Perhaps just because they don't like us."

"But do they know who it is? Her killer?"

"It's hard to tell. We have a... difficult relationship with them. They tell us very little, and they don't like it when we try to find out for ourselves."

"Do you know how close they are to catching someone?" she says, taking a bite of cake. It crumbles onto the napkin on her lap.

He shrugs his shoulders, a slow expressive movement. His mouth turns down as his shoulders rise. He says nothing, fiddling with his coffee cup, waiting for her response.

"But... her family..." It arrives unbidden to her lips. She's thought about the girl's family many times. The pain they must be feeling at their loss. Perhaps she should talk to them. She found the body, they might want to know how she looked. But she shudders at the thought. It's probably the last thing they would want to know.

"I don't know about her family," Jonas says. "We try not to make their lives more difficult, the victims of crime. The police will be in touch with them. If they solve the case, they will tell us."

"Do you think the police would talk to me?"

"It's possible, I suppose, that they will see you. Especially if you can offer them more, as a witness in the case."

Approaching the police seems to be the only route for her. She runs her fingers through her hair in frustration. Nothing seems to have moved on at all.

"I have a question for you," he says, leaning back in his chair.

"Of course."

"You're an intelligent, successful woman, yes?" She inclines her head, waits. "With your own family? Then why are you interested in this girl? She is nothing to you. Not good to find the body, I'm sure, not easy for you. But otherwise, no connection to you."

"No direct connection, that's true."

"So, why?"

"It seems like nobody cares. Recently, I lost someone I loved. My father died. It made me think about her and how her family must be suffering." He raises his eyebrows. A finger of hair slips onto his forehead with his slow nod. He pushes it back and she sees the sympathy in his eyes.

"What do you know about sex trafficking in Lithuania?" he says.

"A little, but only what I could find on the Internet."

He nods, staring into his coffee. "There's not much in the public domain, however hard you look. It's a well-kept secret, and worse than you might think. Not just here but in Russia, Poland, the former Soviet Union countries, the west of Europe, all are involved. The criminal networks are sophisticated and ruthless. It's very dangerous. People make a lot of money. There are links with all kinds of organised crime: drugs, money laundering, smuggling, extortion."

"I realise that, of course, but—"

"So you can't investigate something like this without understanding these things." A warning note rings in his voice and for the first time, he raises his eyes to hers.

She holds his gaze and says, firmly: "Look, I know this.

102

That's why I need help. But if you don't want to help me, that's okay. I can find another way." For a moment, she thinks the conversation is over. But he seems to make a decision. He nods, unwinds the scarf from his neck, puts it on the chair beside him.

"Actually," he says. "There may be a way we can help each other."

*

She looks at him in surprise. She was preparing herself for disappointment, a dead end. Instead, the door has opened a little, he's decided that he can trust her.

"In what way?"

"Let me tell you what has happened since I wrote that story. I believe Margryta Simonis may have been kidnapped, for trafficking."

At last. She's been waiting for this. "Is there any basis for that?"

"Not really. But it does happen here, quite a lot."

"So I understand."

"I've written about it before and sometimes I blog about it."

She waits, wondering if this is going anywhere.

"The police didn't like what I wrote, though I write the facts as I find them, as well as my opinion. Some of it was speculation," he shrugs, his hands spread wide, "but that's what blogs are. They're opinion-based, personal, well, mine is, anyway. But what I said about people trafficking, it was true. They didn't like it. They won't deal with me now about this. About other things, perhaps, but not this."

She's beginning to understand what he might need from her. "I see. And you think I can help?"

"I know the team in the police department that is handling this crime, and the name of the chief investigator. He may deal with you when he won't with me, or any journalist." He looks at her, his eyes questioning.

The door has opened a fraction further. "Well, maybe, but why should they talk to me? I'm a stranger. I found the body, but I saw nothing else. I wish I had. I told them that. Why would they talk to me?"

"Exactly why they might." He looks at her as if he's given her the reason. "You were on the beach. You found her body, and you are a member of the public."

"But I didn't notice much of anything. It was very cold and windy. I don't know what I could tell them." She's beginning to worry that he wants her to lie to the police, fabricate a story to get them to talk to her. However much she wants to know what happened to Margryta, she's not going to put herself on the wrong side of the law, especially in a foreign country.

"But you were there. You could say you've remembered something. They won't be suspicious of you."

It could be her imagination, but he's very focused now, his shoulders tense, waiting for her answer. She begins to wonder if he has a hidden agenda – something he wants from her that he's not saying – and she reminds herself that she doesn't know him, she has no reason to trust him.

"I could… but what are they like, your police? Would I be putting myself into a difficult position with them?"

"No. They might think you're a time waster, but they have to listen to you. You'd have to be a little bit clever, though, to find out more about the case. Tell them your story, about how your father passed away at around that time, how you're concerned for her family. You're a woman with no self-interest. Perhaps they'll open up to you."

She pauses, looking into his face for clues, for something to help her believe in him. He holds her gaze for a moment, then his eyes slide away.

"What exactly do you want to know?" she says.

"There's a gang I'm following. They're traffickers, they run drugs from Russia through Europe, they have brothels, nightclubs, all kinds of illegal trade. A few are Russians, some Lithuanian, one or two western Europeans. I know the names of some of them, but not all. I want to know if this case is linked to them, if they're operating here in Vilnius."

"The police aren't going to tell me that."

"They might tell you that she was trafficked, where she'd been. If you can get them talking, it's possible you might find out something. If you really want to find out more… You don't know if you don't try."

"Let me think about it," she says, gathering her things together. She still doesn't trust this guy. "I'll let you know what I decide to do."

"Okay," he says, disappointment clouding his eyes. He indicates to the waiter. "I will pay."

"Thank you." She stands up, pulling her coat around her shoulders. "And thank you for meeting me. I will be in touch."

He nods, unsmiling. She turns to go, then stops. "One last thing. What, in particular, did you write that the police didn't like?"

"I think the police are corrupt, and I said so. I believe they're protecting these gangs, otherwise why would their arrest record be so bad, and why would this kind of crime be growing by the day? Obviously they didn't like it. They said that I was making it up. But the police have a lot to answer for. I know it."

*

Hi Lazarus,
Sales are going well on the last collection, and I'm preparing for the next season. Can we arrange a meeting in the next week or so? I'd like to run through my thoughts with you before I finalise my plans.

While writing, I wonder if you could give me your views of the police in Lithuania? There is no problem, but I may need to meet them about a personal matter.

Many thanks and I look forward to hearing from you,
Best regards,
Anna

Dear Ms Dent,

Good to hear from you, and I'm glad your plans are progressing. Yes, I'm happy to meet. I'm away until 13th, so perhaps after that. Do suggest a date and time and I will fit in with your plans.

You asked for my views of the Lithuanian police. I hope there is nothing wrong?

My experience of the police here is not extensive. However, their reputation is not entirely good. Certainly in the past police corruption was a big problem, and although the government has put measures in place to improve matters, there are still issues in some departments and with some individuals. In general, the police are not unpleasant, but I would take care. Do not trust them.

Please do let me know if there's anything I can help you with. A knowledge of the language can make a big difference.

Kind regards,

Lazarus

*

She walks along the windy streets of the city for a while, thinking about what Jonas has said. All the trails seem inevitably to lead to the police. Are they corrupt? Colluding with the criminals? If they are, then she's not sure she wants to go near them. Perhaps they're inured to the problem. Or are they overwhelmed by its sheer size, the huge influx of criminal activity from outside the country?

How many other young girls, like Margryta, are trapped by gangs and forced into a miserable, downtrodden life? It's a horrible image, and it could be happening here, right now, in Vilnius, with no one to stop it.

At a pedestrian light, she finds herself gazing at the shop fronts on the far side, the scene changing every moment as people come and go. It takes a few moments for her to realise she's looking at the entrance to a night club. And as she stares, a new trail reveals itself. No, not new – it was there all the time – Jonas had even told her when they first met.

Margryta worked as a waitress in a nightclub in Vilnius.

The doorway announces: *Club Utopia* in large neon lettering. Unlit, the sign looks grubby and unwelcoming. Underneath in smaller letters, it says: *Girls. Dancing. Cocktails*. A couple of steps lead down to a heavy door, which she's surprised to find is open. Peering inside, all she can see is a gloomy stairway leading down to another unmarked door. A single lightbulb is enough to light her way down.

She's surprised to find her heart beating a little faster, her palms clammy as she pulls at the second door, which opens to a large, dark-walled room. Plastic seating crouches around low tables and glasses teeter in a pile on a bar to her left. The room is barely lit by a few humming strip lights; the fancy lamps on the table and on the walls wait like dark creatures watching for prey. Stale smells of old tobacco and alcohol mingle with the chemical tang of cleaning fluid.

There's nobody in the room, but she can hear the splash of water into a bucket from a half-open door behind the bar. A cupboard door bangs and the click and clack of crockery drowns out her tentative: "Hello?" She waits a moment, unsure what to do, then steps behind the bar and knocks on the door.

A startled face appears, a man drying his hands on a dirty dishcloth. Behind him squats a bucket, its mop sitting in a grey soup of dirty water. "*Sveiki*," he says. "Hello."

"Sorry to bother you. Do you speak English?"

"Of course."

She feels slightly ridiculous. "I'm looking for a girl. She might have worked here." It sounds lame, even to her. He shakes his head, indicates the bucket. He's the cleaner, what can he say?

"What time does the club open? When do the staff come in?"

"You want to talk to the girls, you come back tonight,

107

maybe ten, eleven o'clock. After that, too busy." He nods and turns back to the kitchen behind him, as if she's dismissed.

She takes the hint and makes her way back through the dingy room, up to the brightness of the street above.

*

The road to Kaunas, in the centre of Lithuania, runs directly from Vilnius. The linen factory's not far from the town and she has stayed here before on business. She drives carefully, – it's icy outside and a strong wind beats at the car, every gust reverberating through the steering wheel under her gloved hands. Forests and wide, flat areas of farmland pass by. Stork platforms, with their messy nests of twigs and branches, stand proud beside farm buildings. Once on the empty road, she's startled by a stork flapping from the verge in front of her, heavy wings hauling its ungainly body skywards.

She's on her way to see a social worker from the victim support organisation that Mark put her on to. She needs to know how it all works, what it looks like, before she approaches the police.

She finds the flat easily enough. A small, smiling woman greets her at the door and ushers her in, her hand flapping. "Come in, come in, it's cold."

The woman asks in heavily accented English, how was the journey, did she find her way well enough? She's beckoned into a warm sitting room where she waits while the woman bustles about in the kitchen, the aroma of coffee drifting through. She's rehearsed what she's going to ask, but her questions may be the wrong ones.

The woman places a steaming cup in front of Anna, sits opposite her on a dark leather sofa. It squeaks when she moves. She smiles expectantly, so Anna explains again why she's there.

"Thank you so much for seeing me. I know you can't give me any information on specific cases. I need to understand everything about people-trafficking in Lithuania." The woman shrugs, her head to one side, as if to say: *Everything*?

Anxious not to overwhelm the woman, she changes her approach. She explains how she found Margryta, why she's interested. She doesn't mention the police. The woman smiles and nods her sympathy.

Later, Anna walks away from the apartment building close to tears, her feet heavy on the icy pavement.

*

Perhaps Will is right. Here she is, delving into a world she knows nothing about. A world full of danger, deceit and criminal gangs, when she doesn't need to. It does seem fool-hardy, at the very least.

But Will is away, elsewhere in the Baltics, and she feels compelled to carry on. Because if strange things happen and nobody takes an interest, if people die and nobody cares, then the world is a very sad place. Because of this, for now, she will keep going. As long as it's safe. She won't take her search too far; she'll stay within the boundaries and see what happens. Which means seeing the police. As long as she's careful, the worst that can happen is that they say no and send her away.

Hi Jonas,

I've thought about our discussion and I'm happy to help you, as long as it's safe. I won't lie to the police, though, or stretch the truth. I'll see if they will talk to me, and if so I'll find out what I can.

If you're happy with that, send me the details of your police contact and I'll try to see them as soon as I can. I'll let you know what happens.

Regards,
Anna

*

It's later than she intended as she approaches the dark doorway leading down to the basement of Club Utopia. A group of men stands outside, cigarettes cradled in their fists.

There's a flurry of activity as the door opens. A puff of hot air escapes, perfumed with sweat, smoke and the stale whiff of an underground space. The cluster of people opens up as she approaches and she finds herself stepping down towards the open door, drawn as if by an invisible magnet to the secret world inside.

The scene that greets her assaults her senses. She can taste tobacco on her tongue, her throat protesting. Music blares, its deep bass thumping so hard she can feel it through the soles of her feet, and the noise of laughter and conversation mingles with the repetitive riff of guitar and drum. Her eyes, narrowed against the smoke, strain to see through the darkened room, where dim pools of light drip onto small tables surrounded by drinkers lounging on bench seats. The bar is the only part of the room where light blazes, and she edges towards it through a sea of animated flesh, hoping to find a corner where she can lean and watch.

She feels old and underdressed in her jeans and ankle boots, a light scarf around her neck. The women here are young, in some cases, very young. Mini-skirts show off their slim, tanned legs. Long, groomed hair grazes bare shoulders and low-cut tops. Their arms are tattooed, their nails like talons, painted in all the colours of the rainbow. Everything seems to be embellished with sparkle and glitter. They look like porcelain dolls, all manufactured from the same mould. They arrive together in twos and threes and are soon swallowed into the crowd of watchful men.

Squeezing into a tiny space between broad male shoulders, she orders a gin and tonic and retreats to the end of the bar where it's dim and she can lean and look without getting in the way.

The men are older and almost exclusively dressed in black. Black roll necks, black t-shirts over sleeves of tattoos, black jeans, black shoes. Their faces are dark, their hair slicked. They drink shots in small glasses, regularly filled by the bartenders. When they talk to the girls they eye them like predators assessing the kill. They stand close, touching, possessing their trophies, stating their position as alpha male in the pack.

Anna sips her drink, makes herself small in the corner. She won't find anything here, now, it's pointless trying to talk to the waitresses, who come and go to the bar with an endless stream of orders, disappearing back into the crush, deftly balancing trays of drinks as they move. She needs to come back when it's quiet.

She's numbed by the onslaught of music, smoke, the crush of people. She's ready to go when a man, unsteady on his feet, approaches her. He says something to her, a leer on his wet lips, his hand reaching for her shoulder. The smell of aftershave mixed with alcohol is overwhelming. She dumps her glass with a crack on the bar, gives him her most crushing look and sidesteps his flailing hands. To her relief, he shrugs and turns away.

As she steps towards the entrance, a dark door beside the bar opens and a bright bar of light pierces the gloom, casting a yellow stripe across the floor beside her. She catches a glimpse of the inside of the room. Balloons of smoke drift around a group of people lolling on sofas and armchairs, glasses and bottles littering the table in front of them. Shadows of other people creep across the floor. In a moment, the door closes without a sound, as if it never existed.

She's unsure exactly what the room was about, with its air of secrecy, of decadence. Perhaps it was a private party. But she knows who was there in the centre of it, reclining like a king on that sofa, surrounded by smiling young girls.

It was Gavin.

CHAPTER 9

"What do you think?" Will says, gazing at his reflection in the mirror.

"You look great."

"I look trussed up."

He's trying on a suit for the wedding, which is only a couple of weeks away now. He looks uncomfortable, pulling down the sleeves, opening and closing the single button at the waist.

They're in a smart shop in town where the assistants are slick young men with bare ankles, hair crafted into shiny quiffs. They watch with a critical eye as customers browse through racks of colour-coordinated clothing. Anna wonders if their look is specified in the job description: *must have good hair, slim hips, brown ankles*.

"You're just not used to wearing a suit," she says. "Anyway, it's not a formal affair. You could probably get away with a decent jacket."

"Problem is, I don't have one of those, either. All my clothes are like old friends, well worn and just about holding themselves together. I need a proper suit."

"You do? I thought travel journalists were always casual."

"We are, but sometimes we have to meet some quite senior people. It helps to look smart on occasion."

Anna moves aside as a man approaches the rack of grey suits beside her and there's something about him, his shape and size, which jogs her memory. She goes to join Will at the mirror. "You know that guy at the hotel in Vilnius? The one with the wife dripping with bling?"

Will smiles at the description, turning sideways to examine his profile in the suit. "Yep... Gavin. What about him?"

"I thought I saw you at the airport with him the other day."

"Which airport? There are so many." He grins at her in the mirror.

"Heathrow, when my flight was delayed. I thought I saw you in the distance, going towards the gates. You met up with someone who looked like Gavin."

Will's gaze is still on his reflection. He twists and turns his body, lifting his shoulders, studying his back, fidgeting with the sewn-down pockets of the jacket. "As I remember, I couldn't stand the guy."

"So it wasn't you?"

"Not likely. If I'd seen him, I would have avoided him, so it can't have been me. What do you think? Does this make me look serious enough?"

Anna sighs. She hates shopping, even for herself. Shopping for someone else, Will included, is twice as hard. She drifts away, finds a chair and checks her emails.

*

"Well, wasn't that just lovely?" Kate says, sipping at a slender glass.

The wedding guests are gathered in a converted barn-like building, where tall windows watch over acres of fields, rising to hills beyond. Sheep, still as statues, create puffs of white in the expanse of green.

Waiters bring trays of sparkling glasses and platters of delights, tastes that burst on the tongue and melt away too soon, leaving Anna wanting more.

"Mmm," she says, her mouth full. "God, that's divine. Please don't take them away." She lunges after the girl with the tray and scoops up a couple more treats, balancing them

113

precariously in one hand, her drink in the other. "Where did they find this place? It must be a well-kept secret."

"Sai knows the owners. Only available for special occasions. Rave reviews, apparently," Graham says, holding out his glass for a refill.

"Trust them to be in the know. It's a fabulous wedding venue," Kate says.

Sai and Davey arrive, guiding Davey's elderly mother through the guests to a comfortable chair in the corner and settling her with a drink and some friends before coming over.

"Well, we did it!" Delight shines through every feature of Sai's face. "What do you think?"

"So happy for you," Anna says, and means it. "It was always going to happen for you two."

"I don't know what you mean," Davey says, coming up behind Sai.

"Yes, you do. It just seems to work so well for you... commitment, partnership, whatever you call it."

"You should try it, Anna, you never know, it might work for you too." Davey is called away before she can reply. She's glad of the interruption. It's not something she really wants to think about right now, here.

*

At the wedding table, Sai and Davey make an announcement: their dream is coming true, and a little girl will be theirs within a matter of months. They stand side by side, sharing the news, speaking through tears of joy. The room erupts with applause, photo flashes exploding like fireworks.

Will is one of the first to go over, dragging Anna by the hand. She feels the tears well up then. In the midst of all the celebration, that strange sense of isolation. Her own life has turned out very differently from this, and for a moment the flood of regret overwhelms her.

She shakes herself, takes a couple of deep breaths, and offers her congratulations.

They arrive home many hours later. She pulls off her shoes with relief. "Wow. They have some stamina, those boys."

"Indeed," Will says, pouring a glass of water for them each to take to the bedroom. "They'll make great parents." He stops for a moment, staring down at his hands, opens his mouth as if to say more, then hesitates and turns away. Anna watches the muscles tense at the back of his neck. She can guess what he's thinking.

*

Something changes between Anna and Will in the weeks following the wedding. It's not something she can put her finger on, a shift so small that she wonders if it could be her imagination.

But at times he seems remote, more distant than usual, even allowing for the travelling. Not sure whether to be worried, whether to bring attention to it, at first she decides it is in fact her imagination.

She does her best to dismiss it. She's being paranoid, there's nothing to worry about. In all other respects, things are the same: physically it's great, whenever they come together. They both work hard, they value each other's freedom as an individual, domestically and socially they're in line. Surely there's nothing to worry about.

But there is one subject she avoids. Perhaps this is what bothers him, causes this almost imperceptible distance between them. It would make sense if it was triggered by the day of the wedding, that's for sure.

The question of children.

She knows that children are important to him, that he wants a family. At the start, she didn't take the relationship seriously, didn't expect it to last. Even when he moved in, the disruption to her life had been so slight, it meant little to her in the way of commitment.

The age gap was one of the reasons. She hadn't expected him to be interested in her long-term, or indeed, her attraction towards him to grow as it has done. So she assumed that the issue of children wouldn't be a problem. Their relationship would be fun for a while, and then it would be no more.

But Will isn't just any young man. Will is stable, serious, mature, caring. He never mentions the age difference and Anna knows this isn't out of courtesy or sensitivity to her feelings. He simply doesn't regard it as an issue.

And now, she loves him.

Will wants to create a family, a home, a life. Anna, despite herself, despite her lifelong, all-consuming, selfish ambition for success in business, is, inexplicably, beginning to want the same.

When her father died, the chains that tied her to work softened. While she's pretty sure that to most people, even her closest friends, she seems exactly the same, there is a difference and it's important. Perhaps the death of her father has triggered this feeling, but at last Anna's beginning to see – to admit – that she needs a family around her, to love and protect.

Anna wants a baby.

*

The thought takes shape like a rosebud unfurling as she sits alone in her flat. This is different from anything she has ever wanted before. It's as if desire has overwhelmed reason, she's lost control of her senses. She jumps to her feet and strides around the room, fizzing with nervous energy.

At first she can't give the idea any room. She'd be a terrible mother, she'd let everyone down, she's selfish and ambitious and not the caring type, she can't give up her work, her business. She's proved irrefutably in the past that this won't work for her; her marriage failed because she wouldn't, couldn't, commit to anything but her work.

Then, as the shock recedes and her brain starts to function again, logic starts to take over and she begins to understand that this is something profound, something she needs in her life.

If it's not too late.

But Anna is old. She's forty-six now. It's very late to start thinking about a first child. Though her body is still going through its monthly cycle, she has no idea whether it's still possible to conceive. Is it dangerous? Would the baby be at risk because of her age? She has no idea what the repercussions could be, has never needed to find out.

Would it be better not to try? To look at adoption instead?

She picks up her laptop and types in, fingers shaking so much that it takes a few attempts to get it right: *first pregnancy in forties*.

What she reads is terrifying.

CHAPTER 10

She sits at her desk in the office, phone at her ear, half listening to a conference call, her eyes on the screen in front of her. A message, almost lost in the long thread of emails in her inbox, catches her attention.

Dear Anna,
Here are the contact details for the leading investigating officer in the Margryta Simonis case, who will have the latest information, I believe.

I wish you luck, and ask you to let me know what you find out.

Best regards,
Jonas

Dear Mr Bockus,
I believe you are the investigating officer in the case of Margryta Simonis, the girl whose body I found on the beach at Klaipeda in April.

I have heard nothing new about the case for a few months now. I wondered if you have made any progress in finding out how she died and if not, whether I could be of any further help to you. When I was interviewed that day, I was very shocked and unable to remember much about the scene, and it's possible that some things I have recalled since could be useful to you.

I travel on a regular basis to Vilnius on business and

would be happy to fix an appointment with you, if you think it would be useful. I will contact you with dates nearer the time of my trip.

Best regards,
Anna Dent

She stops and rereads the email. It's not exactly lying, or even stretching the truth. It's hinting that she may have remembered something, which is quite possible. Perhaps it'll be enough to pique their interest.

She clicks Send and realises she's been holding her breath.

*

Will is away – it's been two weeks – and Anna's losing sleep. Realising she wants a baby, and not being able to talk to Will, has left her anxious and unsure.

They have never said, out loud, what they want from each other. She knows he wants a family, but whether he wants one with her is another matter. Perhaps he wouldn't want to commit to a woman so much older than himself. Seventeen years. When he reaches forty, she'll already be fifty-seven and showing the signs of age.

Questions battle for position in her mind. What if she can't conceive? Is she prepared to take it further and try IVF? What about adoption? Will she be too old to play with her child when he or she wants to run around all day and she's too exhausted to move? What if they have a child and she and Will break up? Could she cope on her own, and would she want to?

The answer to the last is a firm no, but the rest of the questions swirl and buzz in her head like wasps around a dinner table.

When she speaks to Will – short conversations over a crackly line – she's so consumed by the need to tell him she can barely speak. She comes away each time angry and disappointed with herself, worried that she sounds cold and uncommunicative.

But she mustn't tell him yet. She needs to know what's possible, what her body is capable of. Then she needs to know what he wants, whether there's a chance they might be able to do this together.

Like her hoped-for meeting with the Vilnius police, there's a tightrope to be walked, delicate as spider's silk, before she can move on.

*

She fills her days and long evenings with a huge workload. She's strung out but unable to stop, because if she stops, the wasps start up again.

Jane entreats her to slow down, reminding her what happened when her father died, concerned for her health. The business is doing well, Jane says, extremely well, with profits soaring and a good couple of years ahead. Why is Anna pushing herself so hard now, when it's a rare chance to take it easy and look after herself? Anna insists she's working hard because she enjoys it, all the more because the business is thriving, but she's well aware she's overdoing it. She's on a treadmill for a reason and she's frightened that if she steps off it, she'll break.

As she hurries to the bank between appointments, she catches sight of herself, windswept and unkempt, in a shop window. She sees not herself, but a stranger. It's a shocking reality check. A gaunt, grey face stares out at her. Its eyes are deep in their sockets, grey smudges painted around them, deep lines thrown into strong relief against the pallid skin. Compelled by an urge to study herself at her worst, she preserves the illusion for a few long minutes, staring intently, unblinking, until she's unable to control her brain any longer and the wraith morphs into herself. Late already, she hurries on.

When she's not working, she is with her mum. Perhaps because she coped so well after her husband's death, she's missing him more than ever now that her life has settled into a routine of sorts. While she fills her days well enough, she finds the evenings lonely and long, so she's always happy to see her daughter.

Anna goes there straight from the office. Her mum worries about Anna's lifestyle, has she eaten, did she sleep last night, has she spoken to Will? She says she's eaten, there's no issue with sleeping, just to reassure her.

The pretence is exhausting though. She longs for Will to return.

*

The email that arrives from the Vilnius police late one Friday is disappointing. It's not even from the investigating officer. It's a standard response. An enquiry number, details of how enquiries are managed, no offer of a meeting, not even a chink in the wall.

Disappointed and annoyed, she decides on a new and different tack. She'll do it her way, now, no tiptoeing around.

Dear Mr Bockus,
Thank you for your response. I will be in Vilnius next week, 13–17 July, and will be free on the morning of 14th to visit your office. I would be grateful for an appointment with you or a colleague and will report to your reception desk at 10.00 a.m.
Yours,
Anna Dent

She copies in Vladimir Rostov, the Liaison Officer whose card she was given at the hotel on the spit, just to be sure someone takes notice. She intends to get a meeting if it means calling them every day. She's hoping they'll cave in, if only to get rid of her. She's had enough of waiting.

*

A few days later, having made a nuisance of herself, she extracts a promise to see someone – it is unclear who exactly – on the morning of the 14th.

But in the days before her trip, she begins to wonder what exactly she's going to say. She could easily end up with nothing. She scours her memory of the days she spent at the hotel, the long walks she took along the empty beaches. She walked daily, but saw very little. Sometimes the wind was so strong, she barely looked at the ground around her as she trudged along and back, alone with her thoughts. Every day merges into the next in her memory and nothing stands out. Nothing she can use, anyway.

Her story's too thin. She needs more if she's going to get anything at all from the police. She needs to change her schedule. She needs to go back to the beach.

CHAPTER 11

When she steps off the ferry, the rain has eased and the clouds, low over the horizon in the early morning, have lifted a little, the darkness fading into high white curves. The other passengers drift slowly apart, some heading along the side of the harbour, some striding out towards the forested area in the centre of the spit.

Anna studies a large map beside the ferry station, which shows the routes through the spit. She heads away from the harbour behind her towards the sea on the other side of the long finger of land, the scent of pine trees leading her into the shady forest. The path, soft with fallen needles and forgiving under her feet, leads directly across the centre of the spit. After a while a wooden walkway rises towards the horizon and the ground on each side turns white with sand. When she reaches the top of the walkway, the land falls away into a wide stretch of empty beach, the grey sea beyond.

A strong breeze takes her breath away as she descends the wooden stairs onto the sand. Seabirds call, their cries shrill and urgent as they see-saw on the wind.

It's a long walk to the hotel, but Anna is prepared for this, breathing in the clean air and the solitude. The moulded soles of her trainers make faint patterns on the wet sand behind her. She studies the rising dunes on her left, looking for familiar landmarks, but it's a while before she sees anything she remembers. The bright white shells are there, standing against the breeze, the piled-up sand behind them. A boat sits motionless on the horizon, too far away to see any movement. Wooden stairways rise every couple of hundred metres, becoming less frequent the further she gets. The only other people there as she sets off are far away down the beach, but they're walking away from her and are soon out of sight.

She's alone on a deserted beach, with not a soul in sight, miles of sand in front and behind, sea on one side and thick pine forest on the other. But she feels no threat; this is a place at one with nature, with an aura of peace, where unpleasant things don't happen.

What was Margryta doing here? Perhaps she was never here in life; if her body washed up on the shore, then she could have entered the water a long way away, drowned or already dead when her body was thrown overboard. She must have been on a boat. It's hard to imagine any other way her body would have washed up here.

But what if it didn't wash up here? What if somebody was with her, and killed her here? But surely then she would have been wearing a coat, at least. Or, at a stretch, they could have carried her body here and dumped it in the waves. But why would they do that? It would be a huge risk, even in winter time, with hardly anyone around. Why carry a body any distance at all when it could be hidden in the dense forest? It wouldn't make sense.

Anna stops and looks around her. She thinks she recognises the swell of the sand dunes on the left. Perhaps this is where she reached the limit of her walks, though she would have started a lot further on, at the hotel which has yet to come into view. Behind her the beach goes on and in the far distance a group of buildings squats, white and grey, a power station perhaps. Ahead of her, more beach, more sand dunes and no sign of human habitation.

A little further on there's a pile of driftwood and desiccated seaweed, pushed up the sand into a meandering line of grey detritus, picked at by a groups of crows which appears as if from nowhere.

She carries on, wondering how much further the hotel will be. When she stayed there her walks would be at least three hours – one and a half each way – but she has no idea how far the hotel really is from where she started today. On the map it looked entirely possible to get there on foot, but she didn't check the scale and has no way of measuring the distance she's done. She's beginning to wonder how she'll get back.

The metallic cry of a crow interrupts her train of thought and she watches as it flies up at her approach, landing again a little further down the line of driftwood, joining its fellow, already intent on pecking at something at its feet.

The scene is familiar – the crows, the sea litter, the shells, the froth of the waves on the white sand – this time, though, there's no body, no high-heeled shoe. She sits on the hard, damp sand and stares out at the dark, unforgiving waters of the Baltic Sea.

*

She notices a lone figure some distance ahead, standing at the shoreline. She stands up and walks towards it. As she gets closer, she realises it's a girl, perhaps in her teens. Her coat is buttoned tight to her neck, a woollen hat pulled down over her hair and ears. As Anna approaches, she throws some-thing into the sea and trudges up the beach to a small mound, which rises from the flat expanse of sand. Intrigued, Anna walks towards her. As she gets closer she can see flashes of colour and unusual shapes around the mound. It's some kind of a shrine.

"Hello," she says, and the girl turns with a start. "I'm sorry, I didn't mean to startle you."

"It's okay," the girl says, removing a lock of hair from her cheek with a gloved hand.

"What is this?" Anna says, indicating the shrine. She can see now that the shapes are candles and pebbles laid in a pattern around the mound. Silk flowers have been planted

125

into the sand and ribbons attached, which dance and flutter in the breeze.

"My friend, Margryta, she died. Her body was found near here. My friends and I put this here, for her." Removing her gloves, the girl crouches down, checking with small white hands that the flowers are firm, the sand solid.

When she stands, Anna holds out her hand. "I'm Anna. I found your friend's body. That's why I've come back, to remember her."

The girl flinches at her words, and Anna immediately regrets the business-like manner of her tone. The girl recovers enough to offer her hand. Her fingers are fragile and cold, with a scrape of sand on Anna's palm.

"It's freezing out here." Anna says. "Can I buy you a coffee? I'd like to know more about Margryta."

Wide blue eyes look back at her, uncertain. "My name is Lina," she replies eventually. "Are you walking to the ferry?"

*

At the ferry station they find a small, old-style café, furnished with dark wooden tables and chairs, thick carpets and a warm log fire. They sit by the window looking out over the harbour. The ferry isn't due for a while.

"What was she like, Lina?" Anna says. "Were you good friends?"

The girl nods, looking out at the grey skies towards Klaipeda. "We were in the same class at school. I knew Margryta from when we were small, about six or seven. She was one of my best friends." She sighs, and breaks her cake into small pieces. "I miss her, she was always happy. She loved to party, but she also was kind. She wanted to work with animals one day." The girl's eyes fill with tears and for a moment Anna thinks she will break down but she takes a deep breath and calms herself. She sips her coffee, holding the cup with both hands.

"She took a job in Vilnius, didn't she? Do you know where it was?" Anna says, choosing her words carefully.

Lina shakes her head. "Not really. It was a nightclub I think, in the city, but I don't know the name. She worked as a waitress. She had a boyfriend, she went there with him. Her parents didn't want her to go, but she went anyway, she always wanted to go to the city. It was only supposed to be for the summer, a few weeks."

"Did you know him? The boyfriend?"

The girl's smooth forehead puckers. "No, he was not from here, I never met him. He was older than her, I think twenty-three, twenty-four. He gave her gifts. He drove a nice car. When she started to see him, she was so excited, but she didn't want to go out with us any more. I told her..." A lone tear breaks free and trails down her cheek, her chin trembles.

"What did you tell her?" Anna asks gently.

"I said, she should be careful. Sometimes, the older men, they buy gifts, they flatter, but all they want is sex. She didn't listen to me." She wipes the tears from her cheeks with shaking fingers. Anna reaches across the table to touch her hand.

"You tried, Lina. It wasn't your fault she didn't listen."

"Do you know what happened to her? Did the police find anything?"

"I'm sorry, Lina. I found her, but I don't know anything else."

*

This time, she arrives earlier at the nightclub. Not too early, but early enough for the girls to be talking to each other, chatting to the barman, not taking and delivering orders. The door next to the bar remains firmly shut.

She slides onto a seat close to the bar and smiles at one of the girls, who leaves the group and comes over. It's hard to tell her age. She's heavily made up, with long legs encased in black leggings. A silky top reveals smooth shoulders and an intricate tattoo on her upper arm.

"Hello," Anna says, smiling.

"Would you like a drink?" the girl replies, with barely a trace of accent. "A cocktail, maybe?" She indicates the drinks menu standing on the low table in front of Anna.

"Maybe. Can you recommend something?" Anna opens the menu and flicks to the list of cocktails.

The girl leans forward, blonde hair draping over her face. She tucks one side behind her ear with a red-tipped finger and points at the menu. "Gin fizz, Martini? Or do you prefer vodka? Bloody Mary, perhaps, or a Moscow mule."

"I don't know, and I can't see, I've forgotten my reading glasses. Can you read this one for me?"

The girl sits beside Anna and reads out the ingredients.

"Oh, thank you, that sounds great," Anna says, and before the girl can stand: "Can I ask you something else?"

"Of course."

"How long have you worked here?"

The girl looks puzzled. "A few months? No, almost one year."

"Do you like it?"

She shrugs. There's a golden sheen on her shoulders so when she moves the gentle dip and flow of her skin sparkles in the dim light of the nightclub. "It's okay. The money's good, especially in the summer. I like the girls."

"What about your boss?"

Her smile fades and she glances towards the bar, where a young man is serving a couple of people. Two waitresses stand at the end of the bar, waiting for orders. "He's okay," she says, and starts to get up.

"Wait, that's not what I wanted to ask, I was just interested. I just wondered if you might have known this girl." She takes out her mobile and shows her the picture of Margryta.

The girl takes the mobile, studies the screen. Anna watches her face, but she can't see her eyes.

"No, I don't know her," the girl says. "I need to go, sorry. I will get your drink." She returns the mobile and walks away, fast, towards the bar.

As the room starts to fill up, the thump of music rising, Anna goes to the bar. She shows the barman the image of Margryta. "Do you know this girl?" she asks. "She worked in a club in Vilnius for a while. Her name is Margryta Simonis."

He takes her money, barely glancing at the phone. She waits, the picture casting a light from her hand. When he returns from the till, he nods at the picture. "I know who she is, she died, it was in the paper. It is not your business. It's best you stop asking."

He turns away, leaving Anna's question unspoken on her lips.

*

"Wait!"

Outside the club, Anna turns to see a girl behind her, indicating for her to turn into a small alley at the side of the club. Obediently she steps into the dim space between two buildings. It's just wide enough for a line of bins and access to a side door.

This is not the girl Anna spoke to inside; this girl is smaller, darker and a few years older, late twenties, perhaps. She dips into her pocket, offers Anna a cigarette, then lights one for herself. Her slender fingers shake as she holds the lighter. Then she says: "You have a picture of Margryta Simonis."

"Yes, I'm trying to find out what happened to her." She assumes the girl knows what happened. "Did you work with her?"

"Yes, for a little while. She was one of the good ones. Are you police?" There's no innocence about her face, only the wariness that comes from experience. Disappointment, fear, hardship are written in the lift of her chin, the narrowing of her eyes.

"Not police, no. I was the one who found her."

The girl's eyes widen. "You found her?" She breathes out, her cheeks puffing, and shakes her head. "I am sorry for you."

"I'm sorry for her. Do you have any idea what might have happened to her? Why she left when she did?"

"Margryta was not stupid. She came here for summer work, with one of them." The girl gestures towards the club. "But she realised it was dangerous. She tried to get away at the beginning but they stopped her. Soon it is impossible to leave. Girls come and go, they take them off to other clubs, other countries, then they can't get back. She didn't want that. She wanted to go home."

"So she was trying to get home and they followed her?"

The girl shakes her head, drops the remainder of her cigarette. She grinds the butt into the ground with the heel of her boot. "What do you think? Otherwise she is still alive, eh?"

"And you? Are you here against your will? Are you scared they might take you?"

The girl laughs, a low-pitched, hoarse cackle. "Me? They don't want me. I am old."

She peers around the corner into the street. "I have to go. I hope you find what you want."

*

In the hotel lobby with her laptop and a cup of coffee, working in between meetings, she looks up to see Gavin's bulk bearing down on her, heading for her and nobody else.

A scowl clouds his face.

"Anna, isn't it?" he says. His voice is cold, his words clipped. There's no friendly smile now. A whiff of stale cigar smoke pollutes the air around him.

"Yes," she replies, uncertainly. "We met here some months ago. You're Gavin, aren't you?"

Grey chest hair tufts from the open neck of his shirt, a flush clambers up his already ruddy neck.

"I'll thank you not to ask questions in my clubs," he replies, ignoring her question. "My staff are busy. Don't interfere where you don't belong." And he turns and leaves, each step a thud of anger on the marble floor.

*

The police station is one of those grim, imposing buildings that remain from the Soviet era, not built to please the eye.

Anna strides into the lobby with determination, hoping her air of confidence will have its effect on the receptionist. He looks up from his computer without a smile and waits.

"Anna Dent, I have an appointment at ten o'clock." She gives the name of the investigating officer. The receptionist nods, indicates a register for her to sign and picks up a telephone. She follows his pointing finger to the seats in the corner.

This morning she woke with mixed feelings. She almost cancelled the meeting, but in the end decided that since she'd spent so much time and effort getting this far, she'd do her best to find some answers. If something comes of it, she'll give the information to Jonas and say goodbye; if nothing, then so be it and she can focus on what's become so important to her in recent weeks.

The chairs are uncomfortable and have seen better days, the stuffing emerging in yellow puffs of sponge from the seams of the arms. Rubber flooring, buffed to a shine, gives off a faint smell of disinfectant and the walls are a glossy cream colour that reminds her of school. A cork board hangs on one wall nearby, paper sheets pinned neatly in rows. She wanders over to look. Faces, rendered grainy from the photocopier, with headlines and information below – missing people, perhaps – rub shoulders with printed leaflets hanging by one corner. Notices with headlines in large type, all in Lithuanian, are indecipherable to her, though a few are in English. They're mostly traffic safety notices and advice for tourists. She soon loses interest and sits again in the corner.

People come and go, some in uniform, showing security passes as they pass and punching a code into a keypad by the door at the back of the room. Some look curiously at her. She realises she must look different from the usual visitor and begins to regret her business clothing. Perhaps she should have dressed down. But it's too late now, so she sits and plans her opening lines, her answers to difficult questions, as she's taught herself to do.

*

After a while a young woman in uniform collects her with a gesture. Without a word she takes her through the security door and they follow a series of bright corridors, closed doors on either side, for what seems like a long way. At last the woman stops, unlocks a door, waves Anna into a gloomy room and retreats, leaving her to find the light switch.

The room is completely bare, containing only a small table and four chairs. A window overlooks the street, a venetian blind, its broken slats at awkward angles, half covering it. The light above the table is bright and unforgiving. Anna resigns herself to the waiting game, removes her coat and pulls out her mobile from her bag.

A few minutes later the door crashes open with such force that the metal handle digs into the wall behind it and small piece of white plaster falls to the floor. A huge balding man in a loud checked jacket, his shirt buttons straining over a bulbous belly, strides in. She scrambles to her feet and puts out her hand. It's crushed in a vice-like grip.

"Ah, Mrs Dent," he says. "At your service. Sorry for the wait. Drink?" The young woman behind him, part-hidden by his bulk, looks enquiringly at Anna, who stutters, still recovering from his dramatic entrance: "Tea, please. With milk."

The man advances towards one of the chairs, which he seizes in an enormous fist, lifts and crashes back to the floor. He flings his bulk into it and leans forward. The chair creaks ominously. Anna doesn't know whether to be amused or intimidated.

"Excuse me, I didn't catch your name?" she says.

"Ah, so sorry. I am Vladimir Rostov. Liaison officer." He smiles as if happy to impart this information.

"Good to meet you, but I was hoping to see the investigating officer, Mr Bockus. It's regarding the Margryta Simonis case."

The enormous man nods, sits back in his chair and coughs, a delicate sound like that of a child, his huge hand covering his mouth in a flamboyant gesture. "Ah, yes. He is busy, I apologise. But, Mrs Dent, what is your interest in Margryta Simonis?"

"I'm surprised you don't know," she replies. "I emailed more than once to explain." He nods again and continues to nod, looking at her expectantly, so she soldiers on. "I was the person who found her body on the beach near Klaipeda. I believe I may have useful information about this case. Are you familiar with it?"

"Yes," he says, but Anna's not convinced. There's not a hint of recognition in his eyes.

"I have heard nothing since it happened. Is the case still open?"

There's a knock at the door and the young woman appears, setting a thin plastic cup, containing a muddy grey liquid, in front of Anna. She nods and leaves.

Rostov appears to be waiting for Anna to say something, so she repeats her last question. "Is the Margryta Simonis case still open?"

To her surprise, he stands up and leaves the room without a word, the chair still clattering as the door closes behind him. She's more than a little annoyed by this. Thinking he's abandoned her, she's about to follow when the door crashes open again and he returns, a manila folder in his hand.

He continues as if he hadn't left. "Yes, I believe the case is still open. Progress has been made, but no arrest as yet." He looks at the folder, but doesn't open it.

"Progress?" she says.

"Yes, progress," he replies, smiling.

"Do you know what happened to her? Was she trafficked?"

"Trafficked? Why do you ask that?"

"I… Someone I was talking to about the news story suggested she may have been." She doesn't want to tell him she's been in touch with Jonas Kipras, she might land him in trouble, and it would almost certainly seem an odd thing to do.

"Speculation. People like to make up stories."

She takes a deep breath. This isn't going anywhere unless she forces it. "The reason I came to you is because… well, as you know, I was a witness. I was in shock when I was first interviewed, at the hotel. I wasn't thinking straight, and I couldn't remember much about what I'd seen. I was surprised it wasn't followed up. I wondered if I might be able to help you."

He shrugs, opens the file and starts reading, curving the folder towards him so she's unable to see.

"Yup," he says abruptly, snapping the folder shut and looking at her with intent. "Do you want to write a new statement?"

"I… Well… Don't you want to ask me some questions?" This isn't going quite as she intended.

"No. Do you want to write a statement?" It seems her only option, so she nods. With another crash he leaves the room, taking the folder with him, and in a few moments he returns with a form and a pen.

"Please write."

*

As she walks away from the police station she feels a deep sense of disappointment. All her efforts have led to nothing. She has no answers, no more than she had at the beginning, and despite everything she feels about Margryta and the tragedy of her death, she's starting to feel that persevering will be pointless.

She needs to let the police handle it, as Will suggests, and focus on the rest of her life. There will be no need to hide anything from him any more. He will soon be joining her in Vilnius, and they're going to visit Olga's family. She's looking forward to seeing him.

She tells herself to draw a line under the story. She should email Jonas now, tell him she was unsuccessful and that will be the end of it.

*

Daria lives in a small block of flats with no lift. A grubby staircase, graffiti scrawled on the walls, leads up from the otherwise empty entrance. Anna shivers as they climb; the place feels damp and cold. The doors on each landing are closed and they pass nobody on their way to the fourth floor, where Will turns down a dim corridor with doors on either side.

He stops and knocks. The door is scuffed, brown paint revealing green beneath. There is no letter box. After a few moments they hear movement from inside and a woman's voice calls out from behind the door.

"It's okay, Daria," Will calls through the door. "It's me."

The door opens a crack and a face peers into the gloom of the corridor. A diminutive woman, flecks of grey in her hair, ushers them in. They step into a narrow hallway where a dark wood cupboard, too big for the space, displays a vast array of patterned china dishes.

"Daria, meet Anna. Anna, this is Daria," he says.

The woman's clothes hang in folds from her shoulders, as if she's lost weight. Her feet are clad in frayed slippers which strain over the swollen joints of her big toes. It's hard to tell how old she is. She wears no makeup and the skin on her face has a greyish tinge, as if she never sees the sun. She says, in heavily accented English: "Hello, Anna. You are welcome. Come in, come in."

As she speaks, a door to one side cracks open. A boy peeks out, eyes wide, dark curls framing a pixie face.

"Hello, Sasha." Will crouches down and the boy emerges and hides behind his mother's legs, smiling shyly at Will. Daria takes his hand and ushers them all into a tiny sitting room, where more dark furniture fills every available space. It's no warmer in here than outside, and there's an uncomfortable dampness to the air. A single window on one side looks onto an identical building, which shields the room from the sun and the sky. The smell of cooking – meat of some sort – wafts through from the kitchen, which is linked by a small hatch in one wall.

On a bookshelf beside the sofa is a photograph, in a polished wooden frame. It's of a woman – a much younger version of Daria, and a few pounds heavier – cuddling a little girl, perhaps seven or eight years old. It must be Olga. She looks happy and relaxed, her arm around her mother's neck, smiling into the sun. It's the only adornment in the room, apart from a vase of dried flowers and a simple crucifix hanging on the opposite wall.

Will and Anna perch close together on a sofa while Daria disappears into the kitchen. A toy train sits in the middle of the floor on tiny tracks, attached to carriages of varying shapes and colours. Sasha pushes it around, humming to himself, while Will and Anna watch, trying to keep their feet out of the way as he shuffles around the circular track.

Daria reappears with a heavy tray. At first sight, Anna had thought she was older than herself. But her son is very small, perhaps four or five years old, so she's probably younger than Anna. Anna finds herself wondering if Olga and Sasha have the same father.

"How are you, Daria?" Will asks.

"Sometimes good, sometimes not so good. I was not very well, but at the moment, I am okay. I want to work, but I have to wait until Sasha is at school." She glances at the boy, who continues to play, oblivious.

"What will you do for work?" Will says.

"Maybe cleaning, if I can find the job. Or much better, work in shop, market, a few hours a day. My friend, she sells fruit and vegetables. It's not much money, but at the end of each day, free things, good food for Sasha." Though she smiles, the sadness shows in the tilt of her mouth, the lines at her eyes.

"Can someone look after Sasha for you while you work?" Anna asks.

"He will go to my friend, she has little girl, she comes here sometimes. We can share, work and children."

There's an air of hopelessness about the little flat, with its sad entrance, its heavy furniture, which seems to drain the energy from Anna. She feels deeply sorry for this woman, who's lost her daughter, whose life has such limits.

*

When they leave, Will ruffles Sasha's hair. The boy smiles back and waves from the door.

As they drive through the quiet streets back to Vilnius, Anna stares out of the window, at a blur of grey buildings passing by. "Poor Daria. It must be hard enough living on her own with a small boy, without being ill. What would happen to Sasha without her? Is there a father around?"

He shrugs. "Not to my knowledge."

"How does she cope with Sasha when she's sick?"

"There's the friend, a neighbour. I don't think there's anyone else."

"So you're still giving her money?"

He nods, his face grim. Anna wonders how hard it is for him to see Olga's family, her picture on the shelf, her little brother in the dingy flat.

"We must come back soon," she says, staring unseeingly, thinking about this woman's life and her own.

CHAPTER 12

She sits awkwardly, avoiding eye contact with the receptionist and the young couple opposite her. She needn't worry about them, though, they are oblivious. They lean into each other, silent, holding hands. The girl chews the nail on the forefinger of her free hand; when she takes her hand away, it trembles. Her skin is white and clear, her eyes made up with neat lines of colour and lashes so long they seem to brush her cheeks. She looks like a young alpaca, and Anna expects her to wobble on her high heels when she stands, as if she's just learning to walk. Her partner stares at his feet. His trainers are cobalt blue, unsullied by dust or mud, they're clearly not the tools of a runner. His hair is cut short at the sides, almost shaved, a blonde quiff in the absolute centre. They look clean, neat and affluent; everything about them is new. Anna wonders if by contrast she appears shabby and worn, the years of hard work showing on her face and in her clothes.

She looks away, slumps into the chair. She's sure the receptionist in this smart Harley Street clinic has seen the full spectrum of humanity, including women in their late forties looking for miracles, but that doesn't help Anna, who is more nervous than she can ever remember. All her emotions gather in her stomach, which rolls and rumbles noisily; her hands are cold and damp with sweat.

When she's called in for her appointment, she drops her handbag, knocks her elbow on the door and stumbles into the empty chair that waits in front of a large desk. Facing her is a tall, greying man in his fifties, eyeing her over reading glasses with a sardonic air. For a moment she feels locked in some kind of absurd comedy from which she'll never escape. She shakes the feeling, sits upright in the chair and takes a deep breath.

"What can I do for you, Ms Dent?" His tone is neutral. There is no hint of judgement in the questioning blue eyes, though she searches for it. This won't work if he doesn't take her seriously.

"I want to know if I can conceive."

"Good. Well, that's what we do here. I'll give you a form to complete in a moment, but I'm assuming you have specific questions for me?"

"I'm forty-six, to start with. No children. I want to know what my chances are of conceiving naturally."

*

Now all she has to do is wait. Not for long, but the test results take a few days to come through, then she has to go back to see the specialist and hear his report. To Anna, who hates to wait for anything, it's torture. Despite all the denial for so many years, she wants this so much now that she can hardly bear to think what will happen if the results are not what she wants to hear.

Will is away, which she is relieved about. She could never have kept her anxiety from him. It's hard enough to concentrate on work. She notices Jane giving her an odd look one day as she stares into space and realises her behaviour is out of character. When she can't focus any more, she leaves the office and walks.

From the town centre she can walk into the countryside and back into the town from a different direction. When the weather is good she walks for an hour or two at a time. Her mind follows another kind of path. Her life could change dramatically in a matter of months, for good. Or it could remain the same, though she wonders if that's possible. Perhaps it will never be the same, now she's realised what it could be.

At times, despite her new, deep desire for a child, she shrinks from the idea of being a mother, with all the implications of that ultimate responsibility.

All her life she's been defined by her work. Family has taken a poor second place, she realises with a shock of shame, until her father became ill. That loss has shone a spotlight on her priorities. But without her work, her business, would she even be the same person? She would have to rethink her values, recalibrate her very essence.

Even if she can carry on in some capacity, her life's work won't – can't – be her main focus any more. Knowing what a wrench that would be, how would she cope with being responsible for another human being, so dependent on her? Anna, who's never looked after anyone, not even a pet, in her life?

*

"Is everything okay, Anna?" Jane's face is drawn and pale; worry draws dark lines on her forehead.

Anna, returning from a long walk, miles into the countryside, glances at the clock with surprise. "Sorry, Jane, I didn't realise the time, did you need me?"

"You had a meeting with the IT guys, did you forget?"

Anna stops and turns. "I knew there was something. I'm so sorry, I got distracted. Did you manage to put them off?"

"They were here and waited, but when I couldn't get hold of you we decided it would be better to rearrange. I've pencilled it in for next week." Jane's eyes, wide with concern, follow Anna as she takes off her coat and sits down at her desk. "Anna? Can I ask you something?"

"Of course, anything." Anna knows she owes Jane an explanation. This woman has worked without complaint, spent long hours in the office and taken responsibility for the business when Anna was unwell. She deserves to know what's going on now.

"You've been rather distracted recently."

Anna nods, opens her mouth to apologise. But Jane carries on: "It's okay, I know there's been a lot going on for you. It's just, I've been worrying. You would tell me if you had particular plans for the business, wouldn't you?"

For a moment, Anna can't think what she's getting at. "Plans?"

"I mean, I know it would be a great investment for someone—"

Anna puts up a hand, smiles. "Jane, I'm not selling out. And I certainly wouldn't do anything like that without consulting you."

Jane's cheeks flush pink with relief, or perhaps embarrassment. "I'm sorry, Anna, it's just… this job is important to me." Her voice wobbles slightly and she looks away

Anna feels a deep fondness for Jane. She's humbled by the loyalty of this person who puts her all into someone else's business. "I know, and I do really appreciate what you've done for me over the years. I'm sorry if I've seemed distant. I suppose losing my father hit me harder than I expected. But honestly, don't worry. My plans for the business are the same as ever. I suppose maybe one day in the distant future, I might consider selling, but I promise you now, you'll know all about it. And you won't be excluded, or forgotten, if and when the day comes."

"Thank you, Anna. That's great."

Though the discussion ends there, it leaves her with something else to think about. If she does become a mother, will she want to spend all her time working? What would be the point, if she has no time to spend with her child? Quite apart from having to decide to be a mother first and a businesswoman second, could she really do it? And if she can, what about the business?

*

The results are back and she sits at the consultant's desk again, waiting for him to read his notes. He flips the papers in the file in front of him back and forth as if checking and double-checking, then peers at her over his glasses with a frown. He pushes his chair back from the desk.

"Well, Ms Dent," he says. She can't tell if he's smiling or grimacing. "You've got the reproductive organs of a thirty-two-year-old woman. All's fine and healthy there."

She waits, anticipating the proviso.

"However. In women your age, which is advanced for childbirth, there are fewer eggs available and those that remain could be impaired. There are risks, both to you and to the health of your baby, I'm sure you're aware."

"I am. But I would like to try, if you think there's a chance I could have a healthy baby."

"Let me take you through the risks, and also the tests and treatments that are available, so that you can make an informed decision."

Half an hour later she leaves the consultant's rooms in a daze, clutching a sheaf of leaflets. Her head is spinning but her heart is set.

*

In the coffee shop she bumps into Davey, waiting at the counter. His face breaks into a smile when he sees her.

"It's you! Come here, give us a hug," he says, forcing her to jump the queue. "It's okay, she's with me," he says, smiling at the woman behind him.

"Davey, it's so good to see you, I haven't heard a squeak from you since the wedding! How was the honeymoon?"

"Not long enough. Come and sit down, I was going to take this away, but now you're here I'll take ten minutes."

They find a table in a corner and sit.

"Come on, then, I'm all ears," Anna says. "How is married life? And the Seychelles? Actually, no, don't tell me about the Seychelles, it'll only make me jealous."

"Sun, sand, romance… you can only take so much."

"So it was successful?"

"It was wonderful. I don't think I've ever relaxed so much. At first I was twitchy, so unused to it. I actually felt guilty that I wasn't doing anything. But I did enjoy it, a bit too much, I fear."

"Did you come back down to earth with a bump?"

"Honestly, we were itching to get home to get everything ready for Jenny."

"Your little girl! Of course. When's she coming?"

"Tuesday next week. We can hardly believe it's happening. We've been getting her bedroom ready, buying toys, stocking up the kitchen. There's such a lot to think about."

"Are you sharing child care?"

"At first we'll both take time off, for a few months until the money runs out. Then we'll see how it goes sharing the time. It's worth doing it now though, before we know it she'll be at school."

Anna smiles and nods. She holds her precious secret close.

*

In vitro fertilisation. It sounds to Anna like a farming method: cold and dispassionate.

The specialist recommends it for older women. 'Geriatric mother' is the medical term for her, a woman who decides to conceive for the first time in later life. No holding back for reasons of sensitivity then, she thinks grimly.

Her immediate reaction to his suggestion had been to reject it. If her reproductive organs are healthy, she's still menstruating, then that means she can conceive, and that's enough for her. But her body might have other plans. She must consider IVF as a viable option if she really wants to do this. Whether Will is be prepared to go through the process with her, she has no idea. It's all theoretical anyway, just a fragile bubble of hope floating alongside her. So she leaves that door ajar in her mind, ready to fling it open if the circumstances allow.

Having got this far without telling anyone, she feels a sudden urge to confide, to pour out her insecurities, to ask a million questions. She's never been interested before, though most of her friends have children. It's not in her nature to open her heart to anyone but those closest to her.

She needs to tell Will first. He's the closest, the most important, the person on whom everything now depends. She must prepare herself, find the words.

CHAPTER 13

She takes work home rather than staying late at the office. Will's back, and at last she has the chance to talk to him.

In the kitchen making tea, Will says: "You okay? You seem a bit quiet."

"I know, sorry."

"Something bothering you?"

She takes a deep breath. "I've been thinking very hard about something and I need to talk to you about it."

"Of course. Don't look so worried! Come on then, let's sit down." He turns away to pour water into the waiting mugs.

She feels as if she's risking everything, plunging deep into freezing waters. She closes her eyes and forces herself to speak. "I want to have a baby, Will. I want... I want to have a baby with you." Her voice doesn't even sound like her own, her words falling like pebbles onto sand, landing with a sickening thump.

She watches his back, holding her breath. He tenses, the tea forgotten. He doesn't turn for a few seconds. It feels like an eternity to Anna.

"What?" His voice is choked, the words muffled. Her eyes drill into the back of his head, searching.

"Will, please turn round. What do you think? I want us to have a baby together."

He turns then, with a huge, sparkling smile. She almost collapses with relief.

"Anna, I don't believe it… I thought… you said, in no uncertain terms—"

"I know." Tears threaten and she can't keep her voice steady. "I changed my mind."

"Come and sit down, let's talk about this. You're shaking."

They sit together. He holds her trembling hands in his, as if to steady them by force.

"You changed your mind… Was it Sai and Davey who turned you?" How young he looks. Barely a line crosses the smooth skin of his face. His hands in hers are soft, the fingers slim and long.

She frees a hand, rubs her forehead in the effort to get the words right. "No, not them. My father. After he died I felt really unnerved. For the first time in my life, I lost the ground from under my feet. It was a real wake-up call to… to what's important, I suppose. To the fact that in the end my work just isn't enough."

"And?"

"And I love you. And I know you love me too." She swallows, clears her throat. "And I began to think… to wonder what I really want, and what you really want."

He nods, his eyes bright and searching. She takes a breath. "I know you want children. Do you think you might want them, well, one, with me?"

She can barely breathe again, her heart thumping. She's never laid herself open like this before and the fear of rejection and pain is terrifying.

His face is now serious. He cradles her hands in his.

"I think I might."

*

"But, Will…"

"But what?"

She needs to say it now, or it will sit unresolved. "You should think it through. I'm forty-six now, you're barely thirty."

"And?" A smile plays around his mouth.

"No, we need to think seriously about this. It could take a while to conceive. I could be even older by the time it happens, if it happens at all. That means I could be close to sixty with a child under ten years old. I don't intend to slow down, but you never know…" She bites her lip, she wants to say it all, get it out into the open, so he knows what he's committing to.

"Anna."

"And I don't want to be a single mum, especially as I'll be older, so—"

"Anna, stop. The age difference doesn't bother me one bit. I want to be with you, and I want to have a child with you. Anything could happen to anyone, however young or old, and we can't second-guess the future, so let's not even try. I have no intention of leaving you."

"There's another issue. To do with my age."

"The health of the child?"

She nods, wishing it weren't true.

"You'd have all the tests, wouldn't you? So we'd know, at least."

"Of course. I want to have a child naturally if I can. I saw a specialist, and he said it's possible, though there are risks."

He draws her close, looks deep into her eyes. "But I would care for you and our child gladly, whatever problems we might have. I want this, Anna. I want to create a family, I want to look after you. Whatever you need to do – keep your business, satisfy whatever ambitions you have for it, set up an empire – I'll support you. I'll be a stay-at-home dad if you want. I'll love it."

*

Will's reaction leaves her euphoric; a heady, dizzy feeling that she's leapt into the unknown. When she's not excited, she's terrified, wondering what she's committed to, why she's

147

changing a life which has always been so firmly mapped out in her mind.

After that first evening, when they talked for hours, the plan for a child together triggers a whole new emotional roller coaster in Anna. She's never felt as vulnerable and at the same time as powerful as she does now, now that she's let someone in. Her marriage was never like this, she didn't allow it to be, and since then she has never trusted anyone so completely.

But committing to Will is different. Somehow, because it's him, because of the way he is, she feels able to do almost anything.

They tell no one, not even her mother. They don't want to risk disappointing her. They get on with the business of making a baby in private. They buy all the books, change their diets, sleep and spend long hours in bed. Will works on projects closer to home.

Anna puts out feelers to recruitment agencies, plans how she'll manage her business over the next few years. She decides to strengthen her contracts with two Lithuanian suppliers and sets up a trip to agree terms with each of them.

*

Clutching a cuddly toy and a bottle of champagne, Anna and Will walk through the once-immaculate hallway, squeezing past a buggy and a tricycle. A balloon bounces gently on the floor as they head for the garden, where people have gathered in the warm June air. A tiny girl in yellow dungarees sits laughing on a brightly coloured rocking toy as Sai crouches beside her, taking pictures.

"Davey, she's gorgeous," Anna says as Davey appears beside them. "Doting parents? Sleepless nights? Drowning in nappies?"

"All of that and loving it," he says. "I know you don't get it, Anna, but parenthood is underrated. I've – we've – never felt anything like it. We're full of wonder and awe. We're overwhelmed with love for her."

Anna swallows the unexpected lump in her throat. She squats beside Sai and helps rock the child, who laughs, a trill of bell-like notes.

"Hello, little Jenny," Anna says. "I'm Anna." Jenny stares at her, rocking to and fro with concentration.

"Na," she says, and smiles. Tiny teeth, white as white, emerge from pink gums. Anna experiences something she's never felt before: a deep tenderness for the innocence, the fragility, the sheer newness of this child.

"See, even Anna can't resist her. She's smitten." Sai catches them both on camera and leans towards Anna to show her the result. She looks at the photo and sees a child – relaxed, smiling – staring at a woman with soft, uncertain eyes, a bit like herself. In that moment, they could be mother and child. Her hand begins to wobble and she hands the camera back before she gives herself away.

*

The buzz of her mobile intrudes upon a deep well of thoughts of Will, and babies, and fertility treatment. She watches, fascinated, as it flashes and starts to turn on the glass table-top, as if it's come alive. She pounces on it, fumbling. Without seeing the name on the screen, she presses the green button.

"Karolina's here. I thought you might want to know." It's Kate's voice on the end of the line.

"Karolina?" For a moment, she has no recollection of the name.

"You know, Magdalena's sister, who was kidnapped, the one you thought might give you some pointers about Margryta?"

Anna's at home on her own, working, or trying to work. Kate's sudden entry into her private world brings her up short. She struggles to remember what Kate's talking about, who Magdalena and her sister are. At last it falls into place.

"Sorry, Kate, I was miles away, working on the business plan." The white lie jumps from her tongue with ease. She gives herself a silent reprimand. "Karolina, of course. How come she's here?" Playing for time, she forces herself to concentrate.

"Magdalena offered to help us with the children over the summer holidays, as a thank you. She asked if Karolina could come too, she's been struggling to get over what happened, poor girl. So I said yes, and they're here. They're staying for three weeks, then they're travelling for a week or two before they go back. So if you want to talk to Karolina, now's your chance."

She's vowed to give up on Margryta's story. But at Kate's suggestion her scalp tingles with a tiny thrill of excitement. There's a new element to the story – there's a chance it could even open up its secrets. She can't resist.

"Can I come over, later maybe?" she says.

*

Karolina is a small, pale version of Magdalena. She's dressed in the uniform of girls her age: jeans tight to her slender ankles, T-shirt and long cardigan, sleeves pulled down over bony hands, trainers. Limp brown hair hangs to her shoulders. Her eyes are huge and anxious, flitting from person to person as she follows Magdalena into the sitting room like a shadow. She hangs back, waits to be invited to sit. Magdalena murmurs something to her, her face turned towards her as they huddle on the sofa, her hair brushing her sister's cheek as she sits.

A small person in pink pyjamas appears at the door.

"Mummy. You need to come."

Kate, on her way to the kitchen to get drinks, takes the little girl's hand and says: "Bed time for you, young lady. Anna, I'll get the drinks on the way back. You carry on."

Karolina's eyes widen as she watches Kate's retreating

back, then flick back to Anna, who smiles, hoping to put her at ease.

"It's okay, Karolina," Anna says. "I'm not going to ask you anything difficult."

"My sister's English isn't very good. I will tell her what you say," Magdalena says.

"Tell her not to be scared. I'm just trying to find out about a girl, a Lithuanian, who might have been taken, like Karolina."

Magdalena nods and translates.

"The girl's name was Margryta. Can you ask if she heard that name at all in the house where she was held?"

Magdalena and her sister exchange a stream of Polish. Karolina shakes her head a few times.

"She says there were many girls. She didn't know their names," Magdalena whispers eventually. "She's sorry she can't help you."

Anna nods. This girl looks brittle enough to break with one finger. She doesn't want to frighten her.

"Do you know who they were? The men who took you?" Karolina nods as Magdalena translates. She replies in Polish. Her fingers shake as she pushes her fringe from her eyes.

"She doesn't know who they were, she'd never seen them before. They spoke in Polish, except for one man. They always spoke English to him. She thinks he was the boss."

"The boss? Does she think he was British then?"

"She doesn't know if he was actually British. Perhaps he couldn't speak Polish."

"Did she tell the police about the English speaker?" When Karolina understands the question, she shakes her head and gesticulates.

"No, she's too scared of them."

"Of the police?"

Magdalena nods. "She's been in trouble with them, she doesn't like them."

"Does she know where the girls are taken afterwards, what happens to them?"

Another shake of the head.

She's running out of questions.

"Magdalena, would she look at a picture for me? It might help her remember."

Magdalena asks. Karolina nods, her eyes huge and glassy.

She stares intently at Anna's phone, enlarging the image with slender fingers. There's no sign of recognition. She hands it back, shaking her head, and says something to Magdalena.

"She says she's sorry. She's never seen that girl. She only saw one or two other girls and she's not sure she'd even recognise them."

Anna sighs. "That's okay, tell her thank you from me. It's not a problem."

Karolina asks a question, her voice urgent, her hand on Magdalena's arm.

"She asks was this one of the other girls? What happened to her?" Magdalena says.

"Oh, no, I don't think so. I thought it was possible she was there at the same time, but this girl is from Lithuania and she is missing." This fragile girl doesn't need to know the cruel truth.

*

Dear Ms Dent,

Thank you for the statement you completed with regard to Case No. 1569830, Margryta Simonis. Perhaps you would call in to the police station next time you are in Vilnius. I believe you may be able to help us with something.

Kind regards,
Vladimir Rostov

CHAPTER 14

Anna's marriage had failed, but her relentless focus on work was not the real reason.

Her parents had wanted her to settle down, and she'd found a kind, well-meaning, uncomplicated man who loved her. But to her parents' bewilderment, she hadn't settled down, not at all. It was barely a blip in her relentless work schedule. She wasn't excited, not even about the wedding. She was twenty-seven and not the least interested in the price of the dress or what flowers were on the tables. It all seemed a waste of time, money and effort to her.

And the relationship? If it had ever been right for her, it certainly wasn't once they were married. Perhaps it stemmed from being an only child, the apple of her parents' eyes. Whatever it was that drove her, she continued her life as if he was barely there, on the periphery, and she was sometimes surprised to find him in her space at the end of the day, as if she'd forgotten there was someone else living there. Looking back, she knows she hurt him, remembering his wide eyes searching hers for signs of love, of caring for him and his life. His need for her love irritated her, his presence in her home weighed her down.

Before they married, they talked about children, the future. She told him she wanted children, eventually, one day, but she didn't really think about what she was saying. For him, she realised later, that conversation determined everything, set them on a certain path. But for her the matter of children was so far in the future, so much a matter of *after* everything else she wanted to achieve, that they could have been talking about living on the moon as far as she was concerned. Interesting to think about for the future, one day, maybe. Now, the present, had been far more important, far more exciting, happening right in front of her. Nothing stood in her way.

The marriage ended sixteen years ago. When she proved to him beyond any doubt that she was on her own particular path.

*

They met at a party in London. He was standing in the kitchen, a beer in his hand, leaning against the fridge. He listened quietly as the group around him swayed and laughed and bumped up against him. Every so often someone reached round his back for the fridge door, looking for wine, or milk, or just looking, and he good-naturedly bent his body into the small space left in the crush of people.

She squeezed into the group with her flatmate, a girl called Maxine – tall, beautiful, popular with the boys – and Maxine introduced her to Chris. Anna was intrigued by his quietness in the midst of the fizz of partying people. He listened with good-natured patience to her chatter on about the world of textiles, her dream of running a company. At the end of the evening he offered her a lift home. She felt no threat, no male competitiveness from him, not then and not afterwards when they began to date in a slow, uncomplicated manner. Maybe that attracted her. She felt safe with him. He seemed to like her strength, her way of spotting an opportunity, her confidence.

He was an engineer. Meeting him now, she would be immediately wary, knowing her creativity and drive would grate with his engineer's need for fact, for order, a straightforward life plan. But then she was young and full of expectation. He provided her with the stability she'd always relied on at home, allowing her to fly in safety, knowing if she flew too high there would always be someone there to catch her. She believed she loved him, at first.

But only three short years after their wedding, Anna made the decision that guaranteed the end of their marriage.

*

The irony was that when she found herself pregnant she felt a flush of excitement, joy, even.

She was alone when she took the test, which was a good thing, she soon realised. Chris was out with some old school friends. She'd taken some time to admit to herself the signs: the sudden sickness that overtook her one day at work, the tender breasts. She thought the test would simply rule it out. She was taking all the right precautions, after all, but she bought it on a whim, just in case. Once Chris was out of the flat she sat in the bathroom and followed the instructions, unprepared for the bombshell revealed in blue dye.

The feeling of joy was fleeting, though. It was superseded within moments by a thump of shock which left her damp with cold sweat. Hiding the white plastic pen with its treacherous blue lines, wrapping it in one plastic bag, and then another, she'd rushed outside to hurl it in the dustbin, then gone back and sat, her body balled with tension, on the sitting-room sofa. Every part of her recoiled in terror from this challenge. Her ambitions were set, she was on the path to success, all her plans were in place. This would ruin everything.

It simply could not happen.

That evening, on her own in the flat with her news, trembling with shock, she decided to keep quiet, see how she felt in a day or so. It wouldn't harm to wait.

The day or so turned into a week, then a month, then more. She ignored or hid the physical clues. She started to wear more black, loose jumpers, long shirts. Her body grew, though not as much as she expected. At work and with Chris, she talked about putting on weight, pretended she was on a diet.

She even went for the first scan. She thought it might help her decide, that the tiny floating creature would become a person to her, a living human being that was going to be her child.

The nurse was kind and chatty, expecting her to be happy and excited. Anna was interested, in a detached kind of way, and uneasy.

"Looking good," the nurse said, smoothing the cool gel across Anna's distended stomach. Anna looked on in fascination.

"What gender is it?" she said.

"Hard to say. Do you have a preference?"

"A girl," Anna said, without thinking.

*

In the mirror, she scrutinised herself in the harsh light of the early morning. Her breasts were soft and full, the nipples pinker than before. Her belly, usually so flat and tight, curved outwards so far that she needed to crane her neck to see her feet from above. She took a breath, pulling it in as far as she could; she still looked pregnant. Her whole body looked softer, rounder.

She had to tell Chris.

She was ready to do it. She came home early, cooked dinner, turned off the music and opened her mouth. But nothing came out, the words wouldn't form themselves. A trap had shut somewhere in her brain, kidnapping the announcement she'd prepared.

She stumbled through a story about needing a holiday, wanting to get away somewhere warm. The idea went down well, he smiled and made some suggestions and the plan to tell him the news was in shards around her.

A week later she had the abortion.

It was inevitable that he would find out. Afterwards she knew that, in a way, she wanted him to.

It had all been pretty straightforward; she was in and out of the clinic in a flash. She ignored the inner voice telling her it might be her only chance, she might regret it for the rest of her life, asking her why was she doing it when she was with a loving, kind man. She went back to work immediately, dismissing the advice to rest.

The bleeding started at the office, towards the end of the day. She made an excuse, raced home as fast as she could, hoping Chris would be out.

But he was there when she arrived, shock on his face as she ran to the bathroom, blood running down her legs. At first she ignored him when he yelled at her to open the door, to let him in. But in the end she had to give in. The blood kept on coming, so much of it, she almost passed out as she stood to unlock the door. He called the ambulance, went with her, tried to comfort her. He was confused and concerned, but as yet unaware. She said nothing, turned her head to the wall, squeezed her eyes shut to keep him out.

They had to operate, to clear her womb where traces had been left. It was as if the baby had needed to tell its story.

When she awoke a short time later, she was alone.

*

The only person who knew about the baby, apart from Chris, was Kate.

Anna never told her parents, they were upset enough at the break-up of her marriage. She told them it was amicable, that she and Chris had simply made a mistake, admitted it and gone their separate ways. This did little to comfort them as they liked Chris, his solidity, his ordinariness. They were looking forward to the future, grandparenthood and security for their daughter.

They didn't need to know that she'd denied them a grand-child while betraying her husband in the worst possible way.

In the weeks following the abortion and the break-up, she'd gone through a raft of emotions. When she returned to the flat and realised all his belongings were gone, she was surprised. She hadn't expected him to go so soon. At times she was deeply ashamed of herself. There were moments when a flash of memory would bring her up short, like a slap in the face. The reasons for her break-up with Chris were horrible, like a nasty dream she wanted to forget, and she knew her behaviour had been unforgivable. It was shocking, even to her. She buried what happened, forced it down, to a place where it could be contained, imprisoned and eventually forgotten.

She kept her mind occupied, throwing herself into work, immersing herself in it. She took work back to her new bedsit – she'd given up the flat as soon as she could – and was first at her desk every day. Her career flourished, while her body became thin and her personality brittle.

On a rare visit to her parents, the first since she broke up with Chris, she bumped into Kate at the petrol station. Delighted to see her, she'd agreed to meet for coffee. Kate had not held back, had bombarded her with questions about the break-up. In the end, she found herself unable to sustain the lie, and she'd told Kate, in strict confidence, the ghastly details.

*

When she was about three years old, Anna decided to make a hole in the fence and visit next door's garden. Before her mother even noticed she'd gone, the neighbour returned her, nails broken and bleeding, splinters buried in her tiny hands, triumphant. This extraordinary determination, evident even then, defined her through her childhood and into adult life.

After the abortion, she thought a lot about herself and what made her do it. She decided she was different from other people. She was unable to help herself, simply deficient and lacking in the soft, caring emotions. She was selfish and she couldn't help it. There was nothing she could do about it. Her best plan, therefore, was to follow her ambitions and try not to harm people along the way. She decided she wasn't cut out for proper relationships, other than transient ones or those she could dip into when she felt like it, as she could with her friends. She kept an eye out for danger, allowed nobody to get close, and earned a reputation for being ruthless in business as well as in her private life.

She was certain she'd made the right choice.

She saw Chris again, once. After a few weeks' total silence she received an email stating that he wanted a divorce and that he had started proceedings. No mention of what she had done, no accusations or recriminations. He wanted to meet to say goodbye; he'd accepted a job in Australia. She read this news with a mixture of respect and relief and agreed, reluctantly, to see him.

They met on a bench in the park, on a gloomy March day that matched her mood. Pigeons fluttered around them as they sat an arm's length apart and avoided each other's gaze. She knew what he was going to say, had prepared herself, but no preparation could have made it easy. She tried to pre-empt the question, asked him about the job, but he was having none of it.

"Why? That's all I want to know. Why? Was it so bad being married to me, having a future together? A baby?" His voice trembled with emotion. "How could you not bring yourself to tell me?"

She shook her head and hardened her voice. "I tried. I really did. But I'm not… There's something bad about me. I just couldn't. I'm sorry."

"No, I won't let you get away with that. I knew who you were when I married you, I knew you. I would have loved to have a baby with you, but you didn't give me a chance. You didn't give me…" His voice broke.

"I know," she said. And she did. She knew.

They didn't stay for long, there didn't seem any point. When they parted, she tried to kiss him on the cheek, but he turned away.

*

"What do you mean?" Anna says, staring in surprise at Kate. It's late afternoon and the café is full with mothers and small children, their buggies lining the walls. Anna and Kate have squeezed themselves into the tiny corner space by the window.

"It's sixteen years since you had the abortion, Anna. Margryta was sixteen."

"That's just ridiculous, it's got nothing to do with that."

But even as she says it, doubt flicks into her mind. Has she really been searching for a meaning to Margryta's life, in order to make sense of her own?

The memory of the abortion has remained buried for years, along with the guilt and the shame. She tries not to think about it, never talks about it, even to Kate. It hasn't occurred to her in any way that this obsession, this need to know Margryta's story, has anything to do with her own history.

But Kate's put her finger right on Anna's deepest nerve. Her friend has an uncanny way of seeing through people's smokescreens, their protective layers, and getting to the essence of them, even when they don't want her to. Anna would trust Kate with anything, but sometimes she wishes she wasn't quite so observant.

It seems so obvious, as soon as Kate points it out. The sad story of Margryta and her foreshortened life has touched Anna in the one place she thought was protected like a fortress in her heart. Sixteen years ago she destroyed her child. Margryta was sixteen when she died. It's so obvious.

Kate is unrepentant. "You look as if you've seen a ghost. You really didn't make that connection?"

"You underestimate my ability to bury the past and ignore the obvious. I didn't make any connection, the story struck a chord, but I didn't realise it was that one. But you're right, of course. Perhaps it's atonement, of some sort."

"So now will you stop it? Now you know it's all about you, and not about her?"

*

From the day she had the abortion and her duplicity was discovered, Anna had done her best not to remember. To forget Chris' stricken face, to rationalise her decision to have the abortion, to forgive herself for not telling him. To bury the guilt and forget the loss.

At first it wasn't hard. Apart from her parents, work meant everything. It sustained and fulfilled her. She was proud of her success, her independence, the money that helped her buy her own place and live well. For years, she was able to persuade herself that she'd done the right thing.

But then an odd thing happened. Sitting in a taxi on the way home from a particularly tough meeting, her mind numb from too many hours of concentration, she remembered the date. It was the anniversary of the day of the abortion.

In a few months, her child would have been seven years old.

The realisation hit her like a blow. Reeling, she doubled over, sweat flushing upwards from her chest to her scalp, her breath reduced to sharp, rasping gasps. The driver, spotting her distress in the rear-view mirror, stopped the car, opened the door and offered her some water. Gradually the panic retreated and the driver took her home.

But after that, she thought about the baby often. When she least expected it, a picture would drift into her mind. A little girl – always a girl – dark hair falling down her back in soft curls, doing her homework in the kitchen. Riding a bike, laughing with friends. Every time, she shook herself, did her best to ignore it. And though the vision of this child, her child, did nothing to change her driving ambition, it stayed with her, and every year, on the anniversary of the abortion, she would remember.

*

It's just not happening. Each month she's disappointed and she knows Will's worried too. The more time that passes, the less likely it becomes.

After four months they go to the clinic, together, for tests.

They sit in front of the desk and wait for the consultant to come in. They're both anxious, though they've prepared themselves. They've discussed IVF – he's as reluctant as she is, knowing that failure would be agony – and adoption. They've agreed to keep an open mind. If the natural way isn't possible, they'll go for the next option. They hold hands between the two tub chairs, like teenagers. Her hand is hot in his but she won't let go.

The door opens and the consultant walks in with a confident air, which Anna finds both comforting and irritating. He holds her file in his hand and, spectacles gleaming, checks thoroughly through the papers on the top before he looks up, pulling his glasses off and twirling them, sitting back in his chair.

"Well, it's not the best of news," he says. "But not the worst, either."

There's no obvious reason why they haven't conceived. The tests show nothing untoward. This leaves them with no clear way forward. They can carry on trying for a few months, but because of Anna's age each month is precious. They could opt for IVF straight away, which will immediately start them on a difficult and unpredictable road, or if they're reluctant they can try fertility tablets first. He doesn't recommend leaving it for too long; he does recommend doing everything they can now, before it's too late. They exchange glances and agree to try the short-term option first.

Then, as they stand to leave, he says with an encouraging smile: "Of course, as you know, the fact that you've conceived successfully before, Ms Dent, is a good sign."

*

He says nothing as they walk away from the clinic, nothing as they drive for twenty minutes back to the flat. She's struck dumb, her mind racing.

She'd known it was a risk, of course, not telling him. She agonised over it, tried to imagine telling him, but she couldn't form the sentences, couldn't find the words.

It was a risk, too, asking the consultant not to mention it. He sees so many cases, he can't be blamed for not remembering. Nor for failing to check the note that said: *Ms Dent wants to keep this information confidential*. Perhaps it should have been clearer: *Don't mention the abortion to Ms Dent's partner*. Or maybe they prefer to stay neutral.

Back in the flat, leaning against the kitchen cupboards, he turns to her. "What was that, Anna?" he says.

"I'm sorry, Will. I tried, but I couldn't tell you."

"Come on, I'm a grown man. I know you've had a life before me. Tell me."

"It's bad. You're going to hate me."

"Anna."

She takes a deep breath and walks towards the window, where she can see life going on below. Mothers with buggies, prams, toddlers walking, are everywhere. It's like a Lowry painting, strangely static, though they're all going somewhere.

"Anna?"

"I know, I need to tell you. But I'm ashamed of what happened. So ashamed that I've buried it. That's why I haven't told you."

"What is it, for God's sake? Please, tell me."

CHAPTER 15

When she wakes, he's gone.

They didn't argue, or even discuss what she told him. She gave him the facts, tried to explain her shame, how she had been young and stupid. How she could see now what a terrible thing she did; how she's a different person now. He nodded and held her hand. But he was quiet while she spoke and for the rest of the evening as they ate dinner and sat together for a while, staring at their laptops.

He's probably processing the information, she told herself as they lay in bed together. It will be fine. He fell asleep almost immediately, as he always did, his face softened, his chest rising and falling gently, the sound of his breathing comforting her. She lay beside him for what seemed like hours, her eyes open, unable to settle and not wanting to disturb him, until at last she drifted into a strange, dream-filled sleep, vivid images and strong emotions grasping her in turn until she woke, groggy and exhausted, to see the pillow next to her own empty.

*

She lies for a moment, trying to remember. Did he tell her he was travelling this week? She has a vague recollection of a conversation a couple of days ago, but the details evade her, her mind still in the grip of the night's sleep. She listens, but the bathroom is quiet, the door still open and the light off, and nothing breaks the silence of the empty rooms. She pads through the flat, hoping for a note, a sign that he's slipped out for milk, breakfast, a newspaper. But there's nothing.

Walking back into the bedroom, she lifts the bedspread from the floor, checks his side of the bed for his travel bag, which, when he's home, lives underneath. It's not there. A slow wave of alarm starts to rise from deep inside her. She grabs her mobile, starts to dial, then tells herself she's being ridiculous and cuts the call. She decides to text, her fingers clumsy. Takes a deep breath, deletes it, then sits on the bed and starts again, slowly. *Sorry I missed you. Can't remember where you're going? Xx*

She sits watching the screen for a few minutes, then, angry with herself, takes the mobile into the bathroom and turns on the shower. After a few minutes, when she's in the middle of washing her hair, the phone buzzes and lights up on the shelf above the basin. Ignoring the lather pouring from her hair and the rivers of water from her body soaking the bath mat at her feet, she dries her hands quickly, dropping the towel in her haste.

Belarus. Might call in on Daria on the way back. Home in a week or so. X

*

She tries to be rational. Nothing's changed. Normally, when he's travelling, he doesn't wake her if it's early, he doesn't make a big thing of it. And she takes it in her stride, trusting he'll be back when he says he will, giving him the space to get on with his work as he does for her.

But today feels different. For the rest of the day, she carries on with life as usual, the work day taking over and forcing her to focus on practicalities, decisions, other people. But later, as the light fades and she's alone again, the agitation that's been threatening all day wins over.

Quashing it with logic, she tries to analyse the events of the last few days, the conversation last night and Will's reaction to her confession. He hadn't been shocked or angry, just thoughtful. But that's Will. He's never hasty in his reactions, always contained.

Is this paranoia? An unconscious desire to be punished for what she has done? Possibly. But what had she expected? Perhaps she's making too much of this. He's an experienced, mature person who's perfectly capable of seeing that her actions then were not the actions of the person she is today.

Or maybe he needs some time to absorb what she said, some distance to think about a future with a person whose past behaviour has been so breathtakingly selfish.

*

She stops herself from calling him that night, and the next, and the next. It's not their habit to be constantly in touch when they're travelling, but still she starts to feel angry with him.

On the sixth day she texts him: *Are you okay? X*

What she really wants to say is: Are we okay?

There's no reply, only heavy silence, a blank screen. She calls; it goes straight to voicemail. She leaves a message anyway.

She has to talk it out with him. That's the reason for the sense of disconnect. This revelation, this deep secret that she's so terribly ashamed of, that she's kept from pretty much everyone for so long, needs more, demands so much more attention.

Of course she should have told him about the abortion before; he deserved the bare facts of it, at least. It was even cathartic to tell him – Will, who means so much to her in so many ways. And for him to take her revelations away with him and not give them the chance to air, to unfold, to reveal their full implications, leaves her bereft, halfway up and halfway down, uncertain and incomplete.

Years of denial have made the horrible truth more difficult

to face. While her younger self could rationalise, ignore the demon whispering in her ear, telling her she was a bad person, her older, more mature self, looking the demon in the eye, suffers the full force of all those buried feelings and all that time.

Alone in the flat she stays up late, torturing herself. She forces herself to face the facts, refuses to make excuses for herself, berates herself for being selfish and cruel.

She thinks about the child that might have been, how easily she and Chris could have worked it out. How she didn't even consider the possibility at the time. How that little girl would have changed Anna's life. How her parents – her father, oh, her father – would have adored the child, helped with the childcare, loved the role of grandparents.

And how she, Anna, might have matured into a different, kinder, more selfless person for whom friends and family came first and work second. As it should be.

*

"All set for tomorrow, Anna?" Jane's voice sounds far away, though she's right there at her desk.

"I've emailed you everything – your flight details and hotel reservation – haven't you seen it?" Jane looks concerned at Anna's blank face.

"Yes, yes of course." She's almost forgotten her upcoming trip to Vilnius. She's combining a lot into this trip, planning to make the most of her time there. She has to go to the factory, to a quarterly meeting with the manager. She's promised Daria she will pop in to see her. It's the first time since she went with Will. She's keen to see how she can help.

And she needs to make an appointment with Vladimir at the police station. Though she promised to end her search, his email has tempted her.

And if the police want to speak to her, she must comply, surely.

The trip might distract her from imagining the worst, from the fear eating away at her. The fear that Will is angry and disappointed, changing his mind about wanting a family, a future, with her.

*

She endures the flight in a strange, filmic daze. Once she's on the road to the city, the farmland and forests of Lithuania giving way to the first signs of the suburbs, she rouses herself. Though she hasn't heard from Will, it signifies nothing, and beating herself up is pointless. She needs to get on with her trip, deal with whatever happens. She can't risk another breakdown. And she can't change the past.

After a short nap in her hotel room, she showers, changes her clothes, squares her shoulders and leaves for the factory.

*

The village where Daria lives is about forty minutes from Vilnius, not far from the border with Belarus. It takes a little longer this time – it's rush hour in the city – but it's a straight road and an easy journey and she's soon climbing the steps to the dingy flat.

Sasha is home from school and opens the door, shouting to his mum when he sees Anna. She's brought flowers for Daria and a new toy truck for Sasha. He hops with excitement when she hands it to him.

"Anna, it's so good to see you, thank you so much for the gifts. Say thank you, Sasha."

"Thank you," Sasha says from the floor, where he's already engrossed with the new toy.

Daria has aged in the few weeks since they last met. Her eyes have sunk into deep ditches and the skin on her face looks paper-thin. She coughs into a handkerchief as she leads Anna to the small sitting room.

"Have you been unwell, Daria?"

"Just a cold, small children bring so many germs home from school. But he loves it. He has many friends. And he's learning English!"

"Are you?" she says to the little boy. "Are you learning to speak English?"

"Show her, Sasha," his mum says, drawing him close. "Tell Anna what you have learned."

"How are you?" he says, each word pronounced with care. "My name is Sasha."

"Brilliant!" Anna says, laughing. "How clever are you?"

"How are you, how are you, how are you," he sings, dancing around the room, black curls bobbing.

"Is it better for you, now Sasha is at school?" Anna says. "Are you able to work at all?"

"It is only a few hours, you know," Daria says. "I work when I can. It will be better, when he is older." She pours the coffee from a tall metal jug and offers Anna a biscuit. "How is Will? We love Will so much, and we miss him. Sasha asks about him. Is he busy with work?"

It's an effort to hide her disappointment. She doesn't want to alarm Daria, but she was hoping she might have heard. "He is travelling, working. In Belarus, I think. Has he called you?"

Daria laughs. "He gives me a mobile phone. He is very generous, but I don't use it. It is expensive." She waves a bony hand. "Belarus, you say? A horrible place."

"Why do you say that?" As soon as the words are out of her mouth, she realises her mistake.

"My Olga was taken there. Very bad people in Belarus."

Anna swallows, keeping her voice steady with some effort. "I'm so sorry, Daria, I know what happened to Olga."

Daria touches her arm. "Thank you, Anna. But I am sure Will, he is careful. He is a good man."

"Yes." She doesn't want to think about the reasons why Will might need to be careful. "But Daria, about the mobile, I'm sure he's happy to pay for your calls. You must use it,

Daria. What if something happens to Sasha, or to you? You need to be able to call someone. You could call me, even."

Daria smiles."You are kind, like Will."

"Look, can you turn the mobile on, on a regular day? Sunday nights, perhaps. Then we can check you're okay and say hello to Sasha. Would that be good?"

"Okay," Daria says, but she seems uncertain.

"Okay, get the mobile and we'll turn it on. I'll put my number in for you, and make sure you know how to use it. How about that?"

*

"Ms Dent, good morning to you," Vladimir says expansively, the wall behind the door taking a bashing as he bursts into the room.

Behind him, overshadowed by his enormous torso, is another man, who closes the door carefully behind him. He's smaller and neater than Vladimir, though his black jumper stretches over broad shoulders and she can see the curve of his bicep as he picks up a chair to sit down. His hair is trimmed short; everything about his movements is controlled, efficient, as if he's preserving energy. He looks like the perfect stereotype of a Russian spy.

She shifts warily as Vladimir drops his bulk into the flimsy chair opposite. His leg bangs into the table, causing it to quiver, but he seems oblivious. He turns to the other man suddenly, as if he's forgotten that he was there.

"Ah, Ms Dent, this is Detective Bockus. Investigating officer."

She extends her hand, which is grasped firmly, held a little too long, as she is scrupulously inspected by piercing brown eyes. "Detective Bockus."

Vladimir says, glancing at his colleague as if for approval, "Welcome back to Vilnius, Mrs Dent. I hope you are having a good trip?"

"Thank you, yes. How are you?"

He shrugs expressively and fumbles with the brown folder in front of him without opening it. Bockus sits, arms folded over his chest, impassive, as if waiting for things to get interesting.

"Work, work," Vladimir says. "What can you do? People do bad things, we try to sort it out. Sometimes we succeed, sometimes we don't." He sighs and half closes his eyes, as if he's lost in some distant train of thought.

"Did you succeed with the Margryta Simonis case yet?" she says, hoping he'll get to the point soon.

"No, we haven't yet found the person or persons who murdered Margryta Simonis," he says. "But we think we are getting close." He shoots a look at Bockus, who leans forward and pulls the manila file towards him.

"I hope you can help me," Bockus says. "Please look at these pictures, and tell me if you recognise any of the people in them." He opens the file and draws out some photographs, setting them out in a neat line for Anna to study. He watches her face intently, so that for a moment she feels foolish, as if she's landed unexpectedly in a television drama.

Pulling in her chair, she starts to look at the photos one by one, left to right. Vladimir sits motionless as he waits.

There are six pictures in all, all taken from a distance. She wonders briefly if they were taken from the window of a car, a large black lens surreptitiously snapping. She sees nothing she recognises until she gets to the fourth. It shows a large man looking back over his shoulder towards the right of the picture. His face is in profile, one side in the shadow. He's smartly dressed in suit and tie, his hair groomed and trimmed. His left hand lies on the roof of a dark-coloured car beside him and he looks as if he's calling out to someone. There are two figures walking away from him, their faces partly obscured, their collars turned up against the backs of their necks.

There's something familiar about the profile of the suited man in the foreground, and Anna picks up the photograph to look more closely. As she does, she notices the watch on his left wrist: chunky, ostentatious.

With a shock of recognition she drops the photo back onto the table and looks up at Bockus, who raises an enquiring eyebrow. "Ms Dent? You know this man?"

"Maybe. I... I think so," she says, picking up the photo again. She stands, takes it to the window and studies it. The harsh light of Vilnius brings the image into focus.

"I can't be sure," she says, turning back to the table and taking her seat, still staring at the photo. "Is he a suspect?"

"Who do you think it is?" Bockus has become very focused, staring into her eyes with a disconcerting intensity. Vladimir, too, stares at her as if willing her to reveal her secrets. She feels uncomfortable, unsure of herself.

"Well, as I say, I'm really not sure. But it looks like a man I met here, when the flights were grounded, when the volcano in Iceland erupted. I don't really know him. His name was Gavin."

"Gavin? Last name?" Vladimir takes a notebook from his pocket, fumbles for a pen.

"We only met briefly. Strachan? Strickman? I'm not sure."

"Strickland?"

"Yes, that's it."

"Where did you meet him?"

"Well, I first saw him and his wife in the hotel near Klaipeda but we didn't speak. Then I met them in the bar of my hotel in Vilnius. His wife's called Charlotte." Vladimir writes her name down with a flourish.

"British?"

"Oh, yes, both of them."

"Any idea why they were here?"

"They were here for his work, something to do with clubs and bars. He spends a lot of time here, I think. Is this to do with Margryta?"

"He's a person of interest to us." Bockus sits back and studies her gravely. "Can you tell me exactly where you were when you met him, and what you know about him?"

"Well, it's not much." She reaches down for her phone. "I can tell you exactly when it was, though."

Checking the dates is easy. She tries to remember the conversation she had with Charlotte, but the details are hazy; she remembers the occasion well enough, because it was when she met Will, but she can't recall much of the small talk with the group at the bar. Looking back she knows that Will's arrival had overtaken any interest she might have had in the other people.

She's beginning to sweat in the airless room; her hands and the back of her neck are damp. She lifts her hair from her collar for a moment while Vladimir takes notes.

The detective asks her who else was there, in the group at the bar, and she describes the Russian couple, the sharp-looking man, the young girl. She can't remember their names; she barely registered them in the first place. She excludes Will entirely; he isn't part of this.

"Do you recognise the other men in the picture?" Detective Bockus says.

She picks up the photo again. The man in the foreground looks more than ever like Gavin now with the groomed hair and the expensive-looking watch. Her attention shifts to the background, to the other men partially caught in the camera shot.

A sudden wave of nausea jolts her from her seat and she slams the photo back onto the table. "I'm sorry, I feel…" She tastes the bile in her mouth and rushes out of the room.

Running down the corridor she sees a sign for the ladies. She makes it as far as the first basin before her insides heave, the contents of her stomach forcing their way up through her mouth, spraying onto the white ceramic. She runs the water fast, as her stomach cramps and twists and a grunt of pain escapes as she retches again.

Finally it stops and she gulps water with a shaking hand. She looks up into the cracked mirror above the basin. Her face has turned ashen behind a veil of hair. Her eyes are red-rimmed and teary, with dark bruises beneath them. She takes a few deep, shuddering breaths, feels a little better. She washes her face and a lock of hair that got in the way of her stream of vomit, scrubbing it hard with a squirt of soap to get rid of the smell.

Then she inspects her clothing, wills herself to stop shaking and goes back out to the waiting Vladimir.

CHAPTER 16

Her mum's pale face breaks into a smile. She ushers her in before giving her a hug and a kiss on the cheek. Her skin feels dry and papery against Anna's and there's a gentle whiff of perfume in her hair.

In the kitchen, she bustles about making tea. The routine is comforting; Anna watches as her mother moves about opening drawers and cupboards, barely needing to look at what she's doing. Anna hasn't seen her much recently. She's been avoiding the questions about Will.

It occurs to her that she's good at avoidance; she did it when she broke up with Chris. Many weeks passed before she told her parents he'd gone away, many more before she admitted they'd broken up. She's still doing it now. She avoided telling Will about her past and look where that has got her.

It's making her ill, this state of overstretched nerves, drawn-out not-knowing. It started with the bout of vomiting at the police station in Vilnius and she hasn't felt well since. She'd returned to her hotel that day trembling and exhausted. Vladimir was kind, calling her a taxi and waiting to see her into it, waving aside her apologies and telling her to get better, to ask the hotel to call a doctor if she needed one.

She didn't bother with a doctor. She slept for the rest of that day, right through until the morning, and though she woke feeling weak and wobbly, she ate breakfast, forcing down toast and coffee. She called the police station, apologised again to

Vladimir and told him she hadn't recognised the other men in the photo. Then she left to catch her flight back home.

She went back to work the next day, her stomach delicate and her energy low. But she needed to get her mind off Will.

*

She wants to reassure her mother that everything is fine. Will is just away on business, she tells her, nothing unusual in that. It's happened before and she hasn't worried.

Though she can't help worrying. He's left her in limbo, not knowing how he feels.

And now she wonders if there's another reason why she really must talk to him.

*

Hi Mark,
I'm trying to contact Will – I think he's in Belarus at the moment – have you heard from him? It's been a while since he was in touch and I need to talk to him urgently. If you do hear anything, please ask him to contact me. Many thanks.
  Anna

Hi Anna,
He hasn't contacted me, but I'm sure it's nothing to worry about. Communications from parts of Belarus can be patchy. I'll let you know if I hear anything.
  Mark

The email comes promptly, about an hour after hers was sent. She's in the flat, alone, working, late in the evening and she should be in bed. It's also the time of night when problems threaten her tired mind, festering and growing into monsters.

She must talk to Will. She just can't leave it any longer. She's certain the urgency will have got through to him if he has seen or heard the messages, even though she tried to control her voice and her language. He's too mature to be ignoring her when she's made it so clear that she needs him to get in touch.

The fear that something has happened to him is growing rapidly. Though she knows very little about Belarus, she starts to imagine terrible things. In her research about Margryta, she's read stories of criminal gangs, people trafficking, violence and drugs, and she can't even be sure that the police are safe to talk to. What if he's got tangled up in something dangerous and can't contact her?

She needs to talk to someone.

*

"Kate, I know it's late but can you come over? I need to talk…" She can't control the wobble in her voice; her throat aches with anxiety.

"Of course, are you okay?"

"No, I don't know. Something's wrong. Can you come?"

"Yes. Be there in ten."

For once in her life Anna is genuinely unsure of herself. She's so familiar with sorting things out that asking for help feels alien. Kate's the only person who knows her history, her hidden frailties, the only person she can trust with her terrible, looming suspicions.

When the doorbell chimes she starts, her heart racing.

"Thanks so much for dropping everything," she says, as Kate strides towards the kettle, which she fills and puts on without a word.

"Right," Kate says, when the drinks are done and they're sitting at each end of Anna's small sofa. "Are you in shock? You look as if you've seen a ghost."

"No, I'm not in shock. But I think I've messed up, badly."

"Tell me."

She breathes in, closes her eyes for a moment. She starts

at the beginning: tells Kate about her change of heart over children because of Will, about how much she wants it to work. About the confession of the abortion. How she's beating herself up for not screwing up the courage to tell Will before.

About Will being gone, unresponsive, and her fears that he might be angry with her, or even have left her. That she's terrified he's in some kind of trouble in Belarus.

Kate sits in silence, then she lets out a long, breathy whistle.

"Wow, Anna. Okay, well, let's start at the beginning. You've changed your mind about children? No wonder you seem in shock."

"Call me hormonal, all the clichés about the clock ticking, but yes. It's because of Will. He's the only man I've ever felt able to trust properly."

"He obviously loves you."

"I think so. God, I feel so exposed, so vulnerable."

Kate gives her a lopsided smile. "Not like you at all. But, why on earth didn't you tell him about the abortion before, when you told him you wanted his baby? Surely he would have understood?"

"I don't know, yes, I do. I've buried it for so long. I was so horribly ashamed for not telling Chris I was pregnant, for aborting his baby without his knowledge. He didn't deserve it and I know that. But I don't know how Will feels about me, now he knows what I did. What do I do? Am I being paranoid?"

Kate takes a long sip of her drink and swallows slowly. "Somehow, I don't see Will as the sort of person who would judge, even if he was upset by something. Is he?"

Anna ponders this for a moment. "No, it would be out of character."

"So he might have been a bit upset at you not telling him about the abortion, but I'm sure he's not blaming you. It was a long time ago, and you're sorry for what happened. You did make that clear?"

"Of course I did."

"Okay, so stop beating yourself up. Would he normally have been in touch before now?"

"Well, usually just a text every few days, and I always know where he is. But I've said it's urgent, and he wouldn't leave me dangling like this, I know he wouldn't. There's something strange going on, I'm sure of it."

Kate leans forward, studies Anna's face as if checking she's ready for what she's about to hear. "Listen, Anna, don't take this the wrong way, but I need to ask. Apart from what you've just told me, are things okay between you two? No rows, suspicions? No... violent outbursts?"

Anna recoils, shocked. "No! No, Will would never... not in a million years. How could you even think—"

"I don't. But, you never know. Sorry." She shakes her head, her fringe falling forwards across her brow. She scrapes it away with impatient hands. "Okay. Next difficult question. Is there any reason you know of that he might want, or need, to disappear?"

Anna's starting to feel as if she's drowning, as if the world she knows is seeping through her fingers like sand. "Like what?"

"Oh, I don't know... Does he have any enemies? Anybody who might want to do him harm? Any family problems? Money worries? Anything at all that might mean he needs to lie low."

"My God, Kate."

"I know, I know, but you just... well, you never know. I know you live with him, and you love him. But we never really know someone else. Not properly, not really." Seeing the expression on Anna's face, she puts up her hands and shakes her head again. "Sorry, now I'm being melodramatic. Scrub that comment. Obviously I don't know Will like you do. I'm sure there's nothing remotely sinister in his background. Is there?"

"No, well, there was Olga."

Kate looks startled. "Olga?"

"He had a Lithuanian girlfriend, who he met in Vilnius.

He found out she was being used by a gang of sex traffickers. When she tried to escape, she was killed. It took him a long time to tell me about it. I think it affected him very deeply, so I haven't told anyone about it. It's why he was so against my researching Margryta."

"Poor Will. You don't think…?"

"What?"

"Well, did they find her killer?"

"The police? No, they were useless. He tried to find out who did it, with a friend, another journalist called Mark. But they hit a dead end. What, you think he's gone off to find a murderer in Belarus? God, Kate! Now I'm terrified! Should we tell the police?"

"Don't, for God's sake… It's pure speculation so far."

"You're right, of course. But what if Will's in trouble? I can't just sit here waiting." She gets up and starts pacing again, tidying the room, plumping cushions to occupy her shaking hands. She takes the empty mugs, goes back to the kitchen, boils the kettle, makes more tea, distractedly spilling the water over the work surface, cursing softly as she mops it up.

"Please come and sit down, Anna, I can't think with you fidgeting like that," Kate says. "Look, I'm sorry for suggesting those things, putting them in your head, but you should really think about what you know of Will. What the reason might be that he's not in touch. It could be absolutely nothing. Bad reception or a problem with his phone. But it's worth just thinking through the options, okay?"

Anna does as she's told, sits on the edge of the seat, her hands clasped on her knees, her head bowed. Even her legs are shaking now.

"That's better," Kate says. "Now. What about Will's friend Mark, is he still in touch with him? Do you think he might be able to help?"

"I've already been in touch. He said he'd let me know if he hears anything. He lives in Lithuania. I don't know how much he knows about Belarus, or where Will could have gone."

"Well, you must ask him, talk to him directly. Do you have his phone number?"

She doesn't. It was hard enough to get the email address from Will; she'd won that small battle and left it at that.

"Ask for it. If he's Will's friend, and he's a journalist, he might know more than you do about where he might have gone."

"Good idea." She grabs the laptop from the coffee table and taps out a short message.

"Do you have any idea what Will was working on?" Kate says. "And who for? A newspaper, website, magazine?"

"I have no idea. He keeps everything on his laptop, which he takes with him everywhere. I know he's done some work for some of the national newspapers and various travel magazines. I might be able to remember the titles if I search online, but we'd have to call them all to see if they know anything. Do you think we're at that point yet? It could take days…" Her hands are sweaty again, shaking as the panic begins to rise. "Oh, God—"

"Hold on, Anna, stay calm. Let's think this through. Any regular writing jobs, any friends here who might know more?"

"I think the most regular work comes from *The Times*, the travel section. I could try them."

"Well, that's a start. Let's make a list."

She's grateful for Kate's help, for the practical activity. But there's one thing she can't bring herself to mention, that makes no sense at all. That photo at the police station.

*

She wakes early, agitated and nervous, unable to contain her impatience. She tells Jane she'll be working from home and asks for all work-related calls to be held. Without much hope, she texts Will again: *I'm worried. Please call. X.* She phones him again. Straight to voicemail. Perhaps there really is no signal where he is.

181

She bites her lip as the results come up. She's never thought of doing this before and already it feels like the worst betrayal, though she tries to persuade herself it's for a good reason. It's not because she's beginning to question her judgement. Or Will's honesty.

The search brings up pages of results. There seem to be a lot of men called Will Russell. She types in *Will Russell journalist* and another set of results pops up: a professional profile, not her Will, and other journalists with the same name. In the images, there he is, a head-and-shoulders shot of him, looking very young. She smiles at his face. It's odd but they've never taken pictures of each other, together or separately. Perhaps an indication of how their lives have been, until now.

She goes back to the results and finds his by-line in travel reports. There are quite a few references in *The Times*, as she expected, as well as a travel magazine, a trade publication. They cover the Baltic countries, Ukraine, Russia, Poland, some western European countries too. There are a few lines attached to his profile, but they tell her nothing new. She goes deeper into the results, searching and finding more pieces by him, case studies of holidaymakers in trouble, travel companies going out of business, flights delayed, mundane business stories about the travel sector. She finds his news items on the reaction to the volcanic eruption, from when they first met, a country report on Lithuania, another on Poland. The same photo comes up again and again. He seems ageless online, a Peter Pan amid other, more prolific writers.

She works through the list of magazines and newspapers. But after hours of fruitless calling, sending messages and searching online, she's no further ahead. At every turn, she's frustrated by a wall of circuitous phone systems, bored switchboard operators and out-of-office messages. She begins to wonder how anybody ever gets through to the media. She must be missing something.

She checks her emails, her phone. There's nothing from

Will. A short message from Mark, with his mobile number, but nothing more. She's wondering at what point she should call the police when her mobile buzzes.

"Anna," says Kate's reassuring voice at the other end. "I've checked with the airlines. There were a couple of people I know through work I thought would be worth asking. Apparently Will was in Vilnius for a couple of days, then took a plane on to Minsk."

"When was that?"

"Nine days ago. Sorry, Anna, but there's nothing after that. No further evidence of him flying anywhere. I'll keep checking."

"Okay... thanks. Do you think I should contact the embassy in Belarus?"

"You could, but they might just think you're being melodramatic. I'd wait until you hear from Mark. He sounds like your best bet at the moment."

"But... if I wait, and he comes up with nothing? I feel so helpless, so far away—"

"Honestly, Anna, I'm ninety-nine per cent sure he'll be fine. He'll turn up soon and wonder what all the fuss has been about. Hang on in there."

When she puts the phone down, her hand shakes so much she can't type.

*

As the day passes into the early evening, her agitation grows. Unable to bear it any longer, she puts on her trainers and heads out for a long walk, hoping to work through the worry and stress by exhausting her body.

On her way back to the flat, she makes a decision. She just can't hang about any more. She's going to get over there and do her own searching.

She'll start by flying to Vilnius and from there to Belarus – perhaps go and see Mark – and Daria, too, if she's no

183

further forward. Even if it all comes to nothing, she has to try. If Will's in trouble, and nobody does anything, she will never forgive herself. And he has no one else to call on in a crisis, nobody she knows, anyway, except a brother in Australia — which is even further away.

Two hours later she's organised it all: emailed Jane with details of her trip and booked the first flight to Vilnius the following morning.

She packs her bag without thinking. Usually she's methodical, packing according to her work schedule; this time she picks things out at random, uncertain how long she'll be away, what she'll need.

Rummaging around in the wardrobe, a thought occurs to her. She hasn't looked through Will's things. It's not something she'd normally do. She's always been careful to respect his privacy. But she's been snooping around the internet, so this seems like the logical next step.

She empties the drawers: socks, underwear, t-shirts. She pulls them through her hands to be absolutely sure there's nothing there, feels in the empty drawers, top and bottom, peers under the bed for bags, boxes, anything that might betray his secrets. She even looks under the mattress, cursing him for disappearing like this, cursing herself for suspecting him.

She runs around the flat, inspecting the coats by the door, the tray in the kitchen where they keep any unpaid bills. She rummages through the bathroom cabinet, where there's barely any trace of Will, returns to the living room where she tackles a pile of newspapers and magazines. She pulls books from the shelves to see if there's anything secreted behind them. She drags the drawers right out of the sideboard and tips them onto the sofa, careless of the dust and detritus on the cream linen covers.

At last she sits amid the mess of her once-immaculate sitting room, her sudden burst of energy ebbing away, leaving only frustration. She's not sure whether to be relieved or disappointed.

As she clears up, her eye catches a flash of gold. It's a matchbook, with a gold tiara on the cover and the words: *Princess – Clubs, Bars, Casinos*.

*

She sits staring at nothing, and then her mobile buzzes. She jumps as if stung and fumbles it from her pocket onto the bed. It's an unknown caller. Not Will, then.

She grabs it and, consciously moderating her voice to sound normal, answers the phone.

"Ms Dent," says a deep voice. She slumps with disappointment.

"Vladimir."

"How are you? I hope you have recovered since we last saw you?"

"Oh, yes, thank you, I have. What can I do for you?"

"We would like you to come back so that we can finish our meeting, please. We were interrupted last time…"

"But I spoke to you on the phone," she says, trying to keep the irritation from her voice. "As I said, I didn't recognise those other men. I don't know how I can help you."

"We just have a few more questions. Would you be able to come back in?" The way he says it, though infinitely polite, makes it sound less like a question, more a command.

"I… Yes, I suppose so. In fact, I'm flying to Vilnius tomorrow, from London. But—"

"Good. Can you get here before five o'clock?"

He leaves her little choice. "Yes, I can. I'll be with you around four."

"Good. Just in case, may I ask where you'll be staying?"

A tiny alarm bell rings. They've never asked this before. Is she under suspicion? She can't exactly lie.

"My usual hotel… The Narutis."

"We will see you tomorrow."

CHAPTER 17

This time it's a different room, as soulless as the last, but with a large meeting table, mismatched chairs gathered around it and more stacked in the corner. A projector sits at one end, its single eye staring at a blank wall, its trail of wires disappearing through a hole in the table behind it. Two bottles of water, unopened, sit in the centre of the table with some tumblers. She takes one and opens it, drinks the first glassful down in one go, pours another.

A sleepless night has left her drained. Her overworked mind would not calm down, imagining dangerous scenarios. After an hour or so trying to sleep she'd given up, risen from the bed and got dressed. Then she sat on the sofa and tried to list her options. It was a very short list.

The morning brings little respite. She feels doubly exhausted by the early start and the usual chaos at the airport, where security seems to take longer than ever. She's uncomfortable, bloated from the flight, her stomach churning. She hopes fervently that she can get through the meeting without a repeat of the last time. She goes over to the window and opens it, letting the cool air waft over her. It soothes her a little. In the distance are the roofs of the old town, church spires interspersed with red-tiled gables, the tall belfry of Vilnius Cathedral standing proud among them.

She waits, her heart racing, anxiety building, because she doesn't know what she's going to say to these policemen.

It's only a short wait until they arrive, shaking hands

without a smile, Vladimir cradling a laptop under his arm. He sits close to the projector and a few minutes pass while he connects it to the projector. He opens up the laptop and stares at the screen in silence while Bockus sits making notes in a file, protecting it from Anna's view with the cover. Moments pass. She notes the handwriting on the front, a case number. Then: *Margryta Simonis*, followed by a sentence in Lithuanian. She wonders what it says. Murder? Kidnap? Trafficked? Body on the beach? Perhaps, at last, they've made some progress with the murder investigation and Margryta's killer will be brought to justice. If they have, then that must be a good thing. But it doesn't explain why they need her.

Vladimir finally finds what he wants and turns the projector on, its light sudden and dusty, its hum disturbing the quiet seriousness of the room.

The picture comes up suddenly, large and overwhelming, Gavin's features sharper than in the printed photo. This time she's sure it's him. They ask for her confirmation, she gives it. Then Bockus says: "Please look at the men in the background. Do you recognise either of them?"

Her mind races. What does the photo of Gavin mean? Was he involved somehow in Margryta's murder? Why are the police asking her? She barely knew him. What is a 'person of interest' to the Lithuanian police, anyway?

It takes a huge force of will to keep calm. The enlarged photo has made the figures in the background less clear, the dark edges of their clothes and heads blurred. "It's hard to see, exactly. One of them may be the man I met in the bar where I spoke to Gavin, but I'm really not sure."

After a short exchange in Lithuanian, they stand and beckon her to the door.

"We have software to enhance the faces. Please come."

They walk through brightly lit corridors to another room, where two men sit with multiple screens in front of them. Vladimir, Anna and Bockus stand in a group behind one of them while Bockus gives instructions. The man taps at his keyboard until the photo appears on the large screen in front of him. He creates a box around the two figures in the background, enlarges the heads and starts to work on one of the averted faces. As he does so, features begin to appear: an eyebrow, part of an eye, a cheek, the hint of a mouth. With rapid fingers he takes the section of the picture and transfers it to another screen, brings up a grid, rotates it and creates a complete face from the partial image. Anna stares. A knot forms in the centre of her stomach, just below her ribcage, as if she's swallowed something too large to go down. It aches and throbs, and threatens to betray her.

"Do you recognise this one?" Bockus says.

"No, that's not the man I'm thinking of," she replies. The other man is worked on and soon a second face is generated and enlarged. She can almost feel the heat of Bockus' gaze on her cheek as the features on the screen emerge before her.

"No, I'm sorry," she says, her voice steady. "I've never seen this man."

*

An hour later, back in the characterless interview room on her own, she begins to wonder what's going on.

When they'd enhanced the photo and she'd told them she didn't know the men, there'd been a strange interaction between Vladimir and Bockus; a look, a sharp interchange in Lithuanian, then she'd been ushered out and back along the corridor to the room where they'd started. She'd expected them to join her but they waved her in and closed the door. She wishes she'd stopped them, asked them if she could leave. That would be the obvious next step if she can't help them, surely. But they made no eye contact with her and said nothing.

Perhaps they're dealing with something urgent and will be back shortly to let her go. She presses her fingers into the knot in her stomach, massaging it to relieve the pain.

The room offers nothing to distract her, nothing to read,

no pictures on the walls. From the window she can see very little of the street below. Automatically, almost, she reaches for her mobile and flicks through her emails. Delete, delete, flag. Delete, delete, respond. After twenty-five minutes there's been no sign of anybody. She's irritated at being left for so long, and thirsty. But the water's been removed from the table. She opens the doors of the faded wood sideboard without much hope. It's completely empty.

She wonders what would happen if she were to leave. It probably wouldn't be a good idea, but they haven't arrested her. They haven't asked how long she's got, or whether she needs to get anywhere. She could always make something up if they spot her leaving, or get in touch once she's gone.

As a first step, she decides to make a foray into the corridor to look for the toilets. At least she might be able to get some water there. She opens the door, hoping it won't make too much noise, and looks out. The corridor is empty, so she takes her bag and her coat and walks towards the stairwell.

A door on the left is open and she hesitates, then walks quickly past without looking. She's only taken a couple more steps when a voice behind her says: "Ms Dent, where are you going?"

With a sinking feeling she turns to see Bockus leaning on the doorjamb, the brown folder still in his hand.

She draws herself up and says firmly: "To the toilets. At least, that's where I was hoping to go. On my way out."

"Out?"

"Yes. Unless you're planning to arrest me?" She forces herself to appear relaxed, confident.

Bockus steps towards her and takes her arm. "No, we're not planning to arrest you. But we still need to talk to you. Please come back with me."

"But, surely I can visit the toilets?"

"Not right now. Please come."

She finds herself being propelled back along the corridor, her feet reluctantly following her upper body as he guides

189

her. She removes her arm pointedly from his hand and walks stiffly back into the room.

This time, he sits down in front of her and leans forward, staring into her face. This is too much.

She places both hands on the table. Summoning as much authority as she can. "Please explain yourself," she says. "You've left me in an empty room for upwards of half an hour with no explanation, and now you tell me I can't even go to the toilet. If I'm not under arrest, I believe I'm free to leave."

He ignores her, opens the file and slams the photo down in front of her, his index finger hammering at one of the figures in the background.

"Tell me again, Ms Dent, do you know this man?"

She starts to speak, shaking her head, but he interrupts, his voice metallic and loud in the stark emptiness of the room.

"Please think carefully about your reply. It's important that you tell us the truth now."

*

The floor trembles under her feet and the walls close in. The knot in her gut resumes its ominous ache.

Bockus' flinty eyes bore into her head as if tracking her thoughts, seeing her discomfort, watching her mind wriggle and squirm as it tries to escape, delving into the deepest, softest parts of her brain.

She opens her mouth, closes it again, tries to stand.

"Please sit down," he says. There's no empathy in his face. He's a statue, waiting.

She sits back down, her mind racing through the options. Does she need a lawyer? Are they just rattling her cage, hoping something drops out? But if they know she's lying, that she knows exactly who the other man in the picture is, then she could end up in serious trouble.

She had a suspicion when she first looked closely at the

photograph, taking it to the window to get a better view. The man in the background could only be seen in profile, his head half turned, his collar hiding the lower half of his face. But there was something familiar about the angle of the cheekbone, the shape of the forehead. She'd dismissed it, thinking she was seeing things. It was only when the face was enhanced and reconstructed that she knew, that her suspicion was right.

Because of course she knew the man in the background. There was no doubt she knew that face.

The man behind Gavin was Will.

*

"Ms Dent?" His voice has the edge of a sharpened knife.

She gives in. "Yes, I know him. His name is Will Russell and he's... We live together. In England. But—"

Bockus cuts in. "So you lied. When you said you had never seen the man in the picture." He sits back in his chair, still holding her gaze.

Anna squirms inwardly. Lying has never come easily to her. "I... Yes, I'm sorry. I lied because Will has nothing to do with this man, or Margryta's murder. It was just... an accident... That he was in the picture with him. He would never... He's a travel journalist..." Her voice fades away as she realises she's defending Will when she has no idea why he would be in a photo with Gavin.

"A travel journalist, you say?" Bockus' voice now has a note of sarcasm. Under normal circumstances she would bridle, object to this implication, but she's completely unsettled by this turn of events, unsure of herself, unsure of Will but still not wanting to contemplate his involvement with... what? A criminal? A murder?

She nods, her mind in overdrive. To her surprise, Bockus stands up and leaves the room without a word.

Relieved at his sudden absence but not knowing how long

her reprieve will last, nor whether she's already in trouble for lying, she sits with her head in her hands, agonising, rubbing her forehead as if forcing her muddled thoughts to organise themselves into some kind of sensible order.

*

She breathes deeply, waits for her racing heartbeat to slow. She may not have very long before Bockus comes back, maybe with others. They will want to know everything she knows about Will and she needs to be prepared before she tells them. Her thirst and her now-full bladder will have to wait.

But what can she tell them, what does she know about him? Kate's words come back to her: *You never really know someone else, not really.* Will doesn't give much away, even to her. She has always respected that about him. And she has always believed he has high moral standards, higher than those of most people she knows, certainly than her own.

But has he? She can't believe it's a simple coincidence that brought Will close enough to Gavin to end up in the same photo. It's hard to imagine Will being involved in any way with Gavin, a man he professed to dislike, and who would be the last person Anna would imagine would be his friend.

Then she remembers. Her arms sting with goosebumps.

When she first met Will, he was sitting with Gavin and his wife in the bar at the hotel in Vilnius. He'd claimed not to know them, even though, she remembers with dismay, she'd seen him leave the hotel with Gavin the following day. She'd believed him, having no reason not to. But then there was that glimpse of them together at the airport a few months later. She'd asked him about it, and he'd brushed it off.

If Gavin is a suspect in the Margryta case, then does it follow that Will must be connected too? Surely not, not Will, not the Will she knows and loves. The man she's put her trust in, the man she wants to raise a family with. Is she jumping to horrible conclusions just because of a chance photograph?

But it now seems very plausible that they already knew each other, and they were meeting regularly. And Will didn't want her to know.

That leaves two possibilities. She forces herself to be objective, not to overreact.

The first is that he's still chasing the man who killed Olga. Though he told her he'd given up, and it was a long time ago, it could be the reason he's involved with Gavin. If Gavin is part of a sex-trafficking gang and Olga was working for him, then that would make sense. He could be getting close to the murderer or murderers, collecting evidence, preparing to give them up to the police, who have singularly failed to catch them. It's a logical reason, if frightening for Anna. And it could explain why Will claimed not to like Gavin and seemed to be protecting her from him, why he's been so secretive about his trips. Even why he's disappeared off the radar. He could be getting close to betraying the gang.

It's a terrifying thought that Will could be putting himself in such danger, working with criminals in order to catch them out.

But the second possibility is almost unthinkable. She thinks it through anyway, forcing her brain to work. Will is perfectly placed to bury a life of crime, to fool everybody.

Perhaps everything he told her about his girlfriend, who died at the hands of traffickers, and his efforts to find her, was utter fabrication. Perhaps he's working with criminals, involved in the business, up to his ears in it. What is he doing in Belarus, Lithuania, Poland, for weeks on end? Why isn't he contacting her?

What if everything about him is a sham?

*

She's startled out of this train of thought when the door crashes open again and three men enter the room. Bockus, Vladimir and another man she hasn't seen before.

She pushes away the scenario she's spread out in her mind's eye, forces herself back into the present. As they sit down, she takes a few deep breaths.

"So, you admit that you lied to us about knowing this man, Will Russell." Bockus says.

"Yes, I did. But—"

"It is not a good idea to lie to us, Ms Dent. Why did you lie?"

"I know, I realise that. The reason is I was surprised to see him in the photo. I don't believe he's involved in anything criminal. He's just not... a person who would..." She can't finish the sentence. She's not sure what kind of person he really is, what he's capable of, now.

"Go on."

"When I first met Will, it was in the bar in the hotel in Vilnius. On the same occasion, I met Gavin and his wife. As I said, we were all stranded because of the volcanic ash, it was completely by chance that we were thrown together. To my knowledge, Will and Gavin had never met before."

"To your knowledge?"

"Well, I don't know for sure. But after that, when we saw him and his wife again, Will made it very clear he didn't like him. He called him an arse, and we left so that we didn't have to talk to him."

"How well do you know this Will Russell, Ms Dent?" She jumps as Vladimir's booming voice resonates in the bare room.

"I... Well, I live with him. He... I know him very well."

But she's not at all sure she does.

"You don't sound very certain."

"Yes, yes I am. He's a very decent man. He would never—"

"Never what?"

She takes a deep breath, consciously makes her voice deep and certain.

"You know what I'm saying. I don't even know what you think this man Gavin has done. But Will is not a criminal and he would never knowingly involve himself in anything that would hurt someone. I'm absolutely sure of that."

She holds her breath, praying that she sounds a lot more confident than she feels. There's a pause as they all look at her. Then the sudden harsh tone of a phone sears through the tension in the room. Bockus fumbles in his trouser pocket, puts a mobile to his ear, barks an instruction at the other two and they leave the room as suddenly as they entered.

*

Left on her own again, Anna's mind is in turmoil. She still can't believe that Will is involved in anything, anything at all, criminal, or even remotely unsavoury. He's just too decent. His behaviour towards her mother when her father died was not that of an insincere person, surely.

But when she looks at the facts, it does look as if he was keeping something from her. It looks suspicious – odd, at the very least – that he was seen with Gavin. Photographed with him. Why on earth would he be with him? The police haven't exactly said that Gavin is under suspicion but all the implications are that he is involved in some way with Margryta's murder. Where does that leave Will?

It must be – it has to be – that Will is still be trying to find out who killed Olga. She wants to believe in Will's innocence, but so many questions, so many doubts swirl around in her brain, her head aches with the effort. She can't seem to put the facts into any kind of logical order. She jumps up, paces the room in an agony of uncertainty.

What she does know is that she lied to the police, and they know it too.

Is it a criminal offence? Will she end up in jail? On her own, in a strange country, with nobody to help her? What an idiot she's been. She could be in serious trouble. The knot in her stomach tightens.

*

She whirls round as the door opens behind her. It's Bockus, on his own now, his face grim. "You're free to go, Ms Dent," he says. "But you must leave us your passport and stay in Vilnius."

They're letting her go? Her vision of a Lithuanian prison fading fast, relief washes over her.

"But... I don't understand."

"You don't need to understand. We need to check you are who you say you are, that you are not involved in our case in any criminal way. Then we will give you back the passport."

She starts to scrabble in her bag, then stops. Something seems wrong about this.

"But I do need to understand. I haven't heard from Will for a long time and I'm really concerned now that he might be in some kind of danger. Do you know where he is?"

Bockus shakes his head and makes a gesture with his hand, waving away her question. "That is our concern, too, Ms Dent. I can't tell you any more about our investigations. Your passport please." He holds out his hand, his mouth closed in a determined line.

She finds the passport and hesitates. She knows so little about the police here, except that in the past they were notoriously corrupt. What if they still are and she's meekly handing over her passport? Perhaps she'll never see it again. Bockus glares at her. Knowing she doesn't have much of a choice, she holds it out.

"Please stay in the same hotel. Remember we have your mobile number." Despite her agitated state, the significance of this statement and the implied threat are not lost on her.

"Wait... Don't I get a receipt or something for my passport?"

He smiles a sarcastic smile. It doesn't reach his eyes. No, then, no receipt.

"When will I get it back?"

"When we've done our checks. A few days, maybe more."

He shrugs, opens the door and stands with one arm towards her, ushering her out. A shiver passes down her spine. She's being dismissed, but not entirely.

*

As she walks down the steps outside the police station into the dark street it takes a huge effort of will not to falter. She continues, stiff-backed, until she's rounded the corner, where she sinks onto a bench beneath a tree.

She watches in a daze as the world continues around her. People hurry by, their faces pale in the harsh light of the street lamps, cars moving slowly along the narrow roads. Buildings lit in parts, offices closed, flats occupied for the evening. Gradually the gentle hum and rhythm of the city soothe her and her mind begins to clear. All her efforts to make sense of the situation have exhausted her.

It's more than five hours since she first walked up the steps to the police station. Five hours of agony, an emotional marathon with no resolution.

CHAPTER 18

Dear Mark,

I tried to call you last night but it went to voicemail, apologies, it was probably quite late. I really need to talk to you about Will, urgently. I arrived in Vilnius yesterday and – long story – the police have taken my passport so I can't leave. I might be in trouble, and I'm afraid for Will. Sorry not to say more. I'm not sure I should write it down (or even tell you on the phone), but I need help.

Can you call me as soon as you get this message please?
Anna

Without bothering to wait for a reply, she checks an address on her mobile, grabs her bag and her coat and leaves the hotel.

There's something she has to arrange, before it's too late.

*

"Hi, Anna, it's Mark. I got your message. Are you okay?"

"No, I'm not. I just don't know what to do. Sorry." Her throat is sore with the effort not to cry.

"What's going on? Did you hear from Will?"

"Nothing. But, Mark, I think I'm in trouble. The police…"

Her voice starts to rise with anxiety. She stops speaking before she starts to sound hysterical, but she's choking with tears, her throat so swollen it hurts.

"What's happened? Why did they take your passport?"

"I lied to them. I was trying to protect Will. Mark, do you think they might be listening in?" Bockus' veiled threat rings in her ears.

"What? Why on earth—"

"I'm probably just being paranoid, but I think Will might be in serious trouble." She can't bring herself to say what she really thinks Will might be involved in. Saying it would make it too real.

"What kind of trouble?"

"I can't say, not on the phone, but it's serious."

"Do you have any friends in Vilnius? Someone who can help you with the language? Anyone to talk to? A lawyer? Anyone?"

"No, there's nobody. I don't want to involve a lawyer." She has her business contacts, but not a single one she would call on in a crisis. She has to get Mark to help. "Listen, you know Will, you know what he's been doing, where he might go. You're the only one. Please, can you help me?"

"Okay, just a second." There's a pause and he says something she can't hear, his voice muffled. A woman's voice responds in the background.

He comes back on the line. "I'm going to try to help you. I'll come to Vilnius, tomorrow. I'll see if I can get an early train in the morning. Where are you staying?"

She gives him the name and address of the hotel, weak with relief.

"Thank you so much, Mark. Sorry to land on you. I'll pay, of course."

"Not a problem. Just try not to worry."

He has no idea.

*

"Mark?" Though they've never met before, Anna knows immediately, from his clothes, his demeanour, that it's him.

"Yes. Anna, I presume?"

199

She takes his outstretched hand, which grips hers firmly. He's small and slim, perhaps a little older than Will, his hair thinning at the top. He looks tired, his skin grey and loose, as if he spends too long inside.

"Coffee? I need an infusion," he says, throwing his coat and a laptop bag onto the armchair next to her.

She nods. "Yes, black, please." She hopes the coffee might clear her mind, wake her up after a sleepless night. He goes to the counter and orders. The coffee machine crunches and grinds behind him as he takes the seat next to her, drowning out the piped music and the low hum of conversation from the surrounding tables.

"Right, Anna," he says, fixing her with his gaze. "Are you okay? What's going on?"

She takes a deep breath. "You're going to think I've gone mad." She looks at him for reassurance but he's motionless, waiting. "It's weeks since Will left. Over three weeks, now." Mark shrugs and sips his coffee. The cup they've given him is tiny, with only a mouthful or two of thick brown syrup staining his lips.

"Is that a long time for Will? I have to tell you, I haven't kept up with him much recently. Is it unusual for him to spend so long out of touch when he's travelling?"

"Well, yes, it is. Normally he would at least text, every few days. It's never been this long. I've been leaving urgent messages, voicemails, texts and emails. I had a text, at the beginning, saying he was coming here, then to Belarus. But since then I've heard nothing. It's not like him at all."

"It could just be a problem with the comms. Sometimes, even in parts of England, it can be hard to get a signal."

"I suppose it could be that. Perhaps I'm just being paranoid." But if she is, what about the photo?

"Let's look at what we've got. What did he say he was doing?"

"I know he came to Vilnius for two days, we checked with the airlines. Then he went on to Belarus."

"What is he actually working on there?"

"I… I think he's been doing country reports, some articles on tourism, that sort of thing. That's generally what he does." She bites her lip. Even now she can't bring herself to admit that she has absolutely no idea what the man she has been living with is doing.

"Tourism in Belarus?" He looks sceptical. "Not the most popular holiday destination, certainly from the UK."

"I know." It seems everything he says makes her feel worse.

"Okay. Let's see if my friend in Minsk knows anything, he's a journalist." Mark pulls out his laptop and hunches over the screen.

"How's he going to track him down?" she says. "It's a huge country." They've got so little to go on. Where would anyone look for someone when they don't know why he's there, who he knows or what he's doing?

"Well, exactly," he says, as if reading her thoughts. "But you never know, journalists talk to each other. It's worth a try." He peers at the screen in front of him. Minutes pass while he scrolls and taps.

Anna bites her lip until it's swollen and numb.

He settles back into his chair. "You said you need to talk to him urgently?"

She nods, opens her mouth, closes it again. She doesn't know what to say.

"You haven't said why."

"No," she says, then regrets the sharpness of her tone. "I'm sorry to be abrupt. Just please help me find him."

"So this is why you went to the police?" She's not certain, but there could be a note of disbelief in his voice.

"That wasn't about Will at all. You remember I found that girl's body? Margryta Simonis? I've been trying to follow up, find out what happened to her, how she died. Will warned me off, more than once, and I couldn't work out why. Then, when he told me what happened to Olga, I realised he was being protective, trying to stop me getting into something I didn't understand. I carried on, though. I just felt that nobody seemed to be doing anything about Margryta, nobody seemed to care."

"And the police?"

"I went to them a while ago about Margryta. They just took a statement and left it at that." She swallows; she's going to have to trust this man. At the moment he seems the only person who might be able to help her. "But then they called me in to look at a photo. It was of a man I'd – we'd – met, Will and I, when we were stuck here because of the volcanic ash. A British man, who runs clubs and bars around Lithuania. He'd also been at the hotel on the spit, I recognised him. We knew him as Gavin."

She stops as a waiter arrives to clear the table. She waits until he's out of earshot.

"Is this making sense?"

Mark nods. "So far."

"I was only there because of Margryta, so I assumed – because the police were asking me about him – that this man Gavin was implicated somehow in her death. The thing is…" She hesitates, torn between loyalty to Will and her fears about him. She can barely think it, let alone say it. But she has no option but to trust Mark.

"There were two men in the background of the photo. One of them was a man – I think he was Russian – he was in the bar with Gavin in Vilnius, when we first met him. I don't know his name. The other one was Will."

Realisation wipes the frown from Mark's face. His mouth forms a perfect circle.

"I lied to the police. I told them I didn't recognise him. They must have checked on me though because they knew I was lying. That's why they took my passport. I had no choice. They said they're going to do more checking on me."

"So you were trying to protect Will. But the photo means nothing, Vilnius is a small place and you said you'd both met Gavin before."

"But Will didn't like Gavin when we met him, he made that very clear. Why would he go anywhere near him?"

"He knew him though. Maybe he was being friendly, he's like that. And you don't know that Gavin is involved in anything criminal."

"No, I don't know for certain, but the police obviously suspect him of something to do with Margryta's death. It looks pretty suspicious to me."

"So what do you think Will might have been doing with him?"

"There are two possibilities, both of them terrifying. Either he's still looking for Olga's killers, or…" The words might make it real. They certainly feel like a betrayal.

"Or?"

"He's involved in trafficking girls."

*

His laugh is an incongruous sound amid the fog of her anxiety.

"So because he's in a photo with a dodgy guy, you think Will's a sex trafficker?"

"It is a bit odd, isn't it? Well, isn't it?"

Mark tilts his head from side to side, as if to say maybe.

"But it's not just that. I saw Will with Gavin at the hotel in Vilnius, the day after we met. He'd only just told me he didn't like him. Then I saw them together again, at Heathrow, a few months ago, quite by chance. I'm pretty sure it was him, though I only caught a glimpse. When I mentioned it, he brushed it off as if it hadn't happened."

"And?" The smile still lingers, the amusement in his eyes. Anna feels her anger rise.

"Listen, Mark, I'm not being melodramatic. I'm not imagining things. When we first met him, in the bar, Will called this guy Gavin an arse, he said he couldn't stand him. Why would he meet up with him at Heathrow? Why wouldn't he tell me? And why would Will be with Gavin and his sidekick in a photo the police are interested in? It just doesn't make sense!" She hears her voice rising, pleading with him to believe her, or at least to acknowledge there's something very strange about it.

She tries to read Mark's face. She knows nothing about him, except that he's written about sex trafficking and is a friend of Will's. A finger of fear touches the back of her neck. In her distress, she hasn't stopped to wonder about Mark. What if he too is involved in some shady underworld? She's told him practically everything, trusting him with her darkest suspicions. Is she trampling around on the edges of a hidden world, naive to the point of being a danger to herself?

"Mark?"

He blows out his cheeks and lets the breath go with a coffee-laden puff. He sits forward at his laptop again, his fingers flying on the keyboard. She can't see the screen, only his eyes above it, the soft lines between his eyebrows.

"I'm just checking with someone who might know what Will has been working on recently," he says eventually. "We need to narrow down the options." He waits, tapping his fingers on the edge of the table, still staring at the screen.

"By the way, who's Olga?"

*

It takes her a moment to grasp the question. Her intake of breath is drowned in the general noise of the café, the coffee machine still drumming in the background; her stunned silence goes unnoticed. Mark clicks and types, oblivious to her confusion.

How can he not know who Olga is? Did he not meet Will when he was looking for her, help him in his search? Was he not crucial to Will's discovery of what happened to his girlfriend? She tries to think back to Will's words when he told her about Olga and meeting Mark, but her mind can't seem to put the memory in any kind of order.

Mark glances up, expecting an answer.

"Will's girlfriend who died? In Minsk? I... I thought you'd helped, when he was looking for her. You must remember, you wrote the news story about her?"

"Oh, yes." He doesn't seem to have noticed the shake in her voice. "Of course. I was writing a lot about trafficking at the time, and there were a lot of unexplained deaths."

"There must have been, to forget about Olga." She can't believe he would be so casual about something so important. But she has to control her emotions, she needs Mark's help.

"I remember now. Drugs, wasn't it?"

"Yes, but Will believes she was murdered. By a gang, or an ex-boyfriend..." The headache's growing now, the facts disappearing into a confusing haze. "He told me he'd stopped looking, but now I don't know." She stares miserably into her coffee cup. It all seems so far-fetched. She's close to despair – perhaps she should give up now, go home and wait. Sooner or later she'll find out what's happened to Will. Surely.

"Well, that's it, then, he must have found something new. He's probably still on the trail."

For a moment she feels a flush of relief at Mark's words. Perhaps she's imagined everything, after all. But even if that is the answer, it doesn't help; they're no further forward. If Will is on the right side of the law, but searching for Olga's killer by himself, there's even more reason to worry.

Her tongue feels huge and dry and she sips at the dregs of her coffee, though it's now cold and bitter. It does nothing to help.

Mark peers at the screen, hunches his shoulders as he fiddles with the mouse. "As I said, parts of Belarus can be patchy, particularly in the east. I know he goes to Minsk sometimes but whether he moves on from there or not I don't know. He's probably holed up in some casino somewhere."

She looks at him in horror, her anger spilling over the last vestiges of her control like a river in flood. What's he talking about? Is Mark really not taking this seriously?

"This is hopeless. We're not getting anywhere." She stands and grabs her bag, meaning to go to her room, pack and check out. Though she has no plan, no idea what to do next.

And no passport. Her shoulders sag as the realisation hits her. She's not going anywhere, she can't.

*

As she stands there in despair, her anger trickling away in the face of helplessness, Mark fumbles in his pocket, gets up and walks to the door, his phone at his ear. He stands outside where she can see him, but she can't hear what he's saying.

The problem is, she just doesn't know what to think. Whether to feel foolish, or suspicious. Perhaps Will is absolutely fine, oblivious to her concerns, and he'll turn up at home while she's away, as if nothing has happened. If he'd been away and out of touch this long and she'd been her normal self, tied up with work and not worried that he'd left her, would she be thinking like this? Probably not. In which case she's overreacting.

But what if she's right? Should she trust Mark? He could be stalling, trying to protect Will, telling someone right now that Anna should be stopped, she knows too much. He could be working with Will, part of some dark and complex international crime ring. It sounds melodramatic, even to her. But it could be true.

As Mark walks back into the café, she makes a decision.

"I've sent some messages, spoken to the guy in Minsk," he says, sitting down again. "I think that's all I can do for now, we just need to wait. Don't make any hasty decisions, Anna. I'm sure he'll be fine, he's a seasoned traveller, he knows what he's doing."

"I'm sure you're right. Actually, Mark, I'm really tired and I've got a thumping headache. I'm sorry but I think I need to go and lie down. Thank you so much for coming, and for all your help. Please let me know if you hear anything and I'll do the same." She stands, holding out her hand. She doesn't know what the truth is, but one thing she does know. She just wants him to go, now.

CHAPTER 19

She sits in her room, staring into space, letting her mind wander. She feels less shocked this morning, more able to think with some kind of clarity about what's happening.

It seems that not much has changed about her situation, except that now she's stuck in Lithuania without a passport. Will may have left her; he may not. He may be a journalist; he may be a criminal. Whatever is happening, he's still missing, and that's the important thing.

She cares for him – whatever he's done – and he's part of her life. Nothing will change that.

If he's in trouble, she must try to help. He could be in danger, he could be ill, or he could have been involved in an accident... anything. He could be lying in a hospital in a foreign country, unconscious. How would she know? Would she be contacted? Does anyone know they live together? If not her, then who? Will's brother? Mark, maybe, or Daria?

Daria. Of course, it's unlikely, but she just might know where Will could be. She could even help find him in some way, at least she speaks the language. Anna badly needs an ally, someone who knows Will, who at the very least will listen to her.

And she doesn't need her passport to go to see Daria.

*

It's only forty minutes' drive from Vilnius, and though she leaves immediately, the business of hiring a car and finding her way there takes longer than she hoped. As she nears the village, darkness is falling, and she realises she has no hope of finding her way to Daria's flat from memory in the dark. Everything looks different in the emptiness of a rainy winter's night. A search on her mobile tells her there's a hotel on the main street. She heads straight there and is relieved to find they have a room.

*

It feels strange to be visiting Daria without warning; she doesn't want to alarm her. In the reluctant light of morning she climbs the grim staircase, thinking of Sasha growing up in such a place.

Daria's voice is muffled behind the flimsy front door. "Kas ten?"

"It's okay, Daria, it's me, Anna."

A key rattles in the lock and the door opens. Daria kisses her on both cheeks. "I am happy to see you again so soon, it's a nice surprise. Though you should have said you were coming, I would have prepared cake," she says as she ushers Anna in.

Sasha runs ahead as Anna follows them into the tiny sitting room, taking her hand and pulling her down to the floor to show her his toys. This time, there's no smell of cooking in the room, just a faint trace of stale tobacco.

Daria waves her into the nearest chair and heads for the kitchen. "Now, Sasha, let Anna sit down. Coffee for you?" Soon the tang of fresh coffee drifts through.

"Which car is your favourite? Your best?" Anna says to Sasha, pointing at a line of toy cars that snakes across the floor. He lifts up a red racing car and shows her how the doors open. "Yes, that one's very special."

The little boy grins and runs around the room making racing car noises.

Daria sets down a tray with two steaming mugs of coffee and a little jug of milk. Her hands tremble a little, the bones showing white through papery skin.

"Daria," Anna says, grateful for the warmth of the mug on her cold hands, "how have you been?"

"Not so good," Daria says, shaking her head. She pulls at her thin jumper, shapeless over a cotton dress. "You see, I am so thin. I was beautiful, like you, but not now."

Anna hardly knows what to say. The contrast between them is so great. Yet here she is, a woman who takes for granted all the comforts of modern life, needing Daria's help. "I'm so sorry Daria. I would like to help you, and I will if I can. The reason I'm here is there's something important I need to ask. Have you seen, or heard from Will?"

There's a trace of caution in Daria's voice as she replies. "Will? He is not with you?"

"He's been away for a long time, and I haven't heard from him. All I know is he's here in Lithuania, or possibly in Belarus. I thought perhaps he might have called you, or come to see you…" As soon as the words pass her lips, she knows how unlikely it is that Will would come here, and not call Anna. Yet still, fleetingly, a part of her wants to believe that everything's fine, he's lost his phone, everything will carry on as before. But the fragile filament of hope is destroyed before it's had a chance to settle in her mind.

Daria looks stricken, the lines on her pale face dark against the light from the window behind her. She's about to respond when Sasha jumps up, pulls at her arm, whispers something in her ear.

"One moment, Anna… Sorry." Daria takes Sasha by the hand and they leave the room, talking in rapid Lithuanian.

They're gone for a few minutes and the tension gets to Anna, already taut with anxiety. She can still hear Daria's voice, Sasha's soft answers muffled by the walls between the rooms. She gets up and strides around, looks out of the window at the grey Lithuanian morning, picks up the picture of Daria with Olga. As she puts it back down, she notices a small ashtray, made of beaten metal. It's one of those old-fashioned dishes with grooves in either side to hold the cigarette, sold as cheap souvenirs across Europe.

In the centre is a cigar butt, one end twisted and crushed, like some obscene slug-like creature. It emits the acrid smell of stale tobacco that pervades the room. Around the cigar is a distinctive gold band.

*

She's still gazing at the ashtray when Daria returns, alone. Seeing what Anna's looking at, she stops in her tracks, her eyes wide.

"Daria?" Anna says, picking up the ashtray. "Whose cigar is this?"

"I... Sorry." Daria takes the ashtray from Anna, shaking her head, her eyes averted. "I must throw it away."

"Can you tell me whose cigar this is please?"

A troubled look passes across Daria's pale features and she sits down suddenly on the sofa, as if her legs have given way. She puts the ashtray on the coffee table and pushes it away as if it offends her. "A bad man. Very bad." She shakes her head.

"Daria, it's important you tell me. This man. Who is he and why was he here?"

"This man, he was Olga's boss."

Anna sinks down next to Daria, her mind racing. "Olga's boss, when she worked in Vilnius? Is he Olga's ex-boyfriend?"

Daria nods, her forehead crinkling, biting her lip.

"His name... What is his name?" Her voice comes out louder than she intends, the words tumbling over themselves. Daria wraps her arms around herself and rocks, her eyes closed, pain deepening the lines around her eyes.

Anna swallows and says, more gently: "I'm sorry, Daria, but this is important. Who is this man? What is his name? You must tell me."

"British man. His name is Gavin." Daria pulls a tissue from her pocket and wipes her face with a shaking hand.

Gavin. So it was him. He was the man controlling Olga. Perhaps he was even her killer... The thought makes her shudder. "But why was he here, Daria? Why is he still coming here?"

"We had no choice, Anna. We had no money and Sasha... Sasha was only a baby."

"What do you mean, you had no choice?" Anna resists the urge to shake the woman, to force the truth out of her, right now.

"Daria?"

Daria shreds the tissue in her hands, distraught. "We did a terrible thing. We had nothing, no money, no job. We had the baby to feed. What could we do?"

"Tell me, please. I promise I will try to help you."

"Sasha. He is not Olga's brother, Anna."

"What do you mean?"

"He is her son."

There are so many unknowns now, so many uncertainties, that Anna is beyond surprise. "I see," she says, keeping her voice steady with an effort. "Who is the father?" She's prepared to hear that Will is Sasha's father; she could almost take that in her stride now.

Daria's voice is rough with emotion. "A village boy, a school friend, same age as Olga. When she tells this boy about the baby, he and his family, they leave, never come back." She waves her hand, as if dismissing him, mutters something in Lithuanian.

"But why was this a secret? Why did you pretend he was yours?"

"Because of Olga's work. It was safer for the baby. Olga, she worked for Gavin when she got pregnant. She was hostess in bars and clubs. He was kind, he paid good money, he bought gifts. He said she was beautiful. He did not know she was pregnant.

"But one day he took her to a hotel, told her to sleep with other men, for money. She didn't want. She said she was virgin, to try and stop him, but he raped her and beat her, so

212

badly. It was terrible, Anna, she had many bruises. But the baby was okay."

"So she had to do what he wanted?"

Daria's face contorts with pain, her fingers tightening around the mangled tissue. "She had no choice, she couldn't get away. She had to work. We were so scared. We didn't know what to do about the baby. She wanted to keep it."

"But I don't understand… Why is Gavin still coming here?"

"We said to Gavin, the baby is his." Daria's face collapses and she covers it with her hands.

Anna wasn't expecting this. The dangerous lies this little family is embroiled with, it's worse than she could have imagined. "What? You lied to Gavin?"

"I am ashamed but we had to, Anna! So then Olga is safe. If not his child, then Olga…" She makes a chopping motion with her hand. "Very bad."

"So Gavin believed the baby was his?"

"Olga was so young. It was only way to be safe, for her and the baby. We did a terrible thing, but what could we do?" She hangs her head, the tissue in pieces on her lap.

Anna can't imagine how frightened they must have been. Such a young girl, pregnant already, in the hands of pimps and traffickers, with no hope of escape. They would have done anything to save the baby.

"It's okay, Daria, I don't blame you, I understand. It was a horrible situation for you. But… does he still give you money? Is that why he was here, to see Sasha?"

"Yes, sometimes he comes, sometimes he gives money. When Olga died, he left us alone for a short time. But he believes Sasha is his son and that brings him back. I don't want his money. But if we say the truth now…" Her eyes open wide with fear. "I just want him to leave us alone."

"Daria, the police are looking for him. If they find him, he'll go to prison. You and Sasha will be safe."

"Ah, the police." Daria throws up her hands. "They don't care. They are not good people. They are no use."

Anna seems to have lost track, there's so much to process here. Then she remembers why she's here. "Daria, did Will know?"

She shakes her head vehemently. "That we lied to Gavin about Sasha? No, no, we didn't tell him. We were – ashamed. And we didn't want him to get involved. He knows Gavin comes here, but he does not know why."

"So, he's not Gavin's friend?"

Daria mouth drops open. "You think they are friends? Never. Will asks me about him, I say to him he is dangerous, don't go near him. No, Will doesn't know him."

Anna takes a moment to process all this.

Where is Will in all this mess? Is he involved with Gavin, or trying to bring him down? Daria's response has done nothing to clear the confusion.

A kind of internal mechanism makes her stand, walk to the kitchen and make a fresh coffee for both of them, their mugs now stone cold. Somehow she needs to pause time, in order to cope with what it has thrown at her, and in the mundane actions of boiling the kettle, rinsing the mugs, preparing the drinks, she experiences some respite from the turmoil. She fetches some more tissues for Daria's tears.

As she returns to the living room, a kind of order has returned. It's as if she's entered a new state of consciousness where she can operate on a different level, putting her emotions to one side, to be dealt with at a later time.

"I'm sorry to ask, Daria, but how did Olga die? Did she try to escape from Gavin? Will said she went to Amsterdam."

"Not to Amsterdam, no. She tried many times to escape, but she couldn't leave me and Sasha, and Gavin would not let her go. All those men, it was so hard." She shakes her head, her eyes closed.

"So was it drugs?"

Daria opens her eyes again. They are swollen with tears. "Drugs, yes," she says. "But she never took them! Gavin gave them all drugs, they all used them, but not my Olga.

She loved Sasha too much. All she wanted was to get away, live a normal life. But she was too much trouble for them."

"Do you know for certain that they killed her?"

"The police said it was drugs. She didn't take drugs. Either it was a lie, that she died of drugs, or they…" she points to her neck, indicating a needle. "We will never know, Anna." Her eyes fill with tears again. "We will never know."

*

Sasha's small face peers around the door. Daria calls to him and he runs to her, folding his small body into her waiting arms. For a moment Daria closes her eyes, as if gathering strength from his embrace, then smiles, smoothing a curl of hair away from his wide brown eyes. He listens closely as she talks, then runs to the kitchen and comes back with a box of biscuits, which he puts on her knee. Opening it, she offers the box to Anna, who shakes her head. Sasha takes one, then looks at Daria, his eyes questioning. She nods and he chooses another, skipping back to his toys where he sits nibbling with intense concentration.

"Do you have any idea where Will could be, Daria?"

"I am sorry, I don't know. You say he was going to Belarus?" As she says it, Daria's eyes flick to the ashtray on the table in front of them, where the cigar butt still curls obscenely.

"Daria?"

"Gavin. He came here, to see Sasha, yesterday. Sasha was not here, he was out with my friend, at the park. Gavin was angry. He said he has to go away, to Belarus, as soon as possible, but—"

"Perhaps he knows the police are looking for him. Do you think that's why he has to go away?"

"I don't know, but, Anna…" she grasps Anna's arm with desperate fingers, "he's coming back."

Anna feels the blood drain from her face.

"When? When is he coming back, Daria?"

"I don't know… Soon," Daria says again, her voice urgent.

"He said he's coming back to get the boy. I think today. He wants to take him to live with him and his wife. But I don't want him to have Sasha… He can't take Sasha." At his name, the boy looks up from his toys, his eyes questioning. Daria, her voice reassuring, says something in rapid Lithuanian and he drops his gaze.

"Today?" In a moment, Anna's trance-like calm has turned to fear, Will forgotten in the sudden turn of events. Gavin is coming here, soon? He could be here at any moment.

Daria turns her back on the boy, lowers her voice, leaning in to Anna. "What can I do? Will you help me, Anna?"

She forces herself to breathe, thinking fast. "Of course I'll help you. Do you really think he's coming today?"

Daria nods, her eyes wide with fear.

"Then we have to leave immediately. No… wait. Can Sasha go to your neighbour right now? Will he be safe there for the moment? I need some time to think."

"Yes, he will be safe."

"Right, take him to her, right now. Pack a bag for him, for the night, just in case. Quickly." The little boy looks startled as Daria takes his hand and they run to get his things.

Her mind racing, Anna looks around the flat for something, anything, to help her. At the window, all she can see is the next building along, a small patch of concrete down on the ground. The kitchen reveals even less. It seems the entire flat faces away from the street. Gavin could arrive at the door at any moment and they would have no warning.

A few moments pass before Daria reappears with Sasha, carrying a red backpack, its straps trailing. Anna smiles reassurance at him as he leaves, relieved to know that he's safe for the moment. But they don't have long. Gavin won't be put off again if he finds Sasha gone, he will surely beat down the doors of every flat in the building to find him. She strokes Sasha's hair and smiles at Daria, then closes the door on them with relief.

One second later, her mobile rings.

*

His voice is distant, the words distorting in the wavering signal. "Anna, it's me."

The shock is almost too much to bear. She claps her free hand over her left ear, bends forward in an effort to catch what he is saying. "Will? Will, where are you? I've been so worried… Will?"

A rumble of buzzing and clicking is all she hears in reply. Her first instinct is to run to the window, to clear the line. "Hello? Are you there? Will?"

"I'm here. Anna, I'm sorry I couldn't contact you. I'll explain everything. But…" The crackling begins again and she lays her forehead against the windowpane, squeezing her eyes shut in an effort to hear through the broken buzz of the airwaves.

"Will? Are you okay? Will?"

"Yes, I'm—" But the line goes dead. She stares at the screen, willing it to light up again. Time is running out. She must speak to him. She wants to scream with frustration. She runs to the front door, scrabbling with the latch, and out into the corridor, looking for somewhere, anywhere, where the signal might be stronger. As she reaches the end of the hallway the handset buzzes again.

"Anna? Can you hear me?" Will's voice, that familiar voice she loves so much, is crystal clear now.

"Yes. Are you okay?" The words catch in her throat, tears cloud her vision. Her hand, clutching at the phone, is damp with sweat.

"I'm fine… On a borrowed phone. It's a long story, I'll tell you everything when I get back. It's been a tricky trip, to say the least. Are you at home?"

"No, I'm at Daria's. I need to talk to you. Where are you?"

"You're at Daria's? What are you doing there?"

"I'm looking for you. But I have to go. Gavin's coming here, and—"

217

"Wait, Gavin's going there? You need to leave, Anna. Take Daria and Sasha and get out. If he comes while you're still there, don't let him in. Under any circumstances. I'm in Vilnius. I'll be there as soon as I can."

CHAPTER 20

Her hand's so slick with sweat she can barely dial the number. She wipes it on her jeans, flips the mobile to the other hand. "Mr Bockus, please," she says. "Quickly, it's urgent."

Daria's back, locking the front door behind her. She gazes at Anna, her eyes wide.

"Who is calling?" the voice at the end of the line says. It's too calm, too slow.

"Anna Dent… Please hurry…" She bites her lip until it bleeds, the taste like a warning on her tongue. It seems an age before the voice comes back on the line.

"Mr Bockus is busy at the moment. Can I take a message please?" Already enervated by the softness of the voice, Anna's patience cracks.

"No!" she shouts, then with a huge effort lowers her voice and says, her voice shaking: "This is about a man he's interested in. A man called Gavin Strickland. I must speak to him or Vladimir Rostov. It's urgent. They will want to take my call."

A fumbling sound, then a muffled conversation, then a soft click and an electronic beeping. The wait seems interminable and she paces about, her stomach knotting, gripping the handset until her fingers ache. She's about to ring off and call back when a gruff voice comes on the line. "Bockus here."

"It's Anna Dent. I'm not in Vilnius, I'm with a friend. The family is involved with the British man you're interested in, Gavin, and he's coming here. Soon… Maybe right now."

There's a soft exhalation of breath as if he's breathing out smoke. "He is going there? Explain why you are there and what has happened."

His calm enunciation does nothing to relieve her irritation. She wants to explode, but she has to make him believe her. She responds in as measured a tone as she can muster. "I'm sure you know this man is dangerous. If you're interested in talking to him, he will be here soon. He is threatening my friend. So if you want to stop something terrible happening, I think you need to send someone here, right now."

"In what way is he threatening your friend?"

"He wants to take her little boy. His name is Sasha and he's only five years old. He believes the boy is his son, but he isn't... Look, can you just send someone? There isn't time to explain everything. He could be here at any moment."

"Wait a minute please." The line goes quiet and she controls an urge to scream. Instead she strides from one side of the room to another, thumping her feet at each step. Olga's eyes follow her from the photograph, urging her on.

"Give me the address please."

She retrieves the address from her bag and spells it out. "Will you send someone now? My friend is very frightened. I am too. If Gavin finds me here I don't know what he will do."

There's a long pause until finally, Bockus is back on the line. "I have alerted the local police, they will send someone now. My colleague from Vilnius will be on his way shortly. If you believe you are in danger, you should leave. Can you do that?"

"Yes, I can take them to my hotel, for the moment." She gives him the details, her mind already focused on moving, getting away from the flat as quickly as they can.

"Then you should go, as soon as you can. Can you leave us a key?" She covers the mouthpiece and checks with Daria, who immediately opens the front door again and indicates the floor to the right of the door. "Yes, there's a loose piece of flooring on the right – no, the left – of the door as you approach it from outside the flat. We will leave a key underneath."

"Good. I will be in touch." There is a click on the line and Bockus is gone.

Grabbing her bag, Anna takes Daria's arm, hustling her to the door. "We need to go right now. We're going to my hotel. We'll get Sasha on the way."

Daria's eyes widen at the urgency in Anna's voice. "Yes, okay, I will get my bag."

"Hurry… Bring the spare key."

Daria scrabbles in a drawer for the key, hands it to Anna. The loose flooring is obvious, but it's too late to change the plan, so she crouches and slips the key into the gap between concrete and matting.

*

"So, what have we here?" His voice reverberates around the narrow corridor, powerful and menacing.

She freezes. To her left, a pair of feet clad in expensive leather shoes. To her right, the end of the corridor. They're too late.

Forcing herself to appear relaxed, she stands, her fingers curling again around the key. She turns slowly. There's a sardonic smile on his face as his eyes, deep-set and dark, probe hers.

"Hello, Gavin," she says, keeping her voice as light as she can. Her only thought is to trick him, to delay him somehow. Behind her, out of sight, her hand searches for the door handle. If she can close the door, maybe she can stall him for a few moments. "What are you doing here?"

"I was about to ask you the same thing, Anna." When he says her name, it's heavy with meaning. The two small syllables sound like a threat, as if he wants to pulverise them beneath the heel of his handmade shoe. *An*-na.

"I… I'm visiting a friend." Her fingers connect and the door closes behind her with a small click. He frowns and looks at the door, steps closer. Acrid cigar smoke catches in her nostrils.

221

"Well, well. So am I. That's a coincidence, wouldn't you say?" He takes another step towards her. There's no mistaking his intention. She takes a corresponding step away from him. Her back is now against the door and she's beginning to shake.

"Well, yes. Yes, it is. It's a small world." She can only hope that behind her, Daria has heard his voice, can find somewhere to hide, some way out of this. She draws herself up, tensing for the attack.

"I don't know what you're doing here, but I don't have time for this," he says, his voice harsh and cold. "Get out of my way." He grabs her arm, pushes her to one side, but she is ready for it. She whirls round and jabs the key as hard as she can into his flabby neck. She loses her grip on the key, but not before she feels the soft flesh tear as he recoils from the blow.

With a grunt, he's off-balance and grasping at his neck, struggling for breath. Somehow she manages to unlock the door and get through it before he recovers. She slams it behind her, pushing at a bolt with trembling hands. Daria stands in the tiny hallway, paralysed with horror.

"Quick! Help me." She takes one side of the heavy cupboard in the entrance and, with Daria on the other side, they heave it forward. Piles of plates, cups and saucers slam into a thousand pieces on the floor as the unit tilts and smashes into the opposite wall with a deafening crash, landing at an angle and barring the way. Pulling Daria into the sitting room, she tugs at the sofa and they heave it across the second door.

From outside there are sounds of kicking and thumping, and a torrent of yelling: "Come out here, you fucking whores. I'll kill you, and the boy, too! Open this door, or I'll kick it in!"

Anna's in no doubt that he will kick it in. It occurs to her that he might not be alone. Perhaps there are more people outside, ready to help, and if so, there's no chance they'll escape. From the brief silence that follows the kicking, she guesses he's on the phone, maybe calling for backup. She grabs her own and dials, her fingers shaking.

"Quick," she says to Daria, who's transfixed, trembling,

at her side. "Pile things on the sofa, make it heavy. There... that chair..."

Daria starts to place furniture on the sofa: the coffee table, a dining chair, anything she can put her hands on.

At last the call connects. "Detective Bockus, please... it's urgent... I need to speak to him right now!" Anna yells into the phone, so that Gavin can hear, hoping that he'll stop if he knows she's calling the police, but it's a desperate hope, a slim chance of delaying him.

"Anna..." Daria is rooted to the spot at the deafening sound of Gavin's relentless kicking.

"Shut yourself in the kitchen, quickly!" Anna screams, dropping her mobile to the floor, looking around frantically for some kind of weapon. The only thing she can find is a tall glass vase, heavy at the base and narrowing to a lip at the top, filled with dried flowers and grasses. Tossing them aside, she grabs it with both hands and leaps on to the sofa, holding it high, waiting for any part of Gavin to come through that door.

*

A volley of kicks and thumps gives way to the sound of cracking and splintering as the front door to the flat collapses. He grunts and curses as he smashes his way in and starts on the sitting-room door, just inches from Anna's face. She waits, breathless, holding her weapon high.

Within seconds, a hole gapes and his arm appears, flailing around for the door handle. She hits it as hard as she can with the vase, which catches his arm with a satisfying thud. Briefly his arm disappears, but the hole is bigger now and he adds his shoulder to the yielding wood.

"Get out! Get out! Help, help us!" she screams, making as much noise as she can, hoping to bring neighbours running to the door, though she knows it's a vain hope. Dimly, in the rush of adrenalin that swoops over her, she can hear Daria in the kitchen, screaming too, probably from the window. She braces herself as his head appears, his hair wild, his eyes flashing with fury. The door gives way with a crash, he struggles to heave his weight over the sofa back, and she takes her chance, wielding the vase like a baseball bat at his head.

She lands a glancing blow and the vase smashes into pieces, leaving her clutching a circle of broken glass. The effort of the blow throws her off-balance on the cushioned seat of the sofa, and as she stumbles she sees Gavin reeling but still upright, one leg already slung across the back of the sofa. His face contorts, he lets out an ear-splitting roar and lunges at her. She recoils, trips on the cushions and falls backwards. As she falls, the sharp corner of the sideboard rears towards her and her forehead connects with a sickening blow. White-hot pain stabs at her head and she collapses onto the floor in a daze. She can only watch as his feet thud towards the kitchen door.

"Daria!" With a huge effort she forces herself onto hands and knees. The pounding in her brain doubles as she moves and sickness grasps her stomach in a vice-like grip. She retches over and over and with each cramp the hammering worsens. Gasping with pain, she's dimly aware of other sounds – crashing, Gavin's roar – then, to her horror, his feet step back out of the kitchen, terrifyingly close. She's expecting the stinging blow, his foot swinging back for the kick in her face, her guts, but instead an enormous hand grips her by the throat, squeezing, choking, pulling her upright, her feet scrabbling for the floor. His grimacing face looms into hers, his voice booms in her ears.

"Where's the boy? Where is he? Tell me, or I'll squeeze the fucking life out of you!" His wet lips contort in a grotesque snarl, spittle spraying her cheek as she struggles for breath, arms flailing.

"Gone. He's gone." Even through her fear, she takes pleasure in the look on his face. He's not a man used to being thwarted.

"I swear, I'll kill you!" She believes him. All she can

224

hope, now, is that she can delay him a few precious minutes, and some miracle will happen to keep her alive.

Her vision starts to distort, pinpricks of light sparkling at the edges. Everything seems to slow down. As if watching from above, she wonders in some strange, calm void, if this is it, this is what her last moment in the world will be. It can't be. It mustn't. This is too soon, too... odd.

Then, as she struggles to keep a grip on reality, she experiences a sudden, intense physical awareness. She feels the scrape of the jeans on her legs, the softness of the jumper on her back. Even the hardness of the rings on her fingers against her skin, the cold smoothness of the glass still clutched in her right hand.

The broken vase.

In that moment of realisation, all her senses gather into a burst of pure energy. Her slipping, kicking feet make sudden contact with the floor. She rears up and lashes out wildly with her right hand. The vicious shard makes contact with the fleshy expanse of his stomach. She digs and twists harder, harder, as the grip on her throat loosens, the fingers giving her one last choking squeeze as they relinquish their deadly hold. There's a scream – an animal howl of fury and anguish, and she collapses back onto hands and knees, retching, vomiting, gasping.

As he falls, his clenched fist lands, hard as rock, on the back of her head.

*

She opens one eye, then the other. She's lying on the floor of Daria's flat, alone, glass shards glistening on the carpet, furniture and splintered wood from the broken door thrown about like confetti. A pool of blood shines wetly only centimetres from her face. Cautiously she lifts her head and shuffles her body away from the bloodstain, her ears straining. All she can hear is the sound of her own breathing and the thump of her heart. Wary of the broken glass, she forces herself to her feet, checking her body for damage.

She's bruised and battered. Her fingers probe her throbbing forehead for damage. She's can feel a nasty gash, but it's clear the blood on the carpet is not hers. Gavin's gone, and instinctively she knows the flat is empty. She checks the kitchen through the open door. There's no sign of Daria, but the window's wide open, rain spattering the floor.

Dreading what she might find, she turns and steps carefully through the tangle of damaged furniture to the remains of the front door, where she crouches low and peers out. There's nobody in the corridor, only a trail of darkened blood leading to the stairway. She inches out, heart thumping, and tiptoes towards the stairs. The doors to the other flats in the corridor remain closed. The air in the stairwell is heavy with foreboding as she creeps down to the first landing and flattens herself against the wall beside the rain-spattered window. She looks down.

A large white Mercedes, its windows blacked out, stands at the kerb, a puff of grey smoke rising from the rear. She glimpses a froth of blonde hair, the flutter of a white coat as a woman climbs into the driver's seat and slams the door. As the car pulls away, its engine racing, puddles splash murky water onto the pavement.

From the back passenger door, a red strap trails on the wet tarmac.

*

She runs like she's never run before, her feet pounding, water soaking her shoes, raindrops clouding her blinking eyes. But the white rectangle of the Mercedes grows ever smaller, then turns a corner and is gone. Cursing and heaving, her chest pumping, she bends forward and holds her knees, pulling breaths deep into her lungs. The searing pain of a stitch cuts into her side as rain beats on her back, runs down her neck and soaks her hair, mixing with the tears of frustration on her cheeks. Though she tried her hardest, she knew from the first it was hopeless. Even as she reached the pavement outside the building, the car was too far away to read the number plate, accelerating too fast for her to gain any ground.

But she's certain that the woman she saw getting into the car was Gavin's wife, Charlotte.

*

At last she can stand. She stares after the car, hands on her head in despair. Someone screams her name, runs up behind her and grabs her by the shoulder. It's Daria, hysterical, sobbing, shaking.

"They took him, Anna, they've got him!"

She holds the trembling woman in her arms with a feeling of utter loss. The rain drums its relentless beat on their heads, as they stand, helpless, on the empty tarmac. Then, as she starts to guide a stumbling Daria back to the flat, not knowing what else to do, she hears a dim wail in the distance.

Anna runs towards the sound, heedless of the rain, listening all the time, willing the police car to appear. There's still time, if they're quick, there's still time for them to find the car, to find Sasha. A black-and-white saloon with a blue flashing light, then another, approaches at what seems like a snail's pace. The first car screeches to a stop beside her, rainwater soaking her feet. She yells through the window. "They've taken the boy! A white Mercedes, that way! They have the boy, Sasha. You must follow…" Then Daria is behind her, gabbling in Lithuanian and the young policeman nods.

"You," he says, indicating to Anna. "You come with us." Without hesitation she has the back door open and scrambles in, pointing in the direction of the fleeing Mercedes. She catches a fleeting glimpse of Daria, standing on the kerb alone in the rain, as the car, its siren blaring, takes off.

CHAPTER 21

The police car races through the narrow streets, its siren blaring, rain spattering the pavements left and right.

The Mercedes, with its precious cargo, has disappeared into the streets without trace and the two young officers talk in a torrent of Lithuanian into the radio. But when they reach the main road out of the village, they don't know which way to turn. There's no sign of movement either way. After a moment of deliberation and an animated three-way discussion with the radio, they turn towards Vilnius. There's a lump in Anna's throat and as they speed away she stares for as long as possible in the other direction in case they've made the wrong decision. She can't bear to think they've got it wrong.

They're following a car, which is miles ahead, doing its best to disappear as fast as possible. Catching up with it seems an impossible task. She bites her lip, knowing she can't interfere. They know better than her, both the town and the mind of the escaping man. From what she can gather from the continuous radio conversation, it seems they're alerting other patrols – she hopes the border police – but that doesn't reassure her. Gavin isn't stupid; he knows the area well. He's a criminal, with his own way of doing things.

They turn a corner and suddenly, shockingly, the Mercedes is there, stationary, its front wheel on the pavement, as if it's been forced to stop. The policemen waste no time. The car screeches to a halt and the man in the front jumps out, his hand flicking open the flap to the weapon at his belt. After a couple of garbled instructions into the radio, the driver is out too, gun in his hand, and they're approaching the car, shouting commands. The driver's door opens a crack and Anna can see Charlotte's hands outstretched, her feet dangling, searching for the ground. The other officer is at the passenger door, his gun pointing into the car, his left hand on his radio.

Without knowing she's doing it, Anna is out of the car and running towards the rear of the Mercedes, craning to see Sasha. The first officer, holding Charlotte up against the car, waves her away, yelling an order, but not before she's seen the great bloom of red splashed across the bright white of Charlotte's coat.

"Get back!" the officer says and she retreats to the police car, though she stands in the road, shielding herself with the car door, just in case. With Charlotte now cuffed and immobile, his weapon still on her, the officer gently opens the back door and bends towards the interior. After what seems like an eternity, to Anna's intense relief, a small pair of feet appear and drop onto the tarmac, followed by Sasha, clutching his backpack in both hands. The officer points towards Anna, leans down and says something in the little boy's ear, and then he's running, running towards her.

*

The next minutes pass in a blur of sirens and uniforms. Sasha sits on Anna's lap in the back of the car, her arms tight around him, his head buried against her coat. She watches the scene, weak with relief and unable to move.

An ambulance appears, blaring and garish in the dark of the street; two men run to the Mercedes with a bag, returning to their vehicle almost immediately to collect a stretcher and rush it to the car. Eventually they extract the figure slumped in the front seat and lie him on the ground. They set up a line, settle an oxygen mask over the face, and transfer the inert body to the trolley, raising it to waist height. More minutes pass as they load the stretcher into the open back of the ambulance, and then finally they're gone. Charlotte is nowhere to be seen, swallowed into the back of one of many police cars. Uniformed officers mill about, some of them talking into radios, some inspecting the scene.

At last one of them returns to talk to Anna and Sasha.

"We have them," he says, with a hint of a smile. "Now we must look after you." He looks at Sasha, who returns his stare with huge eyes. Sasha nods and listens as the policeman crouches down and explains something to him in a gentle voice.

"We must take him to the hospital to be checked, just to be sure," he says to Anna.

"Okay," she replies. Though her instinct is to object, she knows it's procedure, and the right thing to do. "Can you get his mother, Daria, to come there?"

"Of course."

On the short journey to the hospital, she realises they're probably following the ambulance that took Gavin. She hopes fervently they'll be well away from him when they get there.

She wishes she'd cut his jugular, now. If only she'd smashed the vase before she hit him. Then they'd never have got near Sasha. She can hardly bear to think what might have happened if they hadn't caught up with the Mercedes.

*

She needn't have worried about seeing Gavin. At the hospital Sasha is given the all-clear by a young doctor who treats him with gentle hands and a smile. A nurse cleans and dresses the wound on Anna's forehead, then leads them to a small room and brings them hot chocolate and snacks. Though she can't face either, Anna encourages Sasha to sip the warm drink and soon, still encircled by her arms, his eyes are drooping.

Overcome with exhaustion, she allows her head to rest on

the wall behind her. There are a million questions, but this is all that matters now. Explanations can come later.

When Daria arrives not long after, she lifts a sleepy Sasha into her embrace, the tears running freely down her cheeks.

*

Back in her room at the hotel with Daria and Sasha curled together in the bed, Anna takes a blanket and a cushion and collapses with a sigh onto the sofa, not bothering to remove her clothes.

As sleep starts to wrap her in its dark mantle, Will's face flits into her mind. A stab of alarm gently tugs at her, but nothing will stop sleep now. She slips gratefully into oblivion.

*

She wakes to the buzzing of her mobile on the floor beside her. When she sits up, the wound on her forehead throbs with pain. She grabs the phone. "Will?" she says, hope rising in her chest. She stumbles to the bathroom, holding her head, while Daria and Sasha sleep on. But it's not Will. It's Detective Bockus, asking her to come to the local police station. He's sending a car; it will be there in minutes. Wearily she gathers her thoughts and her clothes, writes a brief note for Daria and tiptoes out of the room.

*

"Thanks," she says as Bockus hands her a plastic cup, steam rising from its grey-brown contents. "I haven't had the chance to think, or to talk to Daria yet. They're asleep and I'm still confused."

"That's why you're here," the detective says, a smile threatening. "To clear up the confusion."

She makes an effort to order her thoughts. It's like trying

to file paper in a pond. "I'm not sure I can, but I'll do my best." She sips her drink, which tastes like liquid cardboard. "How did Gavin find the boy?" She'd failed to keep him safe, even when she knew danger was approaching.

"Ah. It seems his mother climbed out of the window from her kitchen and into the next-door flat. Then she ran to find the boy. The British woman was watching, waiting for her husband. She followed her."

"So she led her there? Does Daria know this?"

He shakes his head. "No, not yet."

"Please, don't tell her. She's been through enough." Anna can't imagine how Daria might feel, knowing she'd led Gavin to Sasha's hiding-place.

"Okay, I agree there is no need to tell her. But I have some questions for you."

"Of course."

"Were you the one who injured Strickland?"

"I… yes. I was defending myself… He was threatening me, I thought he was going to kill us both." For a moment, she feels defensive. If they're going to accuse her of something, she will defend her actions with all the energy she can muster.

"No, we're not accusing you of anything, Ms Dent. We're just gathering information. The facts."

She sits back. "Do you know how he is? Is he going to survive?"

Bockus gives her a quizzical look.

"I'm not concerned for his health, if that's what you're thinking," she says. "I want him to survive… To be brought to justice."

"Indeed. That is my job, Ms Dent. To answer your question, the doctors say that he will almost certainly recover. Though you fought him off very well. He was badly hurt, needed urgent surgery. His wife thought he was dead, that's why she stopped the car. He was unconscious, not far off bleeding to death. But if you hadn't injured him, we may not have caught up with him. You did a good job." His face cracks into a wry smile, though his eyes are serious. "Anyway, we have him under strict surveillance and we will arrest him when he's well enough. We have many questions for him, too."

"I'm not sorry I hurt him, he deserves to suffer. But I hope he lives." He must live. He must live in suffocating, stinking, excruciating agony and darkness, for all time, for his crimes. For Margryta, for all those girls, for Olga too. Not least for kidnapping a five-year-old boy. "And his wife?"

"His wife, too. Even if she wasn't involved with Strickland's criminal activity, she was part of the kidnapping of the boy. She is in custody."

"I suppose you won't tell me if Gavin was involved in the death of Margryta Simonis?"

"Ms Dent, you know we can't discuss that. But you will know, eventually."

And what about Will? She daren't even mention his name. She has so many questions, but it's only a few hours since Sasha was found, not much more since Gavin attacked her, and her injured head feels as if it's been kicked around a football field. The few hours' sleep has kept her going but now she's feeling the full onslaught of the drama at Daria's flat. She's finding it hard to focus on anything. "I'm sorry, do you mind if we carry on another time? I think I need to lie down."

"Of course. I will get a car to take you to your hotel. But I would like to continue our conversation when you're feeling better. I will be returning to Vilnius today. We can talk there when you return. And you can collect your passport now."

*

Back at the hotel, she delays going up to the room, preferring to leave Daria and Sasha to sleep on.

She orders a coffee, sits in a quiet corner and dials, preparing for another disappointment.

But to her surprise, he answers immediately. "Anna, thank God. Are you okay? Where are you?"

233

At the sound of his voice, so clear he could be in the next room, the events of the past forty-eight hours crowd in. It's all she can do not to break down. "Will." A sob escapes her. "Can you come?"

"I'm on my way to Daria's now. Stay where you are. I'm coming." She stammers out the name of the hotel, tells him to head there instead. She lies back in the chair, her body limp, her eyes closed. He's safe and he's coming, and for the moment, that's all she can think about.

*

By the time he arrives, she's composed herself. She's ordered some toast, and surprised herself by eating it. She feels a little less wrung out and has stopped trying to make sense of the events of the last few days. Gavin is no longer a threat. Daria and Sasha are safe, and Will is going to explain everything.

"Anna, I'm so sorry," he says, with his arms around her.

She holds him tight, to be sure he's real, for so long that in the end he untangles himself from her arms, smiles and says: "It's okay, you know. I'm here."

The sense of relief rises from deep inside her, like coming in from the cold to the warmth of a log fire. She sits and looks at him, drinks him in. His hair a little rumpled, dark smudges underlining his eyes, but the look in them is open, concerned, honest. Remembering her darkest fears of the last weeks, she almost doesn't want to know where he's been, what has happened. None of it seems to matter, now, in this moment, she would forgive him anything.

They sit close, thighs touching, on the sofa. The warmth of him calms her, the tension in her shoulders seeping away. "Are you all right?" he says. She nods, biting her lip to stop it trembling.

"I spoke to the police," he says. "It's all my fault. I should have warned you, I should have been there for you. For you, Daria, Sasha... It could have ended so badly."

She shakes her head. "It wasn't your fault. But where have you been? I was so desperately worried."

"All sorts of things conspired against me. I'm going to get some more coffee for you and tell you everything." He indicates to a waiter, then gently lifts the hair from the dressing on her forehead.

"Your head… You're injured."

"I'm fine, it throbs a bit, that's all. But it's all been so confusing. I thought—" She doesn't know where to start. The blow to her head is not the only reason she's finding it hard to gather her thoughts.

"What did you think? Tell me."

"I don't know what I thought. When you left…" She can't bear to tell him what she'd suspected.

"When I left, I didn't know I'd be away for so long," he said. "I thought a week or so, then I'd be back. I came to Vilnius to find Gavin, only to find he'd gone to Minsk. I'd been in Minsk for maybe three days with no sign of him, though he was expected, they said. So I took off into the country to have a look round, just for a couple of days. I thought I could do a piece on rural Belarus and how it's changed.

"Then all my stuff was nicked. Wallet, laptop, mobile… all gone. Years of experience as a travel journalist and I committed the cardinal sin." He picks up a packet of sugar, a thin sliver of paper, drops it repeatedly on the table. Each time it lands with a soft fizzing noise.

"The dumbest thing I've ever done," he says. "I left them by my side for a millisecond, my bag and my jacket, and they vanished. I was in quite a remote place, not much going on, so I suppose I was lulled into a false sense of security. There was no way of contacting you. No Internet cafés or anything. Anyway, it proved quite tricky getting out of there. I had to get back to Minsk somehow, go to the embassy. It took a lot longer than I expected."

She can hardly believe it, such a simple explanation, and

so obvious. "But, surely, there must have been some way you could have let me know?"

"I suppose there might have been, but I didn't realise you'd be so worried. It didn't seem an unusual length of time, to me. If I'd known, I'd have found a way. I'm so, so sorry, Anna."

She manages a weak smile, shakes her head. How could he know? Normally she'd be at her office, working, not noticing the time passing.

"Anyway, without a passport, I couldn't get a train, so eventually I hitched a lift to Minsk with a friendly truck driver." In Minsk, he'd managed to persuade a hotelier to let him stay on the promise of payment once it was sorted out. "For a few days I just focused on sorting out the mess. Then, all of a sudden, the police turned up at my hotel. I couldn't understand what was going on at first, but they insisted I go with them. I refused at first. I don't know much about how the police operate in Belarus, but they're pretty different from ours. I had no idea what they wanted. But I went with them, and after much confusion and hours of waiting, the Lithuanian police arrived."

*

It must have been a simple job to track Will down. By that time, he'd been in touch with the police and the British Embassy in Minsk. Eventually, after another long delay, they'd got him out of the country and back to Lithuania. He'd endured another series of interviews in Vilnius before they finally let him go.

It takes a few moments for those words to sink in. They let him go, so he's not under suspicion. She feels the tension at the back of her neck, which has gripped her for days, start to ease. "But why were you in Belarus, Will?"

"I should have told you before, and I'm so sorry I didn't. I've been trying to help Daria and Sasha get away from

Gavin. He's the worst kind of gangster, a dangerous man. He deserved everything he got. What he did to Olga... I wanted to sort it all out, finally, because of us, you and me, our plans together, wanting a baby. I'm sorry, Anna. I was trying to keep you out of it."

"You were trying to catch Olga's killer? All this time?"

"No, not all this time. I did give up, initially, when Mark and I reached a dead end. The police had got nowhere with it and it seemed hopeless. But I knew Gavin was involved in Olga's death, he had to be. It was obvious. He was involved in trafficking girls, getting them to work for him, trapping them. He wouldn't let her go. When she became a nuisance, he just got rid of her."

She nods. "I talked to Daria. She told me quite a lot about Gavin."

He looks at her questioningly, but she wants to hear his story first.

"He was still hanging around Daria and Sasha, three, four years after Olga died. I just couldn't understand it, but Daria wouldn't tell me anything. She seemed scared. So I decided to get closer to Gavin. When I met you – that first time, at the hotel – that's why I was there."

He pauses to drink his coffee, his long fingers wrapped around the body of the cup.

"When I heard about Margryta, I realised what had happened. He'd done it again, and he'd probably go on doing it if nobody stopped him. I had to get him away from Daria."

"You were trying to help Daria, and to protect me."

"I had to keep you away from him, I didn't want you to get involved. But then, more recently, I noticed Sasha had new clothes, expensive toys, things Daria could never afford. I began to worry even more. You remember Charlotte said she wanted to adopt? They must have been after Sasha all the time. Daria wasn't well, too poor to look after him without help, unable to protect herself. I was worried for their safety, though I never thought he'd just march in there and take him, even him. So, when I realised the police were on to Gavin, I decided to help them, move things on a bit."

"But why would they involve you?"

"They didn't, it wasn't like that. I'd got to know him a bit, we had a drink once or twice. I pretended I was doing a piece on Vilnius nightlife and interviewed him. That was when you saw us at the airport. I'm sorry for lying. I couldn't tell you. We travelled together, supposedly to see his empire, well at least the part that's in Lithuania. He was beginning to trust me. I was thinking he just needed to make one mistake. So I went back a few times, on the pretext of working. But he seemed to be spending a lot of time in Minsk, so this time, I followed him there. Then at least I could tell the police where he was."

She's horrified. "You went to find him? A man you already thought was a murderer? What on earth did you think you could achieve?"

"I know, it seems mad now. But it's one thing, kidnapping vulnerable young girls, even murdering them in a back alley, in the dark. It's quite another when it's a British national, and a journalist too. I suppose I was relying on that, though he was probably capable of getting rid of me, as well. I just wanted to warn him off Daria, in any way I could. I wasn't aiming to accuse him of anything. But he wasn't there. I checked all his usual haunts. He was expected, but nobody knew when, or where he was. That was probably lucky for me, as it turned out."

Will had decided to wait a few days, then return to Vilnius. But as it turned out, his plans were thwarted.

*

The sky outside the hotel is dark with rain. She's thankful for the privacy of their corner in the lobby, for the time to absorb all this.

"What I don't understand," he says eventually, "is why you were at Daria's. Was it just by chance?"

Anna realises that Will has no idea how frantically she'd searched for him. Doesn't know yet of her meetings with the police, her search for Margryta's story.

"You were gone so long. So much has happened."

He looks up in surprise. "Was I? I can't even remember when I left."

It wasn't such a long time, it's true, now she has some perspective. "I don't even know myself, now." She picks at the skin at the edges of her nail. "But I was desperate, and I couldn't get hold of you."

"Desperate? Why?"

"Because I thought I'd upset you by not telling you about the abortion. You left the day after we saw the consultant, remember? Because you might have thought I was a terrible person for what I did to my husband. I don't know, it all just got to me."

He takes her hand, caresses her fingers. His touch is warm and comforting. "Oh, Anna, that wasn't it. Not at all. I was surprised you hadn't told me, but I understood. I would never blame you for what you did. You did what you felt was right. I'm sorry I wasn't there to reassure you. The trip was all arranged so I went, I thought I'd be back in a few days. You wouldn't normally worry."

She shakes her head. "I know. But I was in a state, Will. Kate came round, we talked, we tried to find out where you'd gone, who might know what you were doing. Belarus just didn't seem like a place you'd go to for work. I even searched the flat for clues, like some mad, suspicious woman, but I couldn't find anything. I left you urgent messages, and you didn't call. I know now, why you couldn't, but at the time it just seemed like you'd disappeared. And then, the police—"

"You called the police?"

"No, not then. But I'd been to see them – the Vilnius police, before all this happened – about Margryta. I know you didn't want me to, and I know why, now, but I just couldn't stop. She was important, to me. A lost child." She meets his gaze for a moment, looking for understanding. "Margryta was sixteen. The same age as my child would have been, if she'd lived. If I hadn't had the abortion. Once I realised that, it really resonated with me. I'd regretted the abortion for years, thought about the baby often, though I tried not to. Tried to tell myself I was fine. But I couldn't help thinking what a terrible thing I'd done to Chris, not telling him about the baby and… destroying it. I felt guilty, all the time, though I tried to bury it. I needed to atone in some way, for my own lost child."

"I can see the link to Margryta. And I was trying to stop you getting involved."

"I was obsessed. Anyway, the police called me back in and asked me to look at a photo. It was Gavin, I identified him. It was related to Margryta's murder, I knew it, he was obviously under suspicion. But they wouldn't tell me why they were interested in him, or anything at all about the case."

She swallows. "The thing is, they wanted to know if I knew another person in the photo. And the other person was you."

He laughs, then, an honest, real laugh, and she knows for certain, now, he's a good man. "Me? They had a photo of me, with Gavin? They must be better at surveillance than I thought. No wonder you were confused."

"I didn't know what to think, Will; on the one hand you seemed to be in cahoots with Gavin, and on the other, you might have been in danger, trying to catch Olga's killer. I just couldn't get my head round it, and the police didn't help. I didn't know where to turn."

*

When he hears about the enormous, terrible lie Olga and Daria had told Gavin – that he was Sasha's father – he is silent for a moment, then he whistles, a long slow exhalation. "So that's why Gavin wouldn't leave them alone.

What a dreadful situation for them. They lied to protect Sasha, but in fact it put him in terrible danger. No wonder she wouldn't tell me."

"Exactly. I was looking for you when I went to her. Apart from Mark, who couldn't help me, she was the only other person I could think of who knew you. By then, I was clutching at straws. I saw one of Gavin's cigar butts in the ashtray – it had to be his, I recognised the brand – and it all came out then. As soon as I realised he was coming back to Daria's flat, I called the police, but it was too late. It was so close, Will, they nearly got away with it."

"But they didn't, Anna, and that's thanks to you. They're safe now. Let's hope Gavin goes away for a very long time."

They sit, their arms entwined, legs touching, trying to soak up as much of each other as they can. So much has happened in such a short period of time.

Daria and Sasha still haven't come down from the room. Though Anna is desperately tired, she wants them to sleep on, to get their strength back after last night's ordeal. There will be a lot of work to do when they get home.

There's also one more thing she needs to tell Will.

*

"So all along, you were trying to protect Daria and Sasha." The more she thinks about it the more obvious it seems.

"I was." He looks at her and she can see the openness in his eyes. Nothing hidden, no falseness.

"So you weren't involved with Gavin in any other way."

"No. No, I promise. It must have looked strange, even suspicious, seeing me with Gavin, but it was all about Olga, and what was happening with Daria. Did you seriously think I might be helping him?"

"No, well, yes, for a short time." Her head hurts and it's not the wound that causing it. Now, it seems impossible that she could ever have suspected him. "I had a kind of epiphany, I suppose. My imagination went mad. Not like me at all, really. When I think what I nearly…" She catches herself, but she knows she has to do this.

"Anna?"

She breathes in, a long, shuddering gulp of air. "I'm going to tell you this, because I never want to hold anything back from you again." Her throat tightens; her voice is a husky croak. "I was in a dreadful state. When I realised you'd gone, I thought you might have left, properly left me." She can't look at him. "I was going mad, Will, I thought you couldn't bear to be with me knowing I'd done such a terrible thing."

She feels the gentle pull of his hand on her arm.

"No, it was a terrible thing," she says, staring into the dark dregs of her coffee. "I'd lived with the guilt for so long, hidden away, it had eaten away at me. I expected you to be shocked at what I did, not to want to stay with me. It was as if I wanted to be punished. But at the same time, I couldn't bear you to leave. So when I didn't hear from you, I couldn't just sit there and wait. I needed to see you, to talk to you."

"I know. I'm sorry."

She shakes her head, determined not to take the cowardly route. "No… there's something else."

"Something else?"

She hesitates, her throat swelling with emotion. "I was sick with worry, I thought I was going out of my mind. I didn't know what I was doing but I had to talk to you, it was getting more urgent every day. Then, when I saw that picture of you with Gavin, I imagined all sorts of things. I'd seen you with Gavin before – in the street and at the airport – do you remember? But you brushed it off and changed the subject. It seemed really strange, especially as you made out you didn't like him. Why would you be with him in a photo and how is that related to Margryta? I had no idea what you were up to, who you were working for, not even which country you were in, half the time. It felt like I'd been asleep for most of our relationship. I thought perhaps I didn't know you at all." She turns to him, willing him to understand.

"Anna?" His eyes search hers, anxious now. "What do you mean, getting more urgent every day?"

*

It had been simple enough. She'd found a clinic nearby that looked professional, for people who could afford to pay. And in Vilnius, she had no concerns about being judged or recognised. She went straight there.

But instead of going in, she found herself sitting outside on a cold bench in the Vilnius drizzle, her thoughts in turmoil.

The mistake she had made sixteen, no, seventeen years ago now, had haunted her for all that time. The biggest mistake of her life. She did a terrible thing. It wasn't because she aborted a child, though she was filled with regret for years, but because she did it without telling the child's father, without giving him any choice in the matter. That was the unforgivable thing. And here she was, at the end of her fertile life, planning to repeat her past, to ruin her last chance to have a child of her own.

Right up until she'd seen the photo of Will with Gavin, she'd known – she was certain – that he was kind, loving and decent, and that he loved her. What they said to her that day had called it all into question.

In her torment, this sleep-deprived, hormonal mess, it was hard to think logically. But sitting there outside an abortion clinic on a damp grey afternoon in Vilnius, she forced herself to work it out.

She could turn left or right. Her choice now would be the direction for the rest of her life. She couldn't even choose to ignore it; there was no third way.

In the end, it wasn't so hard. There was no proof, yet, that Will was a criminal, only a photo, a chance sighting, the wild ravings of her imagination. But far more important: not only was this very possibly her last chance to have a child, it was her last chance to make amends to that first, unborn child. And at last she could prove to herself that she was not a terrible person who didn't deserve to bring a child into the world.

So this time had to be different. She must recognise the father – whatever happened, without question – or enter some kind of grotesque repeating pattern.

This was also Will's child, and she needed, for her own sake, to tell him, to give him the chance to be its father.

She looks into the deep brown of his eyes and sees the goodness in him. There are some truths that are better locked away, for ever.

"Will, I'm pregnant."

CHAPTER 22

British man arrested for murder
Multi-country criminal gang smashed
By Jonas Kipras, Lithuania correspondent, The Times

A British man has been arrested and charged with the murder of Margryta Simonis, 16, from Klaipeda, Lithuania, whose body was found washed up on the Baltic coast.

Gavin Strickland, from Birmingham, was detained by Lithuanian police last week. A number of other suspects – up to twenty people of multiple nationalities, it is believed – known to be associated with him, were rounded up in the culmination of a long and complex police operation.

Suspected of criminal activities spanning many countries over at least a decade, including sex trafficking, drug running and money laundering, Strickland successfully evaded the justice system by running legitimate businesses in the form of clubs, bars and casinos throughout the area. The comprehensive investigation will take place across the Baltic countries and into Belarus.

Margryta Simonis worked as a hostess in a club belonging to Strickland in Vilnius, where she was forced into the sex industry. She managed to escape and travelled to Klaipeda, where her family lived. When she was almost home, she was recaptured by Strickland, taken to his boat and strangled, her body dumped in the sea close to the Kuronian spit.

"This was a young girl starting out in life," Detective

Bockus, Vilnius Police Central, said. "Kidnapped and forced into the sex industry, she died courageously, trying to escape. Because of her, a ruthless criminal gang leader, along with many of his associates, is now in custody and many illegal activities have been stopped. Strickland has been charged with murder and kidnap and we expect a number of other charges to be made in the course of our investigations."

Strickland awaits trial in Vilnius.

*

Anna tears the story from the paper and opens a drawer. She pulls out the plastic folder and adds the cutting to the contents.

How had her friends described her? Lina had said she was happy, she loved to party and she was kind. That Margryta had wanted to work with animals one day. The girl at the club had said she was one of the good ones.

She takes a piece of paper and writes their words, hoping to capture a fragment of Margryta in their voices.

*

"Red or white? Or Pimm's, maybe?" Sai's voice is muffled by the open door of a huge fridge as Anna enters the kitchen.

"Where are you?" she says, laughing. "Ah, there you are. A Pimm's would be lovely. Not too strong, though, please, Sai."

"It's already mixed, but you can top it up with lemonade if you like. It's all there."

On the shiny granite of their kitchen worktops, rows of glasses have been laid out. Jugs of Pimm's, bright with mint and strawberries, stand waiting. Platters cover an entire table top in the dining area: canapés topped with fresh salmon, tiny Yorkshire puddings with tasty-looking centres, sausages dipped in sauce, bowls of fresh strawberries. In the centre is a huge pile of coloured and decorated cupcakes surrounding a birthday cake with *Happy Birthday, Jenny* in pink lettering and three pink candles. Silver balloons hover over the table, bumping gently with the breeze from the open doors. Children's voices echo from the garden outside, where brightly coloured toys litter the lawn.

The fridge door closes, revealing Sai, a large bowl of ice in each hand. He beams as he sees Anna and holds out his arms, still carrying his trophies from the fridge. She kisses him on both cheeks.

"Anna, so lovely to see you! Straight from work, I see. Hang on, I'll get your drink, and then we can go outside, it's such a lovely day. Jenny's having a great time."

In the garden, small children chase each other in and out of a Wendy house which sits in the shade, its windows framed with checked curtains and flower-filled window boxes. There's a little veranda at the front with a tiny rocking chair.

"Love the Wendy house," Anna says. "Is that her birthday present?"

"It is," Sai says. "Isn't it great? She couldn't believe her eyes when she saw it this morning. She was jumping for joy, bouncing all over the furniture."

"Lucky girl." Anna sips her drink and watches as a little boy disappears inside the little hut and the door closes. "Where's Davey? Not on your own with this gang are you?"

"I'm here," says a voice behind her and she turns to greet Davey, who hugs her and plants a kiss on her forehead. He looks relaxed and happy, immaculate in neat grey shorts and white T-shirt. "I see you're being well looked after, anyway," he says. "Is your mum coming?"

"Will's bringing her, they should be here soon. Oh, and here's Jenny's present. Where shall I put it?" She pulls a small package from her shoulder bag. The paper has yellow rabbits and a silver ribbon tied into a bow. "I love presents for little girls. I spent ages deciding, I could have bought half the shop."

Davey smiles. "This from the hard-nosed businesswoman who never liked children. What a transformation. Tell you what, give it to her later, when her friends have gone, otherwise it will get lost in all the excitement. You are staying for supper, aren't you?"

"Of course, wouldn't miss it." As she puts the present back in her bag, there's the sound of voices in the hallway. Kate and Graham appear at the kitchen door waving bottles and grinning, their children running ahead of them towards the garden, disappearing without a glance at Sai and Davey.

"Sorry about my rude children," says Kate. "It's all the parents' fault, no discipline. We brought bubbly to make up for their manners."

As they embrace their friends, Sai relieves them of the bottles, retrieves a wine cooler from a cupboard and empties the bowl of ice around the bottles. "There, we'll have that later when the kids have gone. We're going to need it."

Anna wanders through into the warm sun and sits, cradling her drink, in a swing chair at the edge of the lawn, watching the children playing. How different it all feels from a year ago. How different she is, too.

*

A small boy barrels onto her lap, startling her and spilling her drink.

"Hey, Sasha, slow down," she says, steadying him with her free hand.

"Jenny!" he shouts, and scrambles off, running at top speed to the play house where Jenny and the other children are chasing each other around.

As she stands, shaking the drops of Pimm's from her hand, Will and her mum appear at the back door and join her in the garden.

"Spillage?" her mum says, as Will kisses Anna on the cheek, his arm around her waist.

"A tornado just landed on my lap," Anna says. "Fortunately I managed to save myself. Where's Daria?"

"Just changing the baby. She'll be here in a minute," says Will.

"She's coping so well with all the change. You did a great thing, bringing her here." Her mum is already fond of Daria.

"She's much better," Anna says. "Now she's got a proper diagnosis and the right treatment, she should be fine."

They watch as Jenny and Sasha emerge from the Wendy house and run towards them.

"Will, come, push us on the swing," Sasha says, and Will follows the children to the bottom of the garden.

"It's lovely to see Sasha so happy. He seems to be settling in really well," Anna's mum says.

"He loves Jenny and she just adores him. They're two monkeys together," Anna says.

Sai appears at the doorway. "Kids' tea's ready to go! Can all adults gather up small people and bring them in please. And save room for the birthday cake!"

The adults walk back to the house, Will gathering a crowd of children around him and leading them to a table laden with food. As Will helps Sai and Davey with the drinks, Daria appears at the door, a baby in her arms.

"Here's your mummy, Maggie!" she says, smiling at Anna.

In the few months since they arrived here, Daria has changed. There's a healthy glow to her skin, her hair is neatly cut and her clothes no longer hang loosely from her body. She's a different woman entirely.

"Thank you, Daria." Gathering the baby in her arms, Anna is struck again by the beauty of her child. Grey-blue eyes lock on to hers, an ocean of love behind them. Pink lips curve into a smile, dimpling her perfectly round cheeks, at the sight of her mother's face. Her hair's beginning to grow, a dark lock curling onto her forehead.

"She's beginning to look like Will." Kate comes up

behind Anna and kisses her cheek, smiling down at the baby in her arms.

"I think you might be right. That's not so bad."

Avoiding the mayhem of the children's tea, they head together for the sitting room, where it's quiet. Anna holds the baby on her lap, drinking in the soft smell of her hair. Still she marvels at how perfectly the shape of her baby fits into her body, how profound is her feeling of completion.

"You seem so content, with her."

"It's overwhelming. I never understood the power of motherly love before, but it's so... so natural. It feels like she's always been here, waiting to introduce herself."

Kate smiles. "I think she probably has."

*

It's the same room, though lighter today, as if familiarity has made it more welcoming.

The questioning seems to go on for an eternity, though when she checks the time, she's surprised to see it's only a couple of hours since she arrived. The detective is painstaking and patient, taking copious notes and checking each time that he's understood her answer correctly. Eventually he seems satisfied, gathers his papers together and excuses himself.

When he returns, Vladimir is with him.

"Ms Dent, we meet again," he says, crushing her hand in his enormous grip. "I understand you've been giving us your statement."

"I have. Hopefully this will be the last one," she says, smiling.

"Indeed, I hope so too. Just one thing, Ms Dent. Some advice, no, some friendly recommendations." She nods. It's not hard to guess what he's about to say. "You can trust us to do our job. It can be dangerous to get involved. We knew you were protecting Mr Russell. It would have been best to tell us the truth."

"I know that now. My apologies and thank you."

"Thank you for your help, Ms Dent," Bockus says, opening the door. "You're free to go home now."

She stands to go. "Can I ask… Is it possible to keep me informed about your progress with the case?"

"We will certainly be in touch," Bockus says, holding out his hand.

She puts on her coat and heads for the door.

*

The wind whirls, twisting her hair into dancing snakes around her head. White shells stand to attention, tiny sand drifts holding them straight with military precision. The beach beneath her feet is rippled into deep, hard ruts, barely shifting with her weight. Further up the shore, the pale sand softens, lifting and undulating with the changing winds.

She stares out over the expanse of grey sea, the far horizon a perfect line against a dappled sky. No ships interrupt the vastness of the water, no evidence of life above the ocean, hiding its dark secrets below. Above, a single seagull cries its haunting summons. There's no answering scream.

Bending down, she places a small bouquet of flowers – roses, freesias, gypsophila – on the white sand. She watches as one by one the blooms part from the bunch and lift into the wind, skittering along the beach, catching in the foam at the edge of the water until at last they disappear into the distance.

ACKNOWLEDGEMENTS

Thank you to all my family and friends for supporting me, and also to the following:

My agent, Philip Patterson, at Marjacq.

My editor, Lauren Parsons, and the rest of the team at Legend Press.

Andrius Nikitinas, Commercial Attache at the Lithuanian Embassy, London, for all his help with background information on Lithuania.

Jan Stannard, my partner in crime, who came to Lithuania on my research escapade and walked with me along the Kuronian Spit.

The Lithuanian people for welcoming us to their beautiful country.

The marvellous Scribblers writers group, who were a huge support and help in getting this book finished.

Special thanks to Sharon Bloom for helping me disentangle the plot of this novel.

And to all my readers, thank you.

We hope you enjoyed *The Truth Waits* as much as we did here at Legend Press. If you want to read more thrilling crime stories from Susanna Beard, take a look at her debut novel:

DARE TO REMEMBER

Reeling from a brutal attack that leaves her best friend dead and her badly injured, Lisa Fulbrook flees to the countryside to recuperate. With only vague memories of the event, she isolates herself from her friends and family, content to spend her days wandering the hills with her dog, Riley.

However, Lisa is soon plagued, not only by vivid flashbacks, but questions, too: how did their assailant know them? Why were they attacked? And what really happened that night?

As she desperately tries to piece together the memories, Lisa realises that there's another truth still hidden to her, a truth she can't escape from. A truth that may have been right in front of her all along.

BOOK CLUB QUESTIONS ARE AVAILABLE ON
WWW.SUSANNABEARD.COM

COME AND VISIT US AT
WWW.LEGENDPRESS.CO.UK